Born in England in 19[...]
the first ten years of he[...], where
her father founded Penguin Books in Canada.
She was educated in Montreal, England and
Paris, then worked for publishers worldwide
until she left publishing to devote her time to her
family and her writing. Clare Harkness lives
with her husband and four children in West
London. Her two previous novels, *Time of
Grace* and *Monsieur de Brillancourt*, are also
published by Black Swan.

# Old Night

## Clare Harkness

**BLACK SWAN**

OLD NIGHT

A BLACK SWAN BOOK : 0 552 99590 8

First publication in Great Britain

PRINTING HISTORY
Black Swan edition published 1994

Set in 11/12pt Linotype Melior by
County Typesetters, Margate, Kent.

Black Swan Books are published by Transworld Publishers Ltd,
61–63 Uxbridge Road, Ealing, London W5 5SA,
in Australia by Transworld Publishers (Australia) Pty Ltd,
15–25 Helles Avenue, Moorebank, NSW 2170,
and in New Zealand by Transworld Publishers (NZ) Ltd,
3 William Pickering Drive, Albany, Auckland.

Reproduced, printed and bound in Great Britain by
Cox & Wyman Ltd, Reading, Berks.

To
*Myrtle Neel, Penny Doody and Jackum Brown*
with love

## *Author's Note*

This novel is set in Montreal; and, since the opening scenes take place in 1962, I have used the terminology, street names and English spellings that my characters would have employed at that time. Thus, I have referred to 'Ogilvy's' department store, though the apostrophe and 's' are no longer legally permitted; and I have used the English street names in what were the largely English-speaking areas, but the French names in the French areas.

Similarly, I have referred to the 'Square Mile' – a term which, though rarely heard nowadays and almost unknown to the young, was very much in use at the time. Originally employed to describe the area in which the upper classes and *haute bourgeoisie* lived (an English-speaking, élitist, very rich enclave in the midst of a predominantly French-speaking city and province: an area where, around the turn of the century, three-quarters of Canada's millionaires lived), it came to represent an idea as much as a geographical entity, and was as often used to designate the area's old-established inhabitants as it was to denote the physical area of that name – so much so, that when those same families at a later date moved into Westmount, they continued to be known (except by a few purists) as 'the Square Mile' or 'the Square Milers'.

What is known as the 'ground floor' in England is called the 'first floor' in Canada, thus my characters go up four flights to reach the fifth floor.

Place Ville-Marie is not a square, but a huge modern tower: a commercial centre containing shops and offices.

I should like to stress that this is a novel and

therefore a work of fiction, and that all its characters are purely imaginary. I have tried to choose names which sound Canadian and have therefore chosen mainly Scottish names for the English (the long-established English-speaking families being generally of Scottish descent), so, inevitably, the surnames I have chosen must abound — but to such an extent that they cannot be unique to any one person. In the same way, I have chosen French-Canadian names that are exceedingly common. If I have, by accident, combined both the Christian name and surname of any actual individual(s), living or dead, it is a coincidence which I have done my utmost to avoid.

I would like to thank the following people who have helped me immeasurably in the research and fact-checking which was required for this book. They have, in many cases, put themselves out beyond the call of duty or friendship:

In particular, I must thank Michael Anthony and Myrtle Neel, both of whom have gone to enormous pains, driven huge distances, and spent a lot of their valuable time in checking details for me simply out of friendship; but I would also like to thank very sincerely: Dr Elizabeth Letsky, *MB Durham, FRCP, MRC Pathology*; Mr Colin Sims, *FRCS, FRCOG*; the staff of Queen Charlotte's & Chelsea Women's Hospital; Docteur Lionel Yvenou, *CES Cardiologue*; Penny Doody, Brian Busby, Françoise Derray, Jack Craine (*Director of the Canadian Broadcasting Corporation, Europe*), Nicholas Hoare, Audrey Copplestone, Trewin Copplestone, Ursula Hoare, Alice Lewes; and, above all, my husband and children for so willingly allowing me the time to write. I am also deeply indebted to my publishers who have, as always, been painstaking, patient and enormously helpful.

'. . . A shout that tore Hell's Concave, and beyond
    Frighted the Reign of Chaos and old Night.'

> John Milton, *Paradise Lost*

'Let me assert my firm belief that the only thing we
have to fear is fear itself.'

> Franklin D. Roosevelt,
> *First Inaugural Address, 4 March 1933*

'Who is the third who walks always beside you?
When I count, there are only you and I together
But when I look ahead up the white road
There is always another one walking beside you.'

> T.S. Eliot, *What the Thunder Said*

# Chapter One

Her first words were, 'I always knew I would die in Paris. I knew as soon as I came here.'

'But you're not dead,' the doctor had replied. 'You're alive and you're going to be fine.'

A few minutes earlier she had been floating in space. Everything had been clear, blue emptiness. There was nothing. Just space: empty and clear, like a summer's day.

She was hot and terribly thirsty. She wanted to be cool like the blue nothingness all around her.

She knew that if she could just float a little further away, further out, she would be cool at last. She wanted to float away. Away from what? As far as the eye could see, there was nothing – just endless, eternal, vast, blue nothing.

Then she saw it. In the distance, thousands – possibly millions – of miles away: a tiny sphere, also blue, but darker and solid. She studied it with interest. What was it? She knew it had been important, but she did not know why. It was called 'the Earth'. She knew that much. But what was it? Why had it been important? She had no idea. It seemed ludicrous that this tiny, infinitely distant sphere, so many millions of miles away, should ever have mattered.

One thing she did know, though, was that she must get further away from it if she was ever to stop being so hot.

Then she felt her cheeks being slapped, and she heard the man's voice.

'Open your eyes!' he was shouting in French. 'Come on, wake up! Make an effort, *nom de Dieu!*'

11

Suddenly she remembered mimosa: the smell of mimosa; the Mediterranean and the sound of the sea. She wanted to see the sea and smell mimosa. She was being dragged back.

Shout. Slap. Shout. Slap. Why did he have to shout? He sounded furious. She tried to concentrate, to understand the words.

'My nurses have been with you day and night!' he yelled. 'Day and night! They have been up all night with you ever since you arrived! Why should they stay up with you, if you won't help? You've got to make an effort. No-one can save you, if you don't make an effort. You've got to do it yourself. You've got to try. Come on, open your eyes!'

The smell of mimosa was very strong. She wanted to see it and the sun on the sea, so she opened her eyes.

'*Enfin!*' said a female voice.

The man was still slapping her face.

'Pull yourself together!' he shouted. 'You've got to pull yourself together. We can't do it for you.'

She looked at him, surprised, hurt. Who was he? Then she saw the mimosa in a vase by her bed. Where was she? *Who*, if it came to that, was she? She had no idea. She looked at the bunch of mimosa and was disappointed. It wasn't growing, blowing, bending in the wind. And there was no sea. It wasn't sunny. There was no beach, no sound of water. It wasn't blue any more. It was all white. Lots of white. Lots of people in white. And this man bending over her, shouting and slapping her face.

She was terribly thirsty. She wished they would bring her some water. She brought her eyes back to the man who had finally stopped hitting her. His face was very close.

'I'm sorry,' he said. 'I had to do it. You must try. No, don't close your eyes again. Can't you understand? If you don't want to live, we can't save you. You must understand that. If you don't want to live, there is nothing we can do to save you. We've all been up for

12

days and nights. Ever since you arrived here. It is not fair on my nurses. Why should they stay up, night after night, if you won't help yourself? Think of them for a moment.'

She turned her head slightly and saw tubes coming out of her arms. Bottles and tubes hooked up to stands on wheels. Both arms. Blood in one tube, clear liquid in the other. Blood and water. Water and wine.

'That's glucose,' said the man, as he saw her looking at the colourless liquid. 'You needed food.'

Gradually, things took shape and regained their names. He was a doctor, she realized. She must be in a hospital. She could not remember anything, any people. Not her mother, not her father. No-one.

She was tired. Tired and sad. She had so nearly gone far enough away. She mourned the loss of that immense blue space and the coolness she had so nearly reached.

'I am going to give you an injection,' the doctor said.

She awoke to the smell of coffee. A day later? Several days later? The smell was delicious. Two nurses propped her up and helped her sip from an enormous bowl of *café au lait*. It was the most exquisite thing she had ever tasted. She would remember the smell and the taste of that bowl of milky coffee as long as she lived. She would seek it wherever she went. She would chase it for the rest of her life, but it would always elude her. It would never seem as perfect again.

That afternoon they removed the screen from around her bed, and she was able to see the other people in the ward. Nothing but old ladies, all very frail and very ill. From time to time someone died, and then they were wheeled past her covered in a sheet as if to shroud the fact that they were dead. It gave her the creeps.

There was an empty coffin standing at the foot of her bed. She found it sinister – sinister and frightening. It made her feel gloomy. Eventually she told a nurse that

13

she didn't like all the dying. She didn't like seeing dead bodies being wheeled past her under sheets.

'You were dying when you came here,' the nurse replied, 'so we put you in the same ward as the others who were dying. You're better off here. It's quieter.'

'Well, I hate that thing,' she said, pointing at the coffin. She didn't know what it was called in French.

The nurse looked surprised. 'Does it bother you?' she asked, and then, seeing her eyes, 'Well, we can easily get rid of it,' and she wheeled it out of sight behind a screen.

Another day went by. She was still being given blood transfusions for several hours a day. They made her feel wonderful: sleepy, floating; a drifting kind of life slipping into her veins. But they had removed the drip. They let her sip soup in the evenings, and her *café au lait* in the mornings – that was always the best moment of the day – and they gave her a glass of red wine with her soup. ('Good for the red corpuscles,' the nurses told her, laughing at her astonishment. 'It's full of iron and it's good for the morale. The doctor said you were to have a glass each evening.')

She fell in love with red wine during those long, summer evenings, just as she had done with their milky coffee. She felt it had become, quite literally, her life's blood, and that without it she would not survive.

Shortly after she had regained consciousness, the doctor, on his rounds, asked, 'Do you mind if I sit on your bed for a moment?'

The nurses wheeled back the screen which had just been removed, and the doctor sat down. 'How are you feeling now?' he enquired.

'OK.'

'Well, I'm glad you've got your voice back, anyway. I'm sorry to bother you, but I'm afraid I must ask you a few questions. You've been here for four days, you see,

14

and we don't know who you are. We don't know what happened. Can you tell me anything?'

'I think I had a nosebleed,' she said.

'Your nose was certainly bleeding badly, but there was more to it than that. You were bleeding internally, from your stomach.'

'I had a nosebleed,' she repeated.

'You couldn't have lost that much blood from a nosebleed.'

She did not reply.

'I'm really sorry to have to ask you these questions,' he said after a while. 'I hoped that you were feeling well enough to talk.' He paused, but still she said nothing. 'We must contact your family. We must let them know you are here. Can you tell me where I can get in touch with them?'

She thought for a moment.

'I don't know. I think they might be in Canada. Or in the States. I'm not sure.' She tried to conjure up some image of family, but it remained elusive. She couldn't see any faces in her mind.

'You were within minutes of dying when you arrived here,' the doctor said, watching her intently. 'You had lost a lot of blood. Don't you remember? You found it almost impossible to breathe because of the blood pouring from your nose and mouth.'

'I do remember, yes. They wouldn't let me put my arms above my head. I wanted to lie with my arms above my head, but they wouldn't let me.'

'Do you remember the ambulance?'

'Yes. They tried to suffocate me. They kept holding things over my nose and mouth. I thought I was going to suffocate.'

'They were trying to stem the flow of blood. They were giving you transfusions at the same time. Don't you remember?'

'No . . . No, I don't remember that.'

'You were in the last stages of exhaustion when you arrived. You must have been physically exhausted

15

before you started haemorrhaging. Do you know why you were so tired?'

'I can't remember.'

'Yet you can remember some things. You could be suffering from partial amnesia, but I am not sure if that is the case. Why is it that you can remember some things and not others, do you think? Is it that you don't want to remember the rest?'

She remained silent.

'I'm trying to help,' he said. Then, after a long pause, 'You talked a lot about mimosa.'

'There was mimosa by my bed. It's in the vase, over there. It has a very strong smell.'

'But you like the smell. You kept asking for mimosa. One of the nurses bought it for you because you talked about it so much.'

'I do like the smell, yes. It reminds me of the South of France. It's one of those smells – like eucalyptus, and basil – that I connect with the Midi.'

'Have you lived in the South of France? Is that where you live?'

She thought for some time before answering.

'I must have lived there, I suppose, but I think it must have been when I was a child. I loved it. I know that. I still love it.' She turned her head away and closed her eyes. 'But I don't think I live there any more,' she said eventually. 'I don't know where I live.'

'It seems likely that you live in Paris now, wouldn't you say? We found you here, after all, and you can't have travelled far in the state you were in. It must have happened here, whatever it was that happened.'

'I don't think I live here. I don't know Paris – at least, I don't think I do. Where did you find me?'

'In front of the gare St Lazare. We were telephoned by somebody who saw you collapse in the street. The police called us, too. The ambulance picked you up off the pavement outside the station.'

'Do you think I was hit by a car?'

16

'No. You were coming out of the metro or the station, according to all the people who saw you.'

'I remember now. All those people crowding around and staring at me. I couldn't breathe.'

'Where had you come from? Had you come into Paris from somewhere else? Had you been on a train or on the *métro*? You must remember, surely.'

'*Je ne puis pas*,' she said with a sigh.

He laughed. '"*Peux*",' he corrected her. '"*Je ne peux pas*". Your French is very sweet, very charming, but not very fluent. I don't think you live in France, or you can't have lived here long. How old do you think you are? Sixteen? Seventeen?'

'Sixteen,' she replied, without hesitation. 'I'm sixteen.'

'When's your birthday?'

'The twenty-ninth of June.'

'So you have only just had it?'

'Have I?'

'Come, come. You remember your birthday, I'm sure. Where did you celebrate it?'

'I'm not sure. In Canada, I think.'

'Why Canada? Do you live there?'

'I don't know.'

'You have mentioned Canada before. You said your parents might be there. Are you Canadian?'

'I don't know.'

'How can you be sure of your age and your birthday, if you don't know who you are or where you come from?'

'I don't know.'

'Stop repeating "I don't know" all the time. Try and help. *Think*. Did something frighten you? Did *someone* frighten you?'

She stared at him but said nothing.

'You were very badly bruised,' he said. 'Cut and bruised. You know that, don't you? You've still got the marks. You must feel them. They hurt, don't they? They hurt a lot. I know they do. *Allons, mademoiselle.*

17

Remember, I'm a doctor. Nothing is going to shock me. Were you hit in the stomach?' He waited patiently. 'Try telling me in English, if you prefer. It might be easier. I can understand enough to get the gist of it, if you want to tell me what happened in English.'

He waited in silence for quite some time, but the girl simply lowered her eyes. He watched her hands pulling and twitching at the edges of the sheet.

'What happened?' he asked her again.

She became agitated. 'I had a nosebleed,' she said in English. 'I told you, I had a nosebleed,' and she burst into tears.

The doctor leaned towards her and put his hand gently on her arm. He held it reassuringly until she stopped crying.

'I'm sorry,' he said. 'I didn't mean to upset you. I want to help. Who was he? We might be able to do something about it, if you could tell us what happened.'

Seeing that she was not going to reply, he sighed and rose to his feet. 'If you remember who your parents are, or where they are, please let me know. We should like to get in touch with them.' She was still fiddling with the edge of her sheet, her head bent, her eyes hidden. He put his hand on her head for a moment. 'I'm sorry. You had no papers with you, you see. No handbag. Nothing. So we don't know anything about you.'

He went to the Matron's office and flicked through the pages of the telephone directory. Finding the Canadian Embassy's number, he sat down and dialled.

'I think we may have one of your citizens here. She very nearly died on us. She has suffered some kind of attack. It looks like attempted rape – unsuccessful – and there are marks on her neck, as if someone tried to strangle her. She's very ill, and we must find her family . . . No, not a paper on her. Not a thing in her pockets, no handbag, no keys, not even a bus ticket . . .

'She says she doesn't remember, although I suspect

she remembers rather more than she is prepared to admit. She's clearly suffering from partial amnesia, however. She hasn't a clue who she is or who her parents are. That's genuine, I'm pretty sure . . . Yes . . . Yes, perhaps . . . It had better be a woman, though . . . English Canadian. She's clearly not French . . .

'About five foot six; fair-skinned, fair-haired, grey eyes . . . No . . . Yes . . . Long hair; slight build; weighs about fifty-one kilos, I should say . . . Yes . . . She says she's sixteen. She seems quite sure about that. I would have said sixteen or seventeen, so I should think that's correct. She seems certain that her birthday is the twenty-ninth of June. I don't think she's been in the country long, although I may be mistaken. It's possible she came to Paris from the South of France – she appears to know the South – but she clearly cannot have just stepped off the train or she would have been at the gare de Lyon rather than the gare St Lazare . . .'

He listened to the official on the other end of the telephone. Suddenly, impatiently, he interrupted the man.

'Obviously! We didn't need to inform them, in any case. They were on the scene before the ambulance arrived. They've been unable to come up with anything. They've done the rounds – they've put out radio calls, they've contacted the Alliance Française, the Berlitz, the Sorbonne, the various institutes . . . Nothing so far. No-one missing from any of them . . . Fine . . . Let me know . . . I'd leave it for a couple of days . . . Seriously . . . She's fragile at the moment . . . No, I really cannot allow that. Not at the moment, anyway. I'll tell you when I think she's strong enough . . .'

While they were discussing her, Sally lay staring at the ceiling. She could remember the car – not the make, not the number, but its general appearance – and she could remember the voice; but she could not remember his face.

# Chapter Two

They found out who she was the following day when the people with whom Sally had been staying returned from Burgundy to find her missing, and called the police. It took a further thirty-six hours to trace her parents who were travelling in the States at the time. They had set off from Montreal eleven days earlier and had spent a night in New England before embarking on a leisurely drive across the country, heading slowly in the direction of the west coast.

They had reached the Napa Valley when they were finally informed of their daughter's plight. She had been in hospital for a week by then. The shock was such that her mother never truly recovered from it.

In retrospect, Mrs Hamilton did not know which was worse: being obliged to waste precious time changing planes in New York while her daughter fought for her life on the other side of the Atlantic, or walking into the hospital ward to find that it took Sally a moment or two to recognize her.

Mr and Mrs Hamilton stared at their daughter as she lay, ashen, in her hospital bed, surrounded by an alarming array of medical equipment and with tubes attached to both arms.

'Why is she still having blood transfusions?' Mr Hamilton demanded of the embassy official who had met them at the airport and was acting as their interpreter. 'Ask the doctor. I want to know. She can't have lost that much blood. And what's that other tube for? What's in that other tube?'

'Brock,' wailed his wife, 'we've got to get her out of here. We don't know anything about the blood they're giving her. It may be Senegalese, or anything. I want them to stop giving it to her. The French don't know anything about medicine! For heaven's sake, get her out of here!'

Mrs Hamilton clung to her husband for a second, then sat down and burst into tears.

For nearly an hour the embassy official, editing a little as he went, translated their questions and the doctor's replies.

'I know you are both upset,' he interjected at one point, 'but this is an excellent hospital. I don't know if you realize. She could easily have died. She was unconscious for days, you know. They didn't think they had a hope of saving her – and now look at her. They've worked incredibly hard . . . OK, so she's still having transfusions . . . That other stuff? Yes, it's a coagulant of some sort, he says; her blood isn't clotting properly, apparently . . . Do be reasonable, sir. They can't stop the transfusions . . . Dr Lamotte has already explained that to you, sir. She's taking a long time to build up her own blood. As I understand it, they are trying to increase her haemoglobin – I guess you could say it's a sort of exaggerated anaemia . . . Yeah, well, I'm no doctor either but that's what he's saying . . . OK, ring the American Hospital if you like. You can do it from here. Dr Lamotte says he'd be happy to explain to them and have them give you their view.'

'OK, OK!' shouted Mr Hamilton, half an hour later. 'If the American Hospital says it's the right treatment, I guess I have to go along with that. I'm not happy about it, though. I'd like to move her over there as soon as possible.'

'The doctor says she won't be fit to move for some time. Not for a couple of weeks, at least. He won't let her be moved until he thinks she's well enough. He's adamant . . . I'm sure he's right, sir. He says it would be extremely risky at the moment . . . What? No. He says he hasn't the faintest idea whether the donors were black or white! He says it's irrelevant. The blood group is all that matters. There have been numerous donors, in any case. They've had to give her a lot of blood since she arrived.'

The official decided not to translate what the doctor said next, only continuing when the exasperated Dr Lamotte had calmed down.

'He is pointing out that your daughter happens to have the rarest blood group – probably only about four per cent of the world's Caucasian population have it, apparently, so it's difficult to obtain sufficient quantities for a case like this. He wants you to know that they may have to give her the O group if they run out of her own type ... Yes, it can be given to anyone – provided it's the same rhesus, of course. They're not keen on doing it, particularly not with women, but he wants you to understand that it may be necessary—'

Mr Hamilton interrupted, but was stopped by the embassy official, who put a hand on his arm.

'The doctor wants us to continue this discussion elsewhere. He says you're upsetting your daughter.'

'Come on, Brock, honey. Let's talk about it downstairs,' said Mrs Hamilton, who had been weeping quietly as she held her daughter's hand.

'I want to know how all this happened!' bellowed Mr Hamilton. 'I want to be allowed to speak to my daughter without all you guys hanging around! Will you please leave us? Go on, Louise! You too. I want you all out of here.'

Mrs Hamilton did not move. She continued to weep silently, dabbing at her eyes with a sodden handkerchief.

Sally wished she would stop it. 'Please don't cry, Mum,' she whispered. 'I'm OK now. I'm fine. They've been great. Really kind. They're looking after me fine.'

'I feel terrible, honey,' Mrs Hamilton sobbed. 'I knew we shouldn't have let you come here. I always told you it was a mistake, didn't I?' She turned to her husband. 'Your father was against it, too, weren't you Brock? We should have sent you to Switzerland. I knew we shouldn't have allowed you to come here.'

Sally knew it was her fault. She had insisted on coming to Paris. She didn't want to ruin what French she knew by acquiring a Swiss accent, she had told them, and anyway she wanted to see Paris. She hadn't been in the least interested in going to Switzerland. It was undoubtedly her fault.

At least, she thought, her mother had the tact not to ask her what had happened, unlike her father who was determined to know the truth.

'Come on, Sally,' he insisted. 'What the hell happened? It was a guy, wasn't it? How did you meet him? Was he French? What was his name? Tell us who it was . . . Oh, for Christ's sake, honey, you know it was more than a nosebleed. The doctor says you'd been badly beaten up. You were covered in bruises and cuts, you had marks on your throat, you were haemorrhaging from your stomach . . . Jesus, Sally, be rational! I'm going to get that goddam bastard if it kills me. Did he try and rape you? Is that what happened? Hell's bells, you must remember something!'

The doctor intervened at this point, taking Sally's father by the arm and pulling him towards the door.

'You're upsetting her. Please leave her now. She needs to sleep. She'll remember in time, probably . . .' He led Mr Hamilton, protesting, from the ward.

But Brock Hamilton was not to be deflected. 'She was raped, wasn't she? You're trying to hide it from me. She was raped. I know she was.'

'No,' replied the doctor. 'No. Somebody tried to rape her, but they didn't succeed. I suspect that if they'd succeeded they might well have killed her, but they didn't succeed, I do assure you. The medical evidence is perfectly clear . . . It's impossible, Mr Hamilton. She's still a virgin.'

## Chapter Three

No-one seeing Montreal for the first time today could guess that it was once a city of great fascination and charm. Years of bad planning, incompetence and rampant corruption have combined with the ever-complicated and increasingly unhappy political situation to strip it of everything that made it unique. Its architecture has been savaged, its optimism eroded, its energy stifled and its character destroyed. Gone are many of the historic and spectacular mansions of the once aptly-named 'Golden Square Mile' (destroyed – in at least one case, illegally – to make room for freeways, office towers and apartment blocks without charm). Those that remain have been gutted and turned into 'condominiums', or wings of hospitals, or university faculties; or, at best, have preserved parts of their original interiors and become little-frequented (more often deathly and deserted) private clubs. Major streets have been hacked to pieces, renamed and rebuilt; boulevards ploughed through scores of old buildings; and the most beautiful street in the city, once so elegant and enchanting, is the site of heaps of rubble, broken buildings, gutted churches and high-rise towers. The main thoroughfares are squalid, the shops littered with rubbish for tourists, and the great trees which graced the sidewalks died of elm disease long ago.

It is true that the old French areas, always another world, have succeeded in keeping their architecture largely intact; true, too, that in odd instances a group of magnificent modern buildings has changed the face of a previously uninteresting street; but the heart has gone out of the place, the centre is a wasteland;

business has deserted the province and all money has fled. As a result of stupidity, intolerance, cultural blackmail, fear and greed, this once gracious city now lies in ruins in the stretch of water where the Ottawa and Saint Lawrence rivers meet.

The Montreal of Sally's childhood, however, was not the Montreal of today. As a result of the linguistic and religious differences, a superficially workable (and, from the English point of view, acceptable) form of apartheid reigned. Under the surface, of course, the feud between the two races never ceased; but Sally, like most of the English community, was hardly aware of the French. They spoke a different language; they went to their own schools and universities; they followed another religion (a highly suspect and primitive one, Sally was always told, full of corruption and ignorance, and drunken priests who bled their flocks financially in order to line the pockets of their own soutanes); and they lived in areas of the city where no anglophone set foot. The only French-speaking people Sally ever encountered were janitors, taxi-drivers, street cleaners and the like. She did not meet, or even know of, the old-established French families; their senators, professors and judges lived in a different world from hers.

It was a prosperous town in Sally's childhood – romantic and full of life; and its unique charm was the result of those same cultural and linguistic differences that have since torn it apart. Born of three very different cultures, it gave every appearance of thriving on a combination of old money, New World energy, solid banking, business enterprise, Scottish intransigence, Presbyterian probity and the colossal power of the Catholic Church.

Here, England (or, more accurately, Scotland), France and North America were wed in a triangular marriage which combined the personalities and architecture of all three. A few seventeenth- and eighteenth-century buildings (remarkably similar to their equivalents of the same period in provincial north-west France) nestled, unnoticed until the sixties, among shops and houses, convents and churches of almost every other known style.

The mansard roofs of the Second Empire, the ornate copper roofs of the Baroque Revival, Tuscan pilasters and Doric columns were all common in Montreal. Mile upon mile of the vernacular architecture with its elaborate cornices, art-nouveau glass, many balconies and tangled mass of outdoor staircases (wrought iron, often twisted, and unique to Montreal) gave way in the English sector to Queen Anne gables, neo-Georgian mansions, Second-Empire terraces and nineteenth-century absurdities with castellated turrets and witches' towers.

Streets of terraced, greystone houses stood with quiet dignity alongside the highly ostentatious edifices of the flamboyant, Victorian Eclectic style. These latter, whose wildly ornate façades and impossible mixture of styles were created solely as a display of wealth by the newly rich of the late nineteenth century, never succeeded in overpowering the discreet elegance of the flat-fronted houses tucked away in the neighbouring crescents and squares.

It was a city where *beaux-arts* balconies, stone balustrades and coupled columns with angular capitals lived happily beside Renaissance windows, Gothic Revival buttresses, or the Palladian architecture so much loved by the Scots (who, for most of the nineteenth century, were the local élite). In an astonishingly successful diversity of styles, Romanesque compound arches and squat columns rubbed shoulders with the triangular pediments, colonnades and porticos of ancient Greece and Rome; the neo-classic was shown to advantage against the early skyscrapers, and the scrolls and obelisks of the Baroque Revival seemed as natural among the cartouche of the Second Empire as among the projecting cornices of the Chicago School.

Catholic convents of vast proportions, and religious edifices of all kinds were as much a part of the landscape as the Sun Life building (once the tallest and largest building in the British Empire, where the gold reserves of the British government were housed during the Second World War); and the skyscrapers were as integral to the city as the views across the Saint Lawrence River, or the mountain after which the town was named.

It was an island city whose cheerful cafés and inexpensive bistros snuggled between expensive restaurants, private art galleries and smart boutiques; and where the streets were steep, the views spectacular and the temperatures (both hot and cold) extreme.

Before the Saint Lawrence Seaway was opened, a hush fell on the place in winter: the river was silent, the air dry and icy; and on cloudless days the sun glittered out of an empty blue sky.

In spring, after months of silence, the stillness was broken as ships once again hooted on the river, and ocean liners bravely set off through melting ice to sail a thousand miles to the open sea.

In summer, almost all who could afford to do so deserted the city; but there were always some, even among the rich, who through choice or obligation remained. Those who stayed in town during the hottest months stayed indoors as much as possible; but in the early summer and again in autumn, when the temperatures were bearable, expensively dressed women sat in their gardens, or on apartment balconies, chatting among themselves to the sound of ice clinking against glass; while, in another part of town, old men sat dozing fitfully in rocking-chairs on verandas overlooking unfashionable, picturesque streets.

In the fall, gold turned to copper, pink to orange and then to red; while the mountain became wine-coloured and the sky a deeper blue. Energy returned. Nuns, clutching their breviaries, formed crocodiles and paced about their convent grounds; Franciscan friars with brown, hooded robes and belts of rope put on their sandals and did much the same. Black-robed priests flitted about their business and the children returned to school. Café tables spilled out on to sidewalks, the shops were busy, the restaurants full. Men fell out of their offices and made for the nearest bars; mothers pushed prams along tree-lined streets while children played hopscotch on the sidewalks to the chimes of the angelus bells.

It was a city of many contrasts where, high up the mountain, the rich in monstrous mansions sat while, down below, huge banks that looked like Roman temples and Catholic churches the size of cathedrals glared at each other in ancient rivalry across the leafy squares.

It was to this unusual and haunting city, at the height of the summer, that Sally returned – still in shock – from Paris in 1962. Although pleased to be home, she now viewed the place (as she did the whole world) with a permanently altered and frightened eye.

She was able, for a time, to use the heat as an excuse never to go out; but her parents soon realized that it was not just the temperature in the streets which kept her at home. Though they had not fully appreciated the terror she felt at leaving her hospital-cocoon, it was clear to both of them that the mere thought of the world outside made her feel insecure.

Louise, in particular, was worried. She thought her daughter had become too dependent on her Paris doctor. She had watched her saying goodbye to him and was shocked to see that Sally had tears in her eyes. The doctor had noticed, too, Louise thought, as she watched him put his hand on Sally's shoulder and walk with her to the door. Already unhappy about the bond of affection that she sensed had developed between the two, Louise's misgivings increased when the doctor made what sounded like an impassioned plea to her daughter in French.

What the doctor had actually said to Sally was, 'You must forget what has happened. You must force yourself not to think about it any more. I mean it. It's over and it won't happen again.' He turned her so that she was facing him and looked her firmly in the eye, insisting, 'Whatever it was that happened, you must put it out of your mind. If you do not, believe me, you will destroy your whole life.'

In the taxi, on the way to the airport, Louise asked her daughter to translate what the doctor had said, but Sally shrugged her shoulders, muttering impatiently, 'He didn't say anything – just the usual sort of things people say.'

'You seem to have grown rather fond of him,' her mother was unwise enough to remark.

Sally glared at her. 'I expect you'd feel fond of him if he'd saved your life,' she snapped.

The Hamiltons never found out what had happened to their daughter. They questioned her endlessly once they were back in Montreal, but they soon discovered that Sally was not prepared to let anybody delve. They tried bringing up the subject casually; once or twice they asked her to recount her dreams; they took her to doctors and analysts, but it was all to no avail.

Sally, from time to time, in a nightmarish way, remembered things about which she never spoke. She considered the whole episode private and of no concern to anyone else. In any case, she was unconvinced that her muddled memories of that vague and terrifying incident were not simply something she had dreamt up while she was on the point of dying. (She had hallucinated, after all, about cool, blue, infinite space so why imagine she had not dreamt up all her other outlandish memories?) As if to chide herself for having an overactive imagination, she did her best to convince herself that she had invented the whole thing.

As time went by, the Hamiltons gave up asking

questions and gradually slipped into a tacit agreement to go along with Sally's story that she had simply had a bad nosebleed and had lost so much blood she had nearly died. In order to reassure themselves, her parents turned the memory into a joke, reminding Sally with heavy humour that her veins were no doubt running with the blood of French black Africa.

'Worse, probably,' her father used to say in an attempt to sound light-hearted. 'I expect you're full of some damned Arab's blood. You're just an Arab, honey. That's what you are.' He pronounced the word 'Eyrab', which Sally interpreted as a deliberate attempt to make her feel dirty.

'Why can't he leave me alone?' she demanded of her mother one night, rushing into the kitchen and bursting into tears.

'Oh, come on, honey! It was a joke. You know that.'

'Well, it's a lousy joke! It isn't remotely funny and it's in atrocious taste. What's wrong with Arabs, anyway, and why the hell should anyone care whose blood it is, as long as it works?'

'Come on, sweetheart, be reasonable. Your father is worried about you and his way of hiding it is to make light-hearted cracks. You shouldn't take it so seriously.'

'He thinks I'm dirty, doesn't he? I know that's what he thinks.'

'He doesn't think anything of the sort. Why would anyone think you're dirty?'

She *was* dirty, though, and she knew it. She was an outcast; she felt contaminated, and she was convinced it was her fault. She must have done something to provoke it. She must have asked for it somehow. She despised herself for the fact that it had happened, and it left her terrified of men.

# Chapter Four

Nevertheless, she made slow progress. She finished school, went through university, did a secretarial course and found herself a job; but she was crippled in her daily life by deep, residual fears. She was unable to take a taxi because of her overwhelming terror of finding herself trapped in a car on her own with a man. She could not walk normally if there was anyone behind her; she always turned to see who it was, then either crossed the street or stood back to let the person pass. She walked behind people, but she never walked in front of them (and that, living in a city was quite a feat, as she was well aware). She spent a lot of time with her back to walls, or standing in doorways pretending to look for something in her bag, or emptying an imaginary stone from her shoe in order to allow some harmless pedestrian to pass her. She could not bear to leave her back exposed. In restaurants she always sat against the wall, never with her back to the open room.

Eventually she realized she was going to have to learn to drive if she was ever to feel safe moving around town on her own. She bullied her mother into giving her lessons, then wheedled her father into persuading the examiner to allow him to come in the car with them while she took her test.

Her father tried to persuade her to join his law firm as soon as she started looking for a job but, to his disappointment, Sally refused and chose instead to work for a charity concerned with the protection of battered wives. She worked in an office peopled by women. She felt safe there and it was a job that interested her, but it did nothing to lessen her fear of men.

'Why don't you go and work for your father?' Louise demanded at regular intervals, horrified by Sally's choice of job. 'You'd be much better paid and you'd have decent prospects – there will never be any hope of advancement with that impecunious charity of yours.'

'For heaven's sake, Mum, what would I do with myself in Dad's firm?'

'You studied law, didn't you? So why don't you use it? Why spend your days with all those depressing cases? It's not good for you. You're not cut out for that sort of work.'

'If I went to McEwan & Hamilton, I'd be taken on as a secretary. I wouldn't be practising law.'

'Only at the beginning, while you learnt the ropes. Your father explained all that to you. You'd soon be given something more rewarding to do.'

'But I don't want to go there. I don't want to practise law. I only did it at McGill to please you both – because you made such a fuss about it. It isn't what I want to do at all.'

'Honey, listen to me—'

'No, I won't! You don't give a damn about other people, do you? You and Dad, you're both the same. You don't even want to know what's going on in this horrible world.'

'That's unfair, Sally. Your father wouldn't have taken up the law if he didn't care about other people – and you could help him. You'd be good at it.'

'I wouldn't, because I'm not interested in company law. I'm not interested in helping the rich. Can't you understand? There are women out there being beaten up by madmen! There are women with no homes and no money, who have children to bring up. Those are the people I want to help. I'm going to use what law I learnt for that.'

Sally tried to blot out her memories, but she could not cure herself of guilt and fear. She knew, in a sense, that it was not her fault, yet she still felt herself to be to blame. She told herself that the guy must have been some sort of weirdo and tried to convince herself that not all men were necessarily the same (but lots of them were, she was prepared to bet; he was still loose, the weirdo, somewhere – and plenty of others like him, no doubt). She knew, in her heart of hearts, that she'd done nothing to provoke it – she'd never seen him in her life before, for God's sake – yet she continued to feel, irrationally, that she must somehow have been to blame.

Entirely to blame, in fact: she must have looked easy prey. She must have looked scared, innocent, unable to defend herself. (She had been all those things. She was all of those things still.) She must have given out vulnerable, easy-victim vibes. She still did, she knew. Peculiar and unpleasant little incidents were forever befalling her. Unsavoury creatures of the masculine sex seemed to ooze to life from between the cracks in the sidewalks wherever she set foot. Travelling on the *métro*, visiting apartments to let, walking around supermarkets, men were always making lewd remarks or touching her, squeezing her. Total strangers – always complete strangers. Why? It was her fault. She knew it was her fault. It was something to do with *her*.

The odd thing was that, try as she might, she could *not* remember his face. She had a clear memory of someone in his mid to late twenties – he had seemed old to her – but she could not remember what he looked like.

Well, that wasn't quite true . . . She could remember his size, his build, the smoothness of his fair skin, and the fact that he was French. She remembered that he had lightish hair – not fair exactly, but lighter than light brown – and that it was thick and straight and very well cut. He was faceless, though. She could not fill in the face.

It was his voice that she remembered best; not his voice when he approached her in the café and asked

33

her if she was German, French, Swedish; but his voice later when he whispered terribly gently and sweetly, *'On fait l'amour un peu . . . mais, si, tu verras, on va faire l'amour . . .'*

She couldn't remember his voice in the car, although she remembered what he had said. She had tried to wind down the window to call for help only to discover that there was no handle with which to wind it down. They were driving far too fast for her to risk throwing herself out – in any case, she would have been mangled beneath the wheels of the other cars – so she thumped on the window and shouted, hoping to attract someone's attention.

She thumped and shouted, but he had turned on his car radio. Turning it up until it was blaring, full volume, he said, 'You can make as much noise as you like. No-one will hear you.'

She remembered the place de la Concorde. It was about the only place she was able to recognize. She did not know Paris at all. She had only been there a few days. They were driving incredibly fast, she remembered; but then so were all the other cars. They streamed across the place de la Concorde at high speed, swirling round the traffic cop who was standing in the middle on one of those pedestals, waving his arms around absurdly and blowing shrilly on a whistle. Yes, she could remember that traffic cop. He looked ridiculous in that stupid little round hat – a sort of navy pillbox – and a navy cape. It was the cape that made him look so idiotic. It was very short; and he was flinging it about and waving his *bâton* like some mad conductor directing a symphony.

She had done her utmost to attract his attention, banging as hard as she could on the window and waving and shouting. He looked so damned pleased with himself, she remembered. Showing off to a world that normally ignored him, he noticed her with pleasure as she flashed by in the car. Used to the complete indifference of the Parisian drivers, he could

34

not resist giving her a self-satisfied smile. Returning her wave with a great sweep of the arm, he flung his cape over his shoulder and raised his *bâton* in a magnificent gesture of recognition at her appreciation of his importance.

She knew, then, that it was hopeless. Nobody was going to save her. They hadn't helped her in the café when she was so obviously being pestered. They must have seen that she didn't like it. She hadn't even dared stay to finish her coffee. She had simply left the money and run. Surely they must have seen him running after her? You'd have thought that someone might have helped. She'd run and run until she was completely exhausted but nobody lifted a finger, not even when she fell.

She couldn't remember how she had got into the car. She still had complete blanks here and there. She vaguely remembered picking herself up and running again, then trying to squeeze between a row of parked cars. She remembered that bit because she thought she had lost him at that point. The cars were parked in a line, side by side, and she'd tried to squeeze between two of them but he had flung open the door of one of the cars so that she was blocked between it and the next.

Did he simply steal a car? It couldn't have been his, surely? That would have been too coincidental. Maybe she had made it all up. She must have done. It couldn't possibly have been like she remembered it. And yet she knew she had been in a car with him. Had he hit her on the head? Had he just grabbed her and pulled her in? She had no recollection of that part at all.

Then, another thing: how had she got up all those stairs? She remembered coming *down* the stairs all right. She remembered that bit all too clearly, with her legs like jelly and no idea where she was; but she did not remember going up them. She remembered him stopping his car in a deserted street – God knows what

part of Paris that was – and saying, *'Voilà chez moi!'*
But she didn't remember anything about the building;
she didn't remember the stairs. His room was in the
attic above the fifth floor. She would have had to walk
up six flights of stairs to reach it. She couldn't possibly
have forgotten that, surely? She remembered coming
down them OK. She definitely remembered that.

Had she blotted it out, somehow; or had he simply
knocked her out and carried her up? There was no
image in her mind of walking into the room, of
crossing the floor, of getting on to that bed, whether
pushed there or carried there. Nothing at all between
*'Voilà chez moi!'* and struggling on that single bed and
hanging on desperately to the bar that pegged the
window open. They were in an attic, under the eaves.
The bed was right under the sloping roof, so that she
was able to touch the window-bar just above his head.
It was the only thing she was able to reach, and she
grasped it as hard as she could. It gave her considerable leverage. She would not have been able to
produce anything like the resistance if it hadn't been
for that bar. She hung onto it a lot of the time, pulling
herself up as hard as she could, pushing against him,
trying to force him off her. She bit and scratched and
screamed, too, of course; but none of that seemed to
make much impression on him. It was the bar that had
saved her. She was convinced of that.

The metro. She must have gone on the metro. She
remembered walking, shaking, hardly able to stand
up, and telling herself that if she could find a *métro*
station, she would be able to find her way back to her
lodgings. That was all she could remember. She must
have found a metro and made her way to the gare St
Lazare but she had no memory of it whatever; no
memory of anything until the ambulancemen carrying
her on a stretcher and crowds of people staring down
at her, blocking out the light.

Why had he let her go? She often asked herself that.
They must have struggled on top of that narrow bed

for at least two hours. He had seemed incredibly strong to her; immovable. She had been within seconds of giving up.

It was odd, too, how his mood had changed. Until then his voice had been soft and caressing. Whatever he did to her, no matter how violent, his voice remained gentle. Gentle and terribly sweet. He kept whispering in her ear, softly, sweetly, *'On fait l'amour un peu. Oui, mon amour chéri, on va faire l'amour . . . mais si . . .'*

He never told her to be quiet, or to stop screaming. Nor did he once try to make her stop biting him. She must have hurt him, surely? She had plunged her teeth into his shoulder and hung on as if she were trying to tear off a hunk of his flesh.

From time to time, almost patiently, he pulled her hand away from the window-bar, bending her arm until she thought it would break. As she gasped in pain, her teeth inevitably unclamped from his shoulder and he would then cover her mouth with her own arm which he bent across her face. Lifting himself up, he would lean his entire weight on her, holding her down with his arms while he rammed her stomach and groin with his knee.

At one point he straddled the top part of her body, using his knees to pin down her arms on either side of her head. He was still wearing his trousers (he never took them off). Gripping her throat tightly with one hand, he used his free hand to pull out his penis and brandish it above her face.

Although she had seen her cousins running about naked when they were children, it was the first time she had seen an adult male organ and the sight terrified her. She wasn't sure what she had expected, but she did not expect what she saw. She closed her eyes tightly to avoid watching him masturbate and, all the while, he whispered to her about making love.

She had crossed her legs while he was straddling her in this fashion, taking advantage of the fact that his were occupied kneeling on her arms. She used all her strength to keep her legs crossed after that, in spite of him flaying her with the buckle of his belt, in spite of the beer bottle he smashed against her groin.

She could not bear to think about it any more; but she was still startled at the memory of his sudden change of mood. Just when she had been about to give up he had let out a yell, fallen heavily on her; and then, breathing noisily, had leapt to his feet.

'*Fous le camp!*' he had shouted at her. *Espèce de petite merde! Fous-moi la paix! Fous le camp!*' He pulled her to her feet and threw her towards the door. She fell. Wrenching open the door with unnecessary violence, he dragged her by her torn garments across the floorboards and out to the landing at the top of the stairs. There, shouting, '*Salope!*' he gave one last, almighty heave and kick.

As she rolled down the first flight of steps, she heard the door slam shut above her. Somehow she picked herself up and stumbled down the remaining five flights. She would remember those stairs as long as she lived. She could still hear his voice yelling from the top floor, '*Espèce de petite merde! Fous-moi la paix!*'

# Chapter Five

These memories had not come back all at once. Bits of them suddenly reassembled in her mind, as often as not sparked off by some sound or smell. She could never work out what the connection was, or why a particular noise or odour had provoked another piece of unexpected recall.

As time passed, she became increasingly doubtful about the veracity of it all. Her memory seemed to her to be hopelessly faulty, and so full of gaps that she wondered how reliable the clear parts of her recollections were. She knew she had a vivid imagination, and she wondered whether she hadn't embellished the story in her mind over the years, or whether she hadn't simply invented the whole thing. None the less, however fictitious the memory, and however successfully she buried it or denied it, her behaviour was permanently affected by it.

Insofar as she was able to deal with the masculine sex at all, she felt less threatened by men of her father's age than by men in their twenties and thirties. Even with them, however, she avoided dinners, dances, nightclubs, car drives, trips – anything which involved the dark, the night, being alone with a man, or any possibility of physical contact.

For the first eighteen months after her experience in Paris she turned down all invitations from men; but during the years that followed she slowly gained the courage to accept when friends of her father (men who were, in her mind, substitute fathers and therefore fairly safe) offered to take her out to lunch. As often as not, these lunches included a wife who came along too; and it was then that Sally was happiest for she liked having couples as friends.

Since she did not want to be driven by anyone but herself or another woman, she always insisted, when lunching with a man on his own, on meeting them at the restaurant, just as she always refused the offer of a lift back to work afterwards; but this, in its turn, created another problem, for one of Sally's worst fears was that of entering restaurants, cafés or bars unaccompanied.

The idea of waiting for someone, of having to sit at a table on her own, was a nightmare that haunted her for most of her life and she went out of her way to avoid the possibility of such a situation ever occurring. She developed the habit of arriving very late so that the person inviting her was bound to be there before her. If, for any reason, they were not there, she went away again immediately, sometimes returning later, sometimes not. Frequently she was in such a state of panic as she stood in the entrance, scanning the restaurant, that she failed to notice the person she was looking for and bolted in terror before they could attract her attention. If the other person was late – which happened occasionally – she made sure that she arrived even later the next time; and, as a result of a couple of occasions when she arrived first, developed the habit of telephoning the restaurant to check that the person was there before she set off herself. Once she was assured they had arrived and were waiting for her, she would leave a message to say that she had been held up, but that she was on her way and would be there in no time.

As a result of this elaborate self-defence system, Sally soon became known as someone who was totally incapable of being on time. (In later years this habit of hers was to become so automatic that she no longer thought about the reasons for it. By the time she was thirty, she was routinely late for everything, whether or not she was accompanied by her husband and whether or not there was any conceivable need to be late. By then, to the constant irritation of her friends, she had genuinely become someone who was incapable of being punctual.)

By the time she was twenty-five, Sally was profoundly distressed about her psychological disabilities. In many ways, she seemed surprisingly well-balanced. She was content with her life; she had plenty of friends; she had an interesting and rewarding job; she loved her parents. She also loved her independence, earning her own living, having her own apartment, leading her own life. She was pretty – more than just pretty. She was comic, generous, self-sufficient, popular. Not only did she not mind living on her own: she liked it. Her only serious problem was one to which she could not admit.

In Canada, as in many places, it was unusual for a girl of her age not to have, or have ever had, any sexual relations – particularly in the sixties, when the fashion was promiscuity. Sally was aware of this, and felt ashamed of the fact that she was, as she saw it, completely abnormal. She wanted to be desired. She wanted to be loved. She wanted to be like everyone else.

Through shame and embarrassment, she took to lying to her girlfriends. She invented boyfriends about whom to giggle and gossip whenever they were discussing their sexual adventures. She always made a great mystery of them, saying that she could not tell anyone who they were, so that her friends assumed that she was having affairs with married men. Since she was only ever seen with the opposite sex when she was lunching with one of her father's friends, they had every reason to think of her as someone who only liked older men.

Montreal society has always been kind to its young, with the older generations keeping a kindly eye on the children of their friends, and offering help and advice when needed, cocktails or lunch when nothing more is required. Thus, Sally's parents saw nothing odd about their daughter having lunch with their friends; and the latter invited Sally more out of kindness than anything else, although they were delighted to have the company of a pretty and intelligent girl.

Sally felt safe with her parents' friends, and when any men from this group paid her compliments she knew they were simply being kind. (Had a younger man told her that she was looking pretty, or that her new hairstyle became her, or that they liked the dress she was wearing, she would have been paralysed with fear.)

The day inevitably came, however, when one of the Hamiltons' acquaintances misinterpreted the fact that Sally had agreed to lunch with him for the third time in two weeks, and so he turned up unexpectedly at her apartment one evening. Sally was taken aback when she opened the door and found him standing outside.

Before she had time to react, he walked in, saying breezily, 'Hi! I thought I'd invite myself in for a drink.'

'Well, I'm supposed to be working,' Sally replied nervously. 'I have to write up quite a complicated case history and have it all typed and ready by first thing tomorrow morning . . .' But before she had finished speaking, to her horror, he had put his arms around her and was holding her tight.

'You're very beautiful,' he murmured, but was prevented from elaborating.

Sally screamed, 'Let me go! Just leave me alone!'

'Come on, babe, let your hair down! Let's have a little fun,' he insisted as he tried to kiss her.

'No!' Sally cried in panic. 'Get out of here! Leave me alone! I want you to go!'

Undeterred, the man put his hand over her mouth and whispered, 'Ssh! Don't make such a noise! People will think I'm trying to murder you!' Still with his hand over her mouth, he bent his head and nibbled the curve of her neck where it joined her shoulder. She struggled, making muffled cries through the hand covering her mouth. He thought they were cries of pleasure and, somewhat carried away, bit her harder, bit her much too hard. Suddenly, he felt her go completely limp in his arms, and he lifted his head, intending to kiss her; but as he relaxed his hold, and removed his hand from her mouth, her fists turned to claws, and she scratched him ferociously down both his cheeks.

He took a step backwards, astonished, and his arms fell to his sides. Sally's face was drained of colour. Her legs were shaking; but it was the expression in her eyes which he noticed, nothing else. They stood staring at each other for a second. Then Sally turned and, leaping for the fire extinguisher, ripped it from the wall. Whirling to face him again, she held it in front of her, brandishing it like a weapon; but he was already heading for the door.

He turned as he opened it and looked at her coldly. 'I'm sorry,' he said curtly. 'I was under a misapprehension. It was a mistake.'

A moment later, he had closed the door and was gone.

Sally's terrors did not diminish with the passage of time, and it became increasingly clear to her that the only way to cure herself was to confront her nightmare head on. She must somehow force herself to go to bed with a man; but she had no idea how to set about this, and her task became more impossible when she realized that this hypothetical lover would have to be French. It was an exorcism she was after, and no English Canadian could wipe out her past.

'Have you ever walked around the French areas of Montreal?' she asked a colleague of hers at work one day.

'No,' the girl replied. 'I wouldn't want to, would you?'

'Well, I thought it might be interesting to go and look around.'

She asked her mother the same question. 'I went to a

43

dinner in Outremont once,' replied Louise. 'A Jewish lawyer who worked with your father lived there for a while – I rather think it's where all the Hasidic Jews live. I don't remember it seeming particularly French.'

'I wasn't thinking about Outremont so much as the east end of Montreal. Have you ever been east of the Main?'

'Well, we've driven through the area sometimes, obviously, but I can't pretend to know it particularly. Why?'

'I just wondered. I thought it might be fun to go and look at it – you know, just walk around down there and see what it's like.'

'Well, you know the area around the Bonsecours Market, and you've been to those restaurants in Old Montreal often enough.'

'Yes, but that's different. That's just a fashionable little bit that's been bought up and renovated. It's a tourist attraction; that's not what I call really French. I want to see the parts that haven't been done up, the areas where the English don't go. I want to explore the real French areas – I want to see where they live.'

'I don't think you'd be very welcome, and I'm sure there's nothing of any particular interest to see – although I'm told there's a good fish shop on St Lawrence.'

Sally refused to be discouraged. She set off in her lunch-hour a few days later, and wandered about between boulevard Saint-Laurent and rue Saint-Denis. She felt so frightened, at first, that she was barely able to take in her surroundings; but she was determined to persevere and forced herself to return the next day.

Soon she was spending most of her lunch-hours and weekends wandering round that part of Montreal, though it was months before she dared move more than a few streets away from boulevard Saint-Laurent. She fooled herself that if the situation became more than she could handle, she could save herself by bolting across that cultural divide. However ludicrous she knew the idea to be, and however similar the streets on either side, that main artery dividing the French from the English seemed to Sally to represent the frontier between the terror of Paris and the relative safety of home.

The French she heard around her in these streets was, of course, another French from the one she wished to wipe out. It was the French she had grown up with and heard in this city all her life. It was an inelegant distortion of the pure, poetic language her memory sought; but it was a bastard child of the same, and near enough, she believed, to serve her purpose.

She did not tell her parents about these expeditions. They would have been anxious had they known how she was spending her free time. They were not as anti-French as many of their friends, but it was a moment when the separatists were particularly active, and they would have thought she was taking unnecessary risks. The English had never been popular and, if they continued to despise and distrust the French, their sentiments were returned in spades by the *Québécois*.

Sally knew all this, but she already felt hated and threatened, so the knowledge that she might be regarded as the enemy could not make her feel more menaced than she already felt. She knew that in this province nothing had changed, or would ever change; that they were still the same two solitudes of Hugh MacLennan's novel – two languages, two religions, two ancient cultures that refused to meet. Like ageing siblings who (having hated each other since childhood, when they vied with each other for their mother's love) jointly inherit the parental home and, through lack of other assets, are forced to live out their lives together, squabbling under the same roof until they die, the French and the English in Quebec – as elsewhere – will continue to quarrel as long as they both exist (and one cannot help wondering whether, like rival siblings, they would not miss each other desperately if one of them ever disappeared).

Sally had grown up on this cultural abyss and she wanted to bridge the divide. She believed that if she could find a French-Canadian lover, she would, in the process of becoming a whole person again, simultaneously become a whole Canadian (by which she meant a bi-cultural Canadian; somebody who not only spoke to and understood the other side, but also – by the simple act of living and sleeping with the enemy – actually became one and the same). Whether or not her interest in the French (one might almost say her obsession) was sparked off in the first instance by the episode in Paris, her political leanings as well as her psychological needs made her want to merge into Frenchness until there was no distinguishing her from them. She would become one with the other so there could be no more enemy: only then, she thought, would she be able to live in peace.

# *Chapter Six*

One evening, some months after first venturing into French Montreal, Sally was chatting on the telephone to a friend. 'Do you want to have lunch with me tomorrow?' Gail asked her.

'Sure,' replied Sally, 'but I want to pick up some stuff from Jean-Talon market, so do you mind if we do that first and then find somewhere to eat around there?'

'Jean-Talon? Are you serious? That's miles away, for heaven's sake. Why on earth do you want to go there?'

'Because it's wonderful and it's cheap. It's a bit like a Mediterranean market. I go there all the time to get my vegetables and fruit.'

'You're kidding!'

'You should come and look at it; you'd love it. I'll drive you there if you can get yourself to my office around twelve.'

'Do you think we'll find anywhere to eat around there?' Gail asked uncertainly.

'I'm not sure . . . but if we don't find anything there, we can always drive down Saint-Denis or the Main.'

Sally sounded a great deal more confident than she felt. She wanted Gail to come with her. She had never had the courage to walk into a restaurant by herself in her own part of town and she certainly was not going to try eating in the French sector on her own. But she had to do it, even if it meant dragging someone with her. She had to see.

Gail was enthusiastic when they arrived at the market. 'This is great,' she exclaimed. 'Why didn't I know about it before?'

She felt slightly less confident when they walked into a bistro on rue Saint-Denis. They were clearly the only English in the place and they both felt conspicuous and ill at ease. They ordered in French without too much difficulty, however, and the waiter was perfectly polite.

Gail began to relax once she started to eat. Sally, on the other hand, felt increasingly nervous. She was convinced that everyone was staring at them. She kept her head bent and pretended to concentrate on cutting her steak.

Lifting her gaze, as Gail said something to her, Sally noticed a young man a few tables away. He was watching her. She was sure he had been watching her since they came in. She turned her eyes away and tried to listen to what her friend was saying, but she was conscious that she was still being watched.

A minute or so later she glanced quickly in his direction. The man was looking straight at her. Their eyes met for a second and she felt herself breaking out in a cold sweat. Unable to swallow the piece of steak she had just put in her mouth, she clutched the edge of the table and looked in desperation at her friend.

'What's the matter?' Gail asked her. 'You look awful. Are you OK?'

Sally gulped as she swallowed her mouthful. 'I feel sick,' she said. 'I've got to get out of here. I think I'm going to faint.'

'Why on earth didn't you say so before we ordered? We can't just walk out now they've brought our steaks.'

'I'm really sorry. Do you mind if I leave you to finish and pay? I'll settle up with you afterwards – and I won't go off without you, I promise. I just need some air.'

She rose, adding apologetically, 'Please don't feel you've got to hurry. I'll be by that clothing store on the corner, one block up. I'll wait for you there, OK?'

'Why don't you come back here? I'll only be about ten minutes.'

'I don't want to come back. I'd rather wait for you by the clothing store. I'll see you in a few minutes, OK?'

She did go back, however. Not on that occasion, but a few days later. She was drawn to it like a pin to a magnet. She was unable to stop herself, though she had no desire whatever to return.

She did not go in. She simply peered through the window, looking for the man. To her immense relief, he was not there. It was not that she wanted to see him again; but she was drawn to search for him by something beyond her control.

She went back again and again until one day she saw him, not in the restaurant but further up the street. He must, she supposed, either work or live near there.

Eye contact with strangers is always a dangerous thing. He noticed the expression in Sally's eyes immediately. It was not the casual regard of someone simply passing by in the street. He turned to look at her as she passed, recognized her, and decided to follow her.

The minute she heard his footsteps behind her, she whirled around to face him.

'I remember you,' he said. 'You were in the restaurant that day. You were ill, weren't you? Do you work round here?'

She was unable to reply. She couldn't make a sound. The street was busy. There were plenty of people about; but she knew that people never help you when you're in trouble.

'Do you want a coffee?' he asked.

She stared at him.

'Come on,' he said. 'Let me buy you a coffee.'

He led her to a café a few yards away. She went like a lamb to the slaughter, her mind blacked out, her movements not her own.

He turned out to be a perfectly amiable young man. She felt light-years younger for having managed to have a coffee with him. It did not, for some reason, make it any easier for her to go into cafés or restaurants on her own, but she blossomed at the thought that she had achieved such a major breakthrough – so much so that people kept commenting on how lovely she looked. She had taken on that glow that some women achieve in pregnancy and others acquire at the start of a love affair.

It was absurd, she kept telling herself, to feel like this when all she had done was to have coffee with a stranger; but he was the most threatening person she had ever voluntarily confronted: he was not much older than herself, he was French, she had never met him before, she knew nothing about him; yet, in spite of appearing to like her, he had not attacked her or said anything frightening, or suggestive, or lewd. All he had done was to ask her if she would like to have lunch with him sometime – not dinner, nothing dangerous – and he could not, she told herself, have anything sinister in mind since he'd suggested meeting at a restaurant on Crescent Street, right in the heart of English Montreal. She did not feel secure, but she felt pleased with herself for having made it this far.

She saw quite a bit of him during the next few months and she made sure that all her friends saw her with him, too. She talked about him to everyone and so often that her father (who was not happy about her going out with a French Canadian) exploded at her one evening while they were playing tennis together at the Hillside Club.

'It's Jean-Pierre this and Jean-Pierre that! For Christ's sake, Sally, can't you talk about anything else?' He had difficulty restraining himself from telling her what he thought of her boyfriend. Why couldn't she go out with any of the kids they knew? What on earth was wrong with Pete Fraser, for instance? Or Robin McAllister, or Duncan Wentworth?

Louise, on the other hand, was pretty certain that

Sally had never been out with a boy before and, although privately unhappy about her daughter's choice, did not want to ruin things now that Sally was finally showing some signs of normality. Whatever Brock said about how secretive their daughter was, and however convinced he might be that Sally was having an affair with one of their contemporaries – a married man at that – Louise did not share her husband's opinion. She wished she did. She'd have been a great deal less worried about Sally if she'd believed Brock's theory about their daughter and Jack Whymart. She wondered if Sally was sleeping with Jean-Pierre; much as she disapproved of the guy, it would have put her mind at rest. She didn't think Sally was, though: she was pretty sure she'd never slept with anyone.

Louise was right. Sally had never been to bed with anyone, and she was not sleeping with Jean-Pierre.

The next stage in Sally's route to recovery was her decision to move into an apartment on boulevard Saint-Joseph. (She was living, at that point, on Summerhill Avenue – an address which nobody in her world could fault.) Her parents were appalled and did everything they could to prevent her; and their friends rushed to their assistance, telling Sally that it was insane, that she'd be mugged, burgled, raped. She wouldn't survive a minute, they said; but Sally was adamant. She had to do it. She knew she had no choice.

Sally's move was traumatic. She was so frightened that she made herself ill. She developed shingles and took to her bed for weeks; but she would not give up. Her parents moved her back to their house for a time, but as soon as she was well again, she returned to boulevard Saint-Joseph.

Jean-Pierre lost interest in her while she was unwell, but as soon as she was back in her own apartment he started hanging around again. He was attracted by the fact that he could not persuade her to go to bed with him. It was obvious to him that she was not sleeping with anyone else. He suspected that she had never been to bed with anyone, and a certain conquering instinct made him feel that it would be fun to lay a virgin. An uncharacteristic streak of intuition told him that to lay this one would be a considerable feat. He suggested moving in with her but was turned down.

He was surprisingly patient and this reassured her. Over a period of months, he whittled away at her psyche until she finally agreed to go out with him at night. He took her out to dinner every evening for a week; then, one triumphant Tuesday, after a tremendous struggle, persuaded her to accompany him to a nightclub after dinner.

That was as much as he was able to achieve for quite some time. However, for lack of anything better to do (they did not have much in common, it has to be said), they soon fell into a routine of going to clubs every night. These establishments seemed immensely sinister to Sally at first; but as she gradually, through familiarity, overcame her fear, she discovered a new type of life that she genuinely enjoyed.

She loved dancing, she liked the feeling of being among the French and swaying to the strains of Charlebois and Pagliaro; but more than this, she derived a vertiginous sense of excitement from the atmosphere of primitive sensuality in these smoky, sex-laden dives.

Soon she was dancing cheek-to-cheek with Jean-Pierre: letting him kiss her, and feel her, and hold her closely in his arms. Like an adolescent suddenly discovering the world of sin, she felt she had achieved adulthood, femininity and – more important, because until then it had been submerged – a form of sexuality and of sexual expression.

It was not long before Jean-Pierre, sensing the changes

taking place in Sally, tried again to go to bed with her, and this time he almost struck gold. He succeeded in persuading her to allow him to remove most of her clothes, but then she panicked and refused to lie down beside him. Before he could argue, she was dressed again and asking him to leave.

Night after night, they repeated the same performance. It always ended in the same unhappy débâcle. Finally Jean-Pierre could stand it no longer. He told her she was sick, completely screwed up, a total washout. He yelled at her that she was a ball-breaker, a cock-teaser, a freak.

'You're frigid!' he shouted at her. 'You should go and see a shrink! You really are some kind of nutcase! You're a real freaky bitch! What's the matter with you, anyway? Are you a dyke or something? That's it, isn't it? I should have guessed. Jesus, to think I've been dating a dyke! You disgust me. We're through! I don't ever want to see you again.'

Sally sat with tears pouring down her face, unable to defend herself, unable to explain.

That was the last she ever saw of Jean-Pierre. He slammed the door behind him and vanished from her life.

Sally thought about what he had said to her, though. He was right. She knew that. She obviously *was* screwed up; and, although she didn't think she had any lesbian tendencies, she certainly felt more at ease with women than with men.

A month later, Louise telephoned Sally at work to tell her that her godfather was back in Montreal. 'He's coming to dinner with us tomorrow. Your father and I thought it would be nice if you joined us.'

'OK. What time?'

'We've asked him for seven-thirty, but it would probably be easier for you to come straight from work, wouldn't it, given where you live?'

'Yes, if that's OK with you. I'll be there about six.'

## Chapter Seven

Carson Mackenzie and Brock Hamilton were buddies from way back. Their families had been friends for three generations. They had been to the same day school, the same boarding-school and the same university – McGill – where Brock took a degree in law, and Carson in political science (he had every intention of travelling and chose his career with that aim in mind).

Carson went from university into the Navy until the end of the war; then took up political journalism to become, by the time he was thirty, a foreign correspondent for CBC News. For the next twenty-three years he was based in London, but travelled regularly to Paris, Bonn and Beirut; and made many a brief trip to cover temporary crises here and there.

He was fifty-three when he returned to Montreal, tired of the incessant travelling that he had so loved when he was young and pleased to end his career with Radio International Canada in Montreal. (Had he been more ambitious, or in need of the money, he would have accepted the far more important post the CBC offered him in Toronto but, like all Montrealers, he disliked Toronto intensely and still thought of it as the excruciatingly dreary place he had known as a young man.)

Sally Hamilton was three years old when Carson left Montreal, but he had seen her on and off over the years when he returned on brief visits to see his family and friends. The last time he had seen Sally was at her parents' house in the Laurentians, one very hot summer when she was about fifteen. He had thought, at the time, that she was unusually pretty, but he was none the less surprised, when he arrived for dinner, at how lovely she had become.

Carson was a large man with a forceful personality. He liked to be the centre of attention and he had an incorrigible desire to please women. He saw at once that Sally was frail and, since she was also pleasing to the eye, he felt obliged to make his mark.

He launched off, over dinner, into story after story: recounting how a bullet had flown past his ear on one occasion, in Cyprus; and how he had accidentally been caught up in the street fighting in Paris, during the OAS bombing campaign. Sally would not normally have been impressed by the bravado, but Carson had another card up his sleeve: he was funny and he told stories well.

He was also, as it happened, a very kind man and he felt extraordinarily sorry for Sally. Although, these days, the Hamiltons seldom mentioned their daughter's experience in Paris, he knew as much about it as anyone since Brock had telephoned him at the time to ask his advice in dealing with the French police. Carson was in Bonn when it happened but he knew Paris well, and so was able to give Brock a list of names of people at the Canadian Embassy and at the *Préfecture* who he thought might be able to help. Nothing much had come of these introductions because Sally refused to co-operate, but both the police and the embassy had done their best to be helpful in impossible circumstances.

Brock had had a drink with Carson at the Ritz before bringing him home for dinner that night, and had told him of his worries about Sally. 'She had this French-Canadian boyfriend for six or seven months,' he told Carson. 'He wouldn't have been my choice, I can tell you, but I kept my mouth shut because Louise thought it would help put her back on the rails.'

'How long ago was this?' Carson asked.

'She started going out with him seven or eight months ago. He was very present for a time – then, for no known reason, he suddenly disappeared. Sally's never said what happened. Never mentioned him again.'

'Do you think she has a new boyfriend?'

'Not as far as anyone knows. Louise thinks Jean-Pierre was the only boyfriend she's ever had, and she's convinced Sally never slept with him. She's right, I'm sure. I used to think she was having an affair with Jack Whymart; but I was totally mistaken, I later learned. I don't think she's ever been to bed with anyone. Not that I want my daughter turning into a slut – God forbid – but she's twenty-six, for Pete's sake; and even that wouldn't worry me if it weren't for her seeming so scared all the time. There's no getting away from it. She's scared as hell.'

'You should take her to a psychoanalyst . . .' Noticing Brock's expression, Carson added hastily, 'You know I can't stand the guys – I've never had any time for them – but this case is serious. She needs help, Brock. You must realize that. She needs professional help.'

'My God, Carson, don't think we haven't tried to get her to see someone. We tried for two years! She won't hear of it. She says she's got nothing to tell them. I once introduced her to an analyst we knew – a guy called Fisher – you know him, don't you? I got him to join us at lunch one day at the University Club. Anyway, after he'd left, I told Sally he was a shrink and that he'd be happy to see her any time if she thought he could help. You should have seen her reaction! She hung on to my arm and pleaded with me. "You couldn't ask me to stay alone in a room with that guy," she kept repeating. "You can't! You can't ask me to go and lie on a couch, with some man I don't know in the room!"'

'Well, I can understand that, can't you? Come on, Brock, use your head! You can't expect her to want to be shut in a room with a strange man. Especially not if she's got to lie on a couch, for God's sake! Send her to a woman. It has to be a woman.'

'We tried that, too. We forced her to go to this woman that Angie Belmont suggested and she walked out on her after five minutes. She was furious with Louise for making her go. She said, "How do you expect me to say anything to a person I despise? She's an idiot! Anyway, it's none of her business. I haven't got anything to say to anyone, so just leave me alone!" What were we to do? We couldn't force her. What would you have done?'

'I don't know. Do you want me to try to talk to her?'

'She won't talk to you either, if I know her. But you could try, I suppose. She might take it better from you.'

'I'll invite her out to lunch sometime and see if I can get her to talk.' He paused, then added, 'She was too young to go to Paris, Brock. It's a tough place, and she was only sixteen.'

'We realize that, now. But she was so determined to improve her French – and I think all those holidays we took in the South of France gave her a desire to see more of the country . . . Anyway, it wasn't as if we knew nothing about where she was going: the woman she was staying with was a friend of Annabel Horton.'

'I thought you said she was in a *chambre de bonne* somewhere.'

'She was in the attic room because they didn't have a spare bedroom in their apartment, but it was only one floor up. She was supposed to have all her meals with them and live as one of the family. It was just one of those awful accidents of fate that the grandmother died and they had to dash off to Burgundy the minute she'd arrived. But I guess it would have happened anyway. They couldn't be expected to stay glued to her side every minute of the day.' Brock stared unhappily at his drink for a moment, then added, 'They felt terrible about it, you know. Really terrible.'

At dinner that night, Carson gave Sally his full attention. She was pleased. Although she had always liked him, she had forgotten how entertaining he was.

When, towards the end of dinner, he suggested that they celebrate his return with a lunch, she accepted with alacrity.

'I missed your graduation, your twenty-first birthday and God knows what else,' Carson said to her. 'I've been a lousy godfather, but I'll try and make up for it now I'm back. Do you like shellfish? Oysters? Lobster? Right, we'll go to *Desjardins* and make pigs of ourselves. I hope it's as good as it used to be. Your parents say it's still much the same.'

He offered to drive her home when the time came to leave, but she refused as she always did when men offered her lifts. Brock grimaced at Carson behind her back and said loudly, 'No, Carson, not this time. I always take Sally home at night, don't I honey?'

She turned to her father, looking relieved. 'Yes, you do. Thanks.' Then, feeling that she needed to explain, she turned back to her godfather. 'Dad doesn't approve of where I live, so he always insists on seeing me to my apartment. He thinks Saint-Joseph is full of bandits and murderers and God knows what else.'

'You're living on Saint-Joseph?' exclaimed Carson. 'What the hell are you doing living there?'

'I like the French,' she replied.

'Do you indeed? Well, that's original in this town. Good for you. My god-daughter has guts, would you believe? You should be proud of her,' he said, turning to Louise and Brock. 'I call that real guts!' He gave Sally a broad smile of approval, successfully hiding his doubts.

# Chapter Eight

A few days later, Carson Mackenzie watched Sally eating an oyster and thought what a terrible waste of a young woman's life hers had been. She was delightful company and a wonderful mimic, as well as being touchingly pretty in an other-worldly, strangely haunting way. As she sat opposite him now, giving him a lively account of a funny incident that had occurred at her office, he found it hard to remember the look of terror he had seen on her face as she arrived at the restaurant.

She had been atrociously late and had been walking unsteadily, almost as though she were about to fall, or pass out. She had stopped just inside the door and cast about her frantically with an air of complete panic. He had waved a menu at her to attract her attention, but she stared vacantly about the room without fixing on anything, then turned and rushed out as if all the demons of hell were at her heels.

Carson had leapt to his feet and chased her out into the street. Catching up with her, he put a hand out to stop her as she fled towards a group of women who were about to cross the road. She reacted with astonishing violence as he placed his hand on her shoulder. A shudder like an electric current ploughed through her. He felt her go as taut as the strings of a guitar. She spun round as if whipped, her eyes dark with fear, and hit out at him with a fist that had suddenly turned to steel.

'Sally!' he had exclaimed. 'Sally, what the hell's the matter?'

Her eyes changed colour as if suddenly focusing, then she gasped as she recognized him. 'I'm terribly sorry,' she said. 'God, I'm really sorry. I didn't know it was you.' She looked unhappily at him. 'I didn't hurt you, did I? How awful of me! I'm so sorry. I honestly didn't realize it was you.'

'It doesn't matter,' he said, taking her by the arm. 'It couldn't matter less. Come on. Our table is waiting. Let's go and have lunch.'

He waited until she had finished her oysters, plied her with Chablis, and watched as she attacked her lobster with evident delight. 'It's delicious,' she said. 'It's truly delicious. It's the most wonderful lunch I can ever remember. It's so nice that you're back.'

'Sally, what happened just now? Why did you run away like that? Who did you think I was, in the street?'

She shifted uncomfortably and pretended to be having trouble cracking the lobster's claw.

'Let me do that for you,' said her godfather, leaning across the table and taking it from her. 'Come on, Sally, tell me. I won't tell anybody. I'm not shockable. I might be able to help. Isn't it worth a try?'

She looked at him with a piteous expression. 'Come on, give it a try,' he said again. 'I promise I won't tell a soul.'

For the first time in her life Sally felt tempted to explain, but she did not know what to say. 'It's too complicated,' she said finally, with a sigh.

'Sure it's complicated. It's complicated as hell. That's why you need to talk about it. What are godfathers for, if not to help when things get complicated?'

She smiled at him forlornly.

'Sally, listen, I've been married. I've screwed around. I've been on drunken binges that lasted for days. I've been to whores. I've watched my wife die of cancer. One of my kids dropped out for years and the other got pregnant at the age of fifteen. I've had friends who were junkies; others who hit the sauce. I've seen wars, I've seen death, I've seen kids blown up in front of my very eyes. I failed to save a friend of mine who was wounded and who died because I didn't get him out in time. I have my nightmares, too. There's nothing you can tell me that's going to shock me. I doubt if there's much you can tell me that I haven't heard or seen before.'

'OK,' she said. 'OK, I'll try. But you've got to swear you won't tell.'

'I swear. I've already told you that. I have plenty of faults but I've never yet betrayed a confidence.' He waited, but she started messing around with her lobster again. He filled up her glass. 'Drink some more of that,' he said. 'It might help. It's something to do with Paris, isn't it?'

'Yes.'

'What happened?'

She did not answer.

'Sally, if you could tell me what happened, I am sure I could get you out of this hell. You'll never be free of it unless you can unload it on someone else. Why not unload it on me?'

'Yes . . . but it's difficult. I'm not really sure what happened any more. I think maybe I invented it.'

'OK, so let's assume for the moment that you invented it. In a sense it doesn't matter whether or not it really happened. What matters is the effect this thing – this invention, if you will – had on you; is still having on you. Tell me what you think you remember. You'll feel a lot better if you can make yourself talk about it.'

'You promise you won't tell my parents?'

'I swear to God I won't tell anyone. Not your parents. Not anyone.'

He watched her struggling with herself. Her eyes clouded over and she was shaking. He stretched his arm across the table and put his hand on hers. 'It's OK, Sally. I'm not going to hurt you.'

'He kept saying we should make love,' she whispered finally. She was not looking at him. She kept her head bent. Carson waited.

'Who was he?' he asked, after a moment.

'I don't know.' Suddenly she looked up and there was a tear trickling down her cheek. 'I don't know,' she repeated. 'I'd never seen him before in my life.'

'Where was this?'

'In his room . . . at least, I guess it must have been his room. It was in the attic. You know, one of those *chambres de bonne*.'

'The room where you were staying?'

'No, of course not,' she said impatiently. 'I told you it was in his room. Why would we be in my room? I didn't even know the guy.'

'Where did you meet him?'

'I didn't meet him, I keep telling you – I'd never seen him before.' She began shifting about on her chair in an agitated fashion.

'Calm down, Sally. It's OK. There's no need to be frightened.' He put his hand on hers again. 'How did you get to his room?'

'I don't know how I got there. He took me there, I suppose. I don't remember. There were all those stairs, but I don't remember them.'

'You must remember them or you wouldn't be talking about them.'

'I remember them coming down. I just don't remember them going up. Like I said, his room was in the attic. There were five flights of stairs before that last flight up to the attic. I must have gone up them, but I don't know how. I don't remember a thing about it.'

'Did he ask you to go up to his room?'

'No, he just took me there.'

'How? Did he carry you? Is that what you're saying?'

'I don't know. I can't remember that part.'

'Where were you before that?'

'In the street.'

'Outside his house?'

'When we arrived, yes. He said, *"Voilà chez moi,"* so it must have been where he lived.'

'Whereabouts was this? What part of Paris?'

'I don't know.'

'Roughly? You must have some idea what *quartier* this was.'

'No, I don't,' she snapped. 'I don't know Paris. I'd only been there a few days; and, anyway, he drove so fast.'

'He took you there by car?'

'Yes.'

'Well, where were you when you got in his car?'

'In the street.'

'Which street?'

'I've no idea.' Again, she seemed agitated. 'I was running, so I didn't see the names.'

'Why were you running?'

'To get away from him.'

'Where were you when all this started?'

'In a café.'

'Were you having lunch with him?'

'Of course I wasn't having lunch with him! I keep telling you, I didn't know him. How could I be having lunch with him? I was just having a coffee on my own. I was about to go and look at Notre-Dame. It was somewhere round there.'

'Was he in the café?'

'Yes. He came over and started pestering me. You know ... asking me if I was English, or German, or Swedish. That kind of thing. He sat down at my table and he wouldn't leave me alone. Nobody helped. Nobody helped me from start to finish. Not even the policeman. I don't want to talk about it any more.' She burst into tears.

He let her cry for a while. 'Sally,' he said eventually, 'is this the first time you've told anybody?' She nodded. 'Well, you're doing fantastically. Don't give up now. I know it's difficult; but I promise you, it'll be a relief to get it out. This isn't the best place to talk, though. Would you rather come back to my apartment and tell me the rest there?'

He realized immediately that he had made a mistake. She leapt to her feet with that blind look again. He

63

rushed after her as she raced towards the door. 'I'm sorry,' he said, catching her by the arm. 'Don't go. Please don't go. I shouldn't have suggested it. It was incredibly stupid of me.' He held on to her arm as she tried to pull it away. 'Look at me, Sally. Do I look like someone who's going to hurt you? Come back and sit down. Let's have some coffee.' He felt her relaxing. 'Come on. Come and sit down.'

'Everyone's staring at me,' she whispered as she fumbled in her pocket for a handkerchief.

'So what? What do you care? It's nothing to do with them. But we can go if you like. We can have a coffee somewhere else.'

'I'm sorry,' she said as he led her by the arm back to their table. 'I didn't mean to be rude. It's just that . . .'

'You don't have to explain. It's perfectly understand- able. And it wasn't rude. Now, do you want a coffee or shall I ask for the cheque?'

'I would like to leave, please, if that's OK.'

'Fine. Just give me time to pay, all right?'

Once outside, Sally again tried to leave. 'Thanks, Carson,' she said. 'You've been really kind. And it was a delicious lunch. Really and truly delicious.'

'How about that coffee? Let's go to Murray's – unless you want to walk up to the Ritz. They have much better coffee there.'

'It's sweet of you, but I really must go now. There are a lot of things I have to do this afternoon.'

'Why? What sort of things? For Christ's sake, Sally, it's Saturday. You've got the whole weekend to do things in. Come on. Take it easy. I am sure they can wait, whatever they are. Do you want a milkshake or something, instead of coffee?'

'No, thank you. I've really got to go. Bye, Carson, and thanks again.' She set off, walking briskly, but Carson continued to walk beside her, determined not to let her go before she had finished telling her tale. He sensed that if he could not persuade her to tell him everything she remembered, now she had started, she might block again and become incapable of ever unburdening herself.

'Listen,' he said as they marched up Mackay Street, 'I know you don't want to talk about it but I honestly believe it's important that you tell me the rest. We don't have to have coffee, or go anywhere in particular. We can just go on walking. We could go up the mountain and walk around there, or we could walk to your parents' house, or along Sherbrooke Street, or anywhere you like. I don't mind what we do, but I'm not leaving you until you have talked about it. It's too important. You'll never be free of it if you can't tell me now.'

Sally took some persuading, but she finally agreed to let him keep her company, although she did not mention Paris as they criss-crossed the town. She made him walk past all the places that had mattered to her in her childhood, and he sensed that she needed to relive older memories in order to call back her buried recollections of that incident she was so determined to forget. She made him stand outside her grandparents' house, walk past her old school and past her cousin's old school, cross the campus of McGill, walk in and out of the Redpath Library and sit in the park at the top of McTavish that she had so loved as a child.

They looked at the Sun Life building; they drank tea in Ogilvy's; they walked past the convents that had filled her with such terror as a small girl. They walked up and down Peel Street, Crescent, Drummond, Stanley: they crossed and re-crossed the whole of downtown Montreal.

As if this were not sufficient, Sally then set off along Sherbrooke Street, dragging her long-suffering godfather into Westmount, up Mount Pleasant and along Rosemount Crescent. By the time they reached Cedar Avenue, Carson felt as though he was about to expire.

'My God, Sally,' he panted as they ploughed on up

the mountain, 'have a heart! I'm fifty-three. I'm an old man. I need to sit down.'

'You can sit down when we get to the top. We've got Sunnyside Avenue and those steps to climb first.' However, she allowed him to pause for a moment and catch his breath while she turned to look down on Montreal spread out below them. 'Isn't it beautiful?' she asked. 'I don't believe there's anywhere in the world more beautiful than this.'

They eventually reached the Belvedere, where Carson collapsed on a bench, and Sally stood leaning her elbows on the wall, gazing out across the St Lawrence. She seemed to gain a kind of peace from looking out over the city, with that huge river flowing by and, on the far side, Mount St Hilaire and Mount St Bruno glowing in the last rays of the setting sun.

She liked the fact that Montreal was an island. It made her feel safe. She loved being surrounded by water and being on top of a mountain looking down on it all.

It had become dark by the time she turned away from the view to see her godfather sitting hunched on a bench.

'I'm OK now,' she said. 'I can talk, if you want. We don't have to stay here. We can go somewhere and have a drink, if you like.'

'That's a relief,' he said, smiling. 'I don't know about you, but I feel in need of one. Where do you want to go?'

'I don't know. Where do you suggest?'

Carson thought about it for a moment then said, 'We could go to the University Club, I suppose. There shouldn't be too many people there.'

To his astonishment she said, 'I think your apartment would be better.'

'Are you sure?'

'Yeah, I think so. I don't feel so scared now. I don't know why.'

'OK. Let's try and find a cab . . .' Nobody could have missed the expression that flashed across her face. 'Don't tell me you're frightened of cabs, too? Come on, Sally. You won't be alone. There will be two of us, don't forget. Neither of us is going to attack you with the other one there.'

'I'd rather walk,' she said. 'It's not that far to where you live.'

'Well, it's not what I would call close. However, if that's what you want . . .' He rose from the bench with a resigned sigh.

'You've been very patient,' she said as they set off down the mountain. 'I'm really grateful. I'm sorry to be such a nuisance.'

'You're not a nuisance. It's probably very good for me, all this exercise and air.'

## Chapter Nine

Carson lived in a large apartment in one of the blocks in Westmount Square. Sally seemed perfectly relaxed all the way there and right up to the moment they walked in through the main entrance to the building; but then, to her godfather's exasperation, she panicked at the idea of using the elevator. He hid his feelings, however, simply saying, 'Could you explain to me why, if you feel safe about coming home with me, you feel so nervous about riding in an elevator with me?'

'I have to feel I can get out. I need to be able to open the door. You take the elevator. I'll meet you at the top.'

'Right,' said Carson. 'I'm afraid I'm going to take you up on that. After all the walking I've done today, I'd rather not have to struggle up four flights of stairs if I can avoid it.'

He waited for her upstairs, standing in the open doorway of his apartment. She looked terrified and he was uncertain how to reassure her.

'Do you want to go in first? Do you want me to go in and leave the door open? How do you want to handle this?' He watched her eyes as he waited for her to reply.

'You go in,' she said. 'Do you mind if I leave the door open?'

'Of course not. Do what you like. I'll be in the living-room, just over there.'

He crossed the hall and went into a room on the right. She followed him after a moment, first fiddling with the front-door lock to make sure she could open it from the inside. Reassured, she closed the door after her and went on into the living-room. 'I've closed the door,' she said. 'You won't do anything funny, will you?'

'Of course I won't! Good God, Sally, what the hell do you take me for? Look, I'll sit over here and you can sit right over there and shout at me. I won't move, I promise. But first, if you have no objection, I'd like your permission to get us both a drink. I need one, I can tell you, and I expect you do, too. Is that OK?'

'Yes, of course.' She laughed, but she did not move from the doorway.

'What will you have?'

'What are you going to have?'

'A double rye, which I'd have on the rocks if I dared go and get the ice.'

'Go on, then. I'll stay by the front door while you get it.' She moved back across the hall and opened the front door.

Jesus, he thought, this was going to be something else. Feeling like a murderer in his own house or a psychopath under surveillance, he made his way gingerly to his kitchen and helped himself to ice from the freezer.

'You still haven't told me what you want,' he called. 'Do you want a rye and ginger? A bloody Mary? I make an excellent dry Martini, if you want something to blow off the top of your head.'

'I'll have a rye and ginger,' she called back.

'With or without ice?'

'With ice, please.'

'Fine, here it comes.' He appeared again from the far end of the passage, carrying several bottles of ginger ale and a bucket of ice on a tray. 'The rye and the glasses are in the living-room so I'll give you a shout when I've poured out your drink, OK?' He disappeared into the living-room again and, a moment later, called, 'Right, your drink is on the table by the sofa. I'm sitting with mine at the other end. You can come in now. I won't move again unless you say I can.'

She shut the front door once more and walked

hesitantly into the living-room. He was, as he had said, sitting at one end of the room, clutching a large drink. She went to the other end of the room, picked up the glass he had left there for her and sat down.

'Congratulations,' he said. 'You've gone a long way in an afternoon. You deserve your drink.'

She smiled at him nervously, raised her glass to him, then took a sip.

'So,' Carson said after a moment, 'where had we got to? You were running away, then you got in this guy's car. Why did you do that?'

'I don't know. I don't remember.'

'Did he ask you to go home with him?'

'No.'

'What made you get in his car? Did he offer you a lift home to your place?'

'No.' She took a gulp of her drink. 'At least, I don't think so. I honestly don't remember. I don't know how I got there at all. Perhaps I made the whole thing up. I can't seem to remember anything any more. I must have made the whole thing up.'

'I don't think so, Sally. You ended up in hospital, after all. What was the last thing you can remember before being in the car?'

'I remember falling, and then running again and trying to squeeze between these two parked cars. Then the door of one of the cars opened in front of me and there was no room to squeeze through. He must have been in one of the cars and opened the door. I don't know how he got there. I can't understand a thing about it. I don't even know where I was by then.'

'Well, he must have pulled you in somehow. Maybe he hit you on the head. Do you remember having a sore head afterwards?'

'No.'

'Well, however he managed it, he appears to have abducted you, wouldn't you agree?'

'Yes . . . Yes, I suppose so.'

'OK. So then what?'

'He drove off, really fast. I don't really know where. I remember driving along the *quais* at one point, on the Right Bank; I'm sure it was the Right Bank. We crossed the place de la Concorde – before that, I think – and I was banging on the window, trying to attract people's attention.'

'Why didn't you wind the window down?'

'There wasn't a handle. It had been broken off. I was shouting and thumping on the window and he put on the car radio really loud so no-one could hear. He said, "You can make as much noise as you like. No-one will hear you."'

'Did he say that in English or in French?'

'In French. He was French. He said everything in French.'

'Did nobody notice you banging on the window?'

'Yeah, the gendarme did, but he didn't help.'

'Which gendarme was that?'

'There was this gendarme in the middle of the place de la Concorde. They're not gendarmes, I know – anyway, one of those traffic cops that I always think of as gendarmes. He was standing on a kind of circular thing, a sort of podium or whatever. I don't know what you call it. Anyway, he saw me and waved.'

'He waved at you?'

'Yeah . . . Funny, really, isn't it? He thought I was waving at *him*. He was so ridiculous. We were gone in a flash, anyway.'

'So then he drove you to his place, right?'

'Yes.'

'And he said, *"Voilà chez moi."* Did he say anything else?'

'No. Or if he did, I don't remember it. I don't remember any more until we were upstairs.'

'OK. So what's the next thing you remember?'

Sally looked at her hands, then picked up her drink. She stared at it as if she had never seen it before, tipping it gently from side to side and watching the ice move. Carson waited.

'What's the next thing you can remember?' he asked again after a while.

Sally did not reply. 'Can I have some more ice?' she asked finally.

'Sure. Do you want to get it yourself, or do you want me to get it? It's in that ice-bucket over there on the side.'

'I'll help myself.' She rose and walked to the sideboard, but Carson could see that she was watching him out of the corner of her eye. He did not move. He waited until she was sitting again before he dared pick up his drink. This was the moment, he knew, when she was likely to run. Any false move on his part and he'd blow the whole thing.

Neither of them said anything for a full minute. 'How about some more rye while you're at it?' Carson suggested eventually. 'It looks as if your glass needs topping up.'

'Yes. Yes, I guess I would like some more. Can I get it for myself?'

'You know you can. You just do whatever you want.'

'You need some more, too. Will you stay sitting if I bring it to you?'

'Of course. Look, I'll leave my glass there, on the table. You can always hit me over the head with the bottle if I so much as sneeze,' and he laughed, more from nervousness than from the idea that there was anything droll about his remark.

Sally laughed too, rather uncertainly. 'I know I'm being ridiculous,' she said. 'I'm sorry, I can't help it.'

'Don't give it a thought. It's a wild idea, this. It could become the new party game. It could really catch on.'

Sally laughed again, this time sounding more genuine. She took her glass to the sideboard, helped herself to more rye, then walked towards Carson with the bottle in her left hand. In her right hand she was clutching the opener that she had used to take off the cap of the ginger ale. It was one of those old-fashioned ones that have a sharp, metal-cutting point for opening cans. She was holding it like a dagger. She clearly had every intention, thought Carson, of plunging it in him if he moved.

She topped up his glass, watching him as she did so, then returned to the sideboard, moving with a strange, crab-like walk. She was determined not to turn her back on him, thought Carson. How in hell had the French boyfriend managed her, he wondered. He waited until she was sitting down and then asked, 'You had a French boyfriend, didn't you? Did you treat him like this?'

'At the beginning, yes. Not after a while, when I got used to him.'

'Can I ask you a personal question which is none of my business?'

'I may not answer, but you can try.'

'Did you go to bed with him?'

'No.'

'But he stuck around for quite some time, didn't he?'

'Yes.'

'Did you tell him any of this?'

'No.'

'He must have tried to go to bed with you, didn't he?'

'Yes.'

'Is that why you split up?'

'Yes.'

'Didn't you want to go to bed with him?'

'No. At least, I thought I did in the beginning ... theoretically, I mean. I thought I had to ... I thought, you know, that ...' Her voice trailed away. 'But I couldn't,' she added after a pause. 'I just couldn't, so that was that.'

'OK. Let's get back to Paris. Can you tell me what happened next?' Sally started to fidget. 'Come on, Sally, try.'

She pulled a cushion towards her and clutched it to her chest. 'I can't,' she said in a tiny voice. 'It's so embarrassing. I don't want to think about it. I don't want to think about it ever again.'

'He tried to rape you, didn't he?'

'It was disgusting . . . I feel so revolting . . . I felt filthy. You can't imagine how filthy I feel . . . I don't want to talk about it,' and she started to cry.

He wanted to console her. He wished he could put his arms around her and stroke her head. He watched her clutching her cushion and rocking slightly as she cried. 'There's nothing for you to feel filthy about,' he said. 'He was the one who was filthy. You've got to understand that. Whatever he did to you, it wasn't your fault. Try and tell me what happened. Did he undress you? If you can talk about it, you'll be free. It will be over for once and for all.'

'It's too embarrassing. I can't . . .'

'I told you at lunch, there's nothing you can say that will embarrass me. I'm shocked at what happened, like any normal person would be shocked – appalled – by what happened; but I'm shocked *for* you, not *at* you. I couldn't be shocked at you if I tried. Nobody's judging *you*. You must understand that.'

She continued to rock back and forth, clutching her cushion. 'He hit me,' she said at last, keeping her head down. 'He knelt on my stomach and flayed my chest and my legs with his belt – with the buckle of his belt.' She buried her head in her cushion and whispered, 'It hurt. I don't think he was doing it very hard, but it hurt a lot all the same.'

'What a bastard!' Carson exclaimed. 'Jesus, Sally, I'm sorry.'

'He kept whispering to me that we were going to make love. He had this really gentle voice. You can't imagine how gentle. And he kept whispering these things to me and calling me *"chérie"* and *"mon amour chéri"*. He didn't use words like, well, you know . . . awful words . . .'

'You mean . . .'

'I mean he didn't use *"baiser"* and words like that. He sounded so gentle – really sweet and kind – and he kept whispering, *"On va faire l'amour un peu,"* but all the time he was ramming his knee into my stomach, or kneeling on my arms and exposing himself, or practically strangling me, or hitting me with his belt.' She wanted to tell her godfather about the beer bottle but she was too embarrassed to do so.

'How long did all this go on for?'

'I don't really know. It seemed like forever, but I've always had this idea it was about two hours. I don't know why. Maybe it was only half an hour.'

'Did he rape you? I mean, in the medical sense? Clearly he violated you in every other way.'

'No. He didn't rape me. I think he was intending to, but maybe he wasn't. I wonder sometimes if it happened at all.'

Carson noticed that she was becoming calmer as she talked. She had stopped crying and had finally lifted her head, although she still wasn't looking at him.

'How did you get out of there?'

'I don't know, really. I mean one minute I thought I'd had it – in fact, I thought he was going to kill me – and then the next, he was dragging me off the bed and shouting at me to leave. I can't explain what happened exactly. He just suddenly changed. He stopped sounding sweet and started yelling at me and calling me a *"salope"* and a *"petite merde"* and he dragged me out of the room and threw me downstairs – well, kicked me, really.'

'He didn't try and follow you?'

'No. He kept on shouting insults from upstairs, but he kept the door shut.'

'How did you get to the gare St Lazare? That's where they found you, isn't it? Do you think all this happened near there?'

'I don't think so, no. But I can't be sure. I'm not sure of anything any more. I remember crawling down those stairs and dragging myself to my feet at the bottom; and I remember thinking that I had no idea where I was, but that if I kept walking I must eventually find a *métro*, and then I could work out where I was and how to get back to Madame Bonnard's apartment – that's where I was living. And that's all I remember until the ambulance.'

'Christ, Sally, what a godawful story! Why on earth didn't you tell anyone? They might have found him if you'd told someone at the time.'

'I know, but I couldn't. I can't explain. I felt so ashamed, so incredibly ashamed . . . And, anyway, I didn't remember that much at the beginning. It was ages before I remembered all that I've just told you. It only came back in bits and pieces over a period of two or three years.'

'Well, you've done it; you've managed to talk about it, do you realize? I'm really proud of you.'

'You won't tell anyone, will you? You promised you wouldn't.'

'I promised and I keep my promises. I'm far too flattered that you confided in me to want to spoil it by betraying the confidence. But any time you're scared, here I am. Your Dad is my oldest and closest friend. Your Ma, too. I'd always do anything for them or for you. Just bear that in mind.'

Sally smiled at him, looking him straight in the eye for the first time for half an hour. 'I'm so grateful, Carson. I'm truly grateful. You've been so patient and so very kind. It's just that, you know, I'm so frightened a lot of the time . . . It's awful. I'm so scared . . .' She suddenly burst into tears and flew across the room towards him. He stood up as he saw her coming and held out his arms. She flung herself against him, sobbing hysterically.

'It's all right, Sally,' he said, putting his arms around her and stroking her head. 'I promise, it's going to be all right.' He assumed she needed to cry so he let her go on sobbing against his shoulder. He could think of nothing useful to say but, as her tears finally subsided, he stroked her head one last time and repeated, 'It's going to be all right, I promise you.'

'I need to blow my nose,' she said at last, sniffing and wiping her eyes with the back of her hand.

'There's a box of Kleenex in the bathroom if you want to help yourself. It's down the passage, second on the left.'

He poured himself another drink while she was out of the room. He felt worn out by all the emotion and wondered what to do with her next. Should he give her dinner? Should he send her home to sleep? If she wouldn't take a taxi, she certainly wouldn't allow him to drive her home, so how the hell was he going to get her there? He couldn't leave her to go back on the Metro. He'd have to go with her, which was the last thing he felt like doing at that point. He tried desperately to think where there was a Metro stop in her part of town. It was not an area of Montreal he had ever frequented.

'Do you want some dinner,' he asked Sally when she reappeared, 'or would you rather I took you home?'

'I think I'd like to go home, if that's OK with you. I feel frightfully tired suddenly.'

'I'm not surprised. What with all that walking and then all the emotion I should think you're completely exhausted. Now, tell me how you usually get home.'

'Well, I hardly ever go out at night. If I do, I take my car so I can drive myself home. I didn't bring it this morning because I knew I wouldn't be able to park on Mackay and I thought I'd be going straight back afterwards. In the daytime I usually take the Metro. There's a stop almost opposite where I live.'

'I imagine you don't want me to take you home in a cab?'

'I don't mind as long as you come with me,' she said to his surprise.

'My goodness, you've made progress! Well, that makes things easier. I'll call one right away.'

Half an hour later, their taxi pulled up on boulevard Saint-Joseph.

'Shall I see you up to your apartment, or would you rather go in by yourself?' Carson asked.

'I don't mind. I'm OK on my own. I'm used to it. But you can come up if you like.'

'OK. Well, I'll just see you to the door of your apartment. I'll feel happier if I've seen you safely inside.'

He asked the cab driver to wait for him while he accompanied her upstairs.

'Good night, my dear,' he said as soon as she had opened her apartment door. 'Don't forget, I'm there if you ever need anything or if you want to talk any more. You've got my number, haven't you? Maybe you could give me a ring tomorrow, just to let me know you're OK?'

'Of course. But don't worry. I'm fine now. I'm just tired.'

'All right. Well, get some sleep. Goodbye, dear.'

'Bye.' She watched him start down the stairs, then called after him, 'And thanks again.'

# Chapter Ten

Carson woke early the next morning, roused by the chiming of bells. There was no chance of forgetting it was Sunday in this town, he thought. In London, he had never been aware of bells.

He felt stiff from his previous day's exertions. It must have been years, he thought, since he had walked that far. He knew he ought to take more exercise but the thought irritated him – he disliked being reminded that he was not as young as he once was.

He lay in bed for a while, thinking about Sally, and hoping she would not feel embarrassed with him now that she had told him her tale. What would make a man behave like that, he wondered; and would the police have found him if Sally had told them what had happened at the time?

He remembered Brock telling him that the French doctor had been convinced Sally's attacker would have killed her if he had succeeded in raping her, but Carson could not see the logic of this any more than he could understand why the man had finally allowed Sally to leave. Was one to assume the guy was impotent, he wondered. Was that why he had let her go? And the doctor must have had some reason for believing Sally would have been killed if she had not managed to avoid being raped. Was that because, in the criminal mind, she would have seemed despicable if she had succumbed? The psychology of it all was beyond him. Perhaps doctors had more experience than one realized of these types of crime and could thus see a pattern in the behaviour of such people which was not evident to anyone else.

It was odd, he thought, that Sally had never told

anyone about it. He had read that rape victims suffered from guilt but had never, for the life of him, been able to understand why. In Sally's case, of course, never having been to bed with anyone, he could see that it must have been even more frightening than it would have been for someone who had already had affairs, but he still could not see why she had refused to tell anyone: he would have thought that her first instinct would have been to make sure the man was caught.

Deciding that it was all beyond him, he abandoned these ruminations and turned his mind to happier matters. He'd see if he could find someone to play tennis with him later, he thought. (He was suddenly determined to get into shape.)

He rose and made himself breakfast. It was a perfect late summer day. The sun streamed in through the window; and across the city, bells were ringing from innumerable steeples and spires. Whenever he heard the incessant chiming of bells, Carson was reminded of the tales he was told as a child about the underground passages which ran between convents and seminaries, churches and hospitals; and the orphanages which were always attached somewhere in between. (These tunnels, which came to light during the building of Notre-Dame church, were – as Carson well knew – originally built as a means of escape from Iroquois attacks; but anti-Catholic sentiment had, in the early nineteenth century, been fuelled by a prostitute's published 'story' of priests raping novices in underground passages and the resulting babies being thrown into the lime pits under Notre-Dame. For all that the author was later discredited, the seed of doubt had been sown, and the suspicions about the behaviour of priests and nuns were never totally wiped from the Protestant mind.)

Once Carson had finished his breakfast, he began to worry about Sally again. By eleven-thirty, when he still had not heard from her, he decided to telephone her.

'Hi,' he said, as soon as she picked up the phone. 'I

just wanted to make sure you were all right after last night.'

'I'm fine, I think. I only just woke up so I haven't had much time to find out yet.'

'What are you going to do with yourself today?'

'I don't know. Nothing much, I guess.'

'Do you want to have a game of tennis this afternoon? I thought I'd go up to the Hillside Club and play a couple of sets.'

'Wow! What energy! I thought you'd be exhausted from all that walking yesterday.'

'I can tell you, sweetheart, I find it a lot less tiring to play a couple of sets of tennis than to climb that darned mountain. Anyway, do you want a game?'

'That'd be great. What time?'

'Around three o'clock?'

'OK. I guess Dad and Mum might be there, too. They often are on Sunday afternoons.'

'Do you want me to ring them and see if they'd like to play doubles with us?'

'Sure.'

'Good. I'll see you there just before three.'

'Hi, Brock,' Carson said, a few minutes later, when his friend picked up the phone. 'Do you and Louise want to come and play doubles with me and Sally at the Hillside this afternoon?'

'Sure,' Brock replied. 'That's a great idea. Let me just check with the boss.' Carson could hear him calling Louise. 'Yep,' Brock said, after a brief conversation with his wife, 'that's fine with her, too. Did Sally make that lunch with you yesterday, by the way?'

'Yes.' Carson wished he'd never told Brock.

'Did she turn up?'

'She was fifty minutes late, but she arrived eventually.'

'Goddammit, she's *always* late! What the hell's the matter with her? I can't get it into her head that it's important to be punctual. I hope you gave her a rocket. Wait till I give her a piece of my mind.'

'Don't, Brock. Don't say anything. It was fine. She's a swell kid. You should be proud of her.'

'Did you manage to say anything to her?'

'I made a lot of helpful noises but whether or not they sank in I don't know,' Carson said, hoping to sidestep any further questions by this remark.

'I don't think much sinks in with Sally on that subject. Still, thanks for trying. Anyway, Louise wants the phone so I'd better get off it. See you at the club around a quarter to three.'

'OK. See you there.'

Louise noticed something different about her daughter the minute she saw her with Carson. There was a complicity between the two of them. She could not put her finger on what it was exactly but she could sense it, none the less.

Carson, she noticed, seemed very concerned with making sure Sally was happy. Well, that was no bad thing, she told herself. On the other hand, she knew Carson of old. He just had to please women, especially when they were young and pretty. She hoped he wasn't out to seduce her daughter.

She told her husband, while they were driving home afterwards, that she wanted him to have a discreet word with his friend. She had never told Brock that Carson used to make passes at her in the old days, but she was tempted to tell him on this occasion when he refused to listen to her.

'Come on, Louise, for Christ's sake! You know she always gets on with our friends. She feels safer with them than with kids her own age.'

'Yes, but this is different . . . Don't shake your head at me. It is! It's different . . . Brock, listen to me. I'm her mother and mothers can tell sometimes. Carson has this strange look when he's talking to her: real tender and concerned.'

'Hell's bells, Louise! Why shouldn't he be concerned? I told you I'd talked to him about it. He's her godfather, isn't he? What the hell do you expect him to be? Indifferent?' Brock was beginning to shout.

Louise was always unsuccessful in calming her husband when he was in this mood, but she could never resist trying.

'OK, OK. Cool it, sugar. There's no need to shout.'

'I'm not shouting!' he yelled at her. 'Anyway, what would be so awful if Carson did fall for her? He's my oldest friend. He's one of the kindest, most honest men on earth. He's got a great job. He's got plenty of dough. He's not short of brains. He's a great guy – and maybe he's lonely since Gail died. Had you thought of that?'

'He's too old for her, honey. Maybe he *is* lonely since Gail died, but he's still too old for Sally.'

'You'd have preferred her to get hitched to Jean-Pierre, would you? You really wanted a dumb, French-Canuck son-in-law and a bunch of Roman Catholic grandchildren, is that right? They would all have had to be Catholics, you realize; she'd have ended up just like all those French-Canadian broads, with no teeth from eating too much sugar pie, and a thousand squawling brats hanging on to her skirts.'

'I didn't say I wanted her to marry Jean-Pierre. I just said Carson was too old for her.'

'Well, there hasn't been a great deal of choice to date, has there? I mean, Jean-Pierre seems to have been the only contender so far. I wouldn't be too picky, Louise, if I were you, or your daughter may end up an old maid for life.'

# Chapter Eleven

Carson was very busy for the next few days and did not have much time to think about Sally. She, on the other hand, thought about her godfather a great deal. She hoped he would ring her but when, after a week, he had not done so, she plucked up her courage and rang him at work.

'I'm sorry to bother you, Carson. I know you're busy, but there's something I want to tell you. Something to do with what I told you the other night.'

'Where are you?'

'I'm at work.'

'Can you talk?'

'No.'

'Do you want to have dinner?'

'Aren't you doing anything?'

He was supposed to be writing a feature for *Newsweek*, but it would have to wait. 'I was going to work,' he replied, 'but it'd be a wonderful excuse to put it off until tomorrow.'

'Are you sure?'

'Positive. It's something that doesn't have to be finished until the weekend. It can wait another day.'

'OK. That'd be nice. I'll bring my car this time so you don't have to see me home. Where do you want me to meet you?'

'How about the Maritime Bar at the Ritz? We might as well eat decently while we're at it. I haven't been there since I got back, in any case . . .' There was a silence at the other end of the line. 'Sally? Are you still there?'

'Yes. Sorry. I was just thinking. I'm not very good at going into restaurants by myself. As a matter of fact,

I've never done it at night. Would you mind if I picked you up at your apartment and we went on there together?'

'Not at all. Come and have a drink first, if you like.'

Sally felt elated as she walked up the four flights to Carson's apartment. A week earlier she would have been incapable of this and now she wasn't even scared.

Carson was not quite sure what to expect. He thought it likely they'd have to go through the same performance as last time but the moment he opened the door to her, he realized that this was not going to be the case.

Sally greeted him with a friendly smile, said, 'Hi, Carson,' and gave him a kiss on the cheek.

He stood back to allow her to shut the door if she felt so inclined. She shut it. Then he waited to see if she would go in to the living-room without any problem. She did, so he followed her.

'What do you want to drink?' he asked. 'How about a cocktail this time? I make a mean daiquiri, if you'd like one.'

'I'd love one,' she said, walking to the sofa and sitting down.

'How's work?' he asked as he mixed the rum, fresh lime juice and melted cane sugar in a cocktail shaker.

'OK. Pretty good, in fact, except that . . .' She left her sentence unfinished.

'Except that what?' Carson asked, adding crushed ice to the mixture and giving it a hard shake.

'Except the men in these cases . . . They're all such brutes. They're so sadistic. You wouldn't believe some of the things they do to their wives. It makes me wonder if any men are normal. I mean, even though we always go in pairs, or even in threes – if we have to see them at all – it's sometimes quite scary. You should have seen the one we had to talk to today . . . We had to get the police to come, in the end.' She paused as

Carson gave the cocktail shaker a last few flicks of the wrist. 'Why *are* men so violent? Can you explain it to me?'

'You mustn't form your view of men from the cases you are handling. Most men aren't at all like that, I do assure you. It's just that in your job you're bound to see a concentration of violent, drunken, abusive types – inevitably – and I have to say, I don't think you should be doing that job. It's not going to help you over your fear of men: it can only make it worse.'

'I know,' Sally replied, 'but I have to do it. I feel I'm kind of paying off a debt . . .'

'A debt? What on earth are you talking about? You don't owe anybody any debt!'

'Well, a duty rather than a debt, perhaps,' Sally murmured as Carson poured out their drinks. 'I mean, I'm alive, when I should be dead, and I've got to stop it happening to anyone else. They need someone to stand up for them, these women . . . It's difficult to explain. I have to do it, that's all.'

Crossing the room with her drink, Carson watched Sally like a lynx, ready to stop moving instantly if she looked at all nervous. She did not seem bothered at the sight of him approaching, so he continued until he was standing beside her, and handed her the glass. Still uncertain of her reactions, he avoided sitting beside her and went instead to an armchair the other side of the room.

'Well,' he said as he sat down, 'what was it you wanted to tell me?'

She looked uncomfortable suddenly, and crossed her legs before answering. 'It's stupid,' she remarked. 'I know it'll seem stupid to you; but now I've told you so much, I feel I have to tell you the rest.'

'Yes?'

'I remember what he looked like, you see, but I can't remember his face. He had this light hair, quite thick, and incredibly well cut – you know, one of those French, stylish cuts; but I can't remember anything about his face. It's crazy. His face was near mine practically all the time, and I can't remember it at all.'

'You've obviously blotted it out.'

'Yes, but it's ridiculous. I can't even remember the colour of his eyes. I mean, sometimes I think he had grey eyes – grey or blue – but then, when I think some more, I know they could have been brown. I don't know if it was a thin face or a fat face; whether it was round, or square, or pointed. He might have had a firm chin or no chin at all. He might have had pimples, or even scars for all I know.'

'I'm sure that's quite normal. You don't want to remember it, so you've wiped it out.'

'But it worries me.'

'Why?'

'Because I want to remember. I want to remember what he looked like.'

'Maybe it's better not to remember.'

'But I have to remember. I have to know who I'm looking for.'

'You're looking for him?'

'Sort of, yes. I'm always looking for him in a way.'

'Why, for God's sake?'

'Because he's out there somewhere, isn't he? He's still out there roaming around. He's going to get me. I know he is. And I want to see him coming. I want to know what he looks like.'

'Listen, Sally, he's in Paris if he's still on the loose, which seems unlikely – you can be pretty certain that he's been locked up by now. People can't behave like that for long without being caught; and, anyway, it's three thousand miles away. He's not going to come to Montreal, is he? It's all a long time ago, Sally. It's nine or ten years ago, isn't it? It's all over. It's in the past.'

'It's easy to say that, but it doesn't feel over to me. Something about me made him do it. It was definitely something to do with me. I'm sure he's still looking for me. I know he is.'

'Don't be silly. He was a freak. He was sick. He'll

have done the same thing to other girls since then, you can be sure – poor, wretched little things. He's bound to have been caught by now.'

Sally stared at the far wall, not listening. 'He wouldn't want me to go around telling people about him, either,' she murmured. 'He'll get me sooner or later. I know he will.'

Carson tried to reassure her, but it was almost as if she had gone into a trance. She was still staring at the wall and her eyes had taken on that cloudy, myopic look again. It was obvious she wasn't listening to a thing he was saying. She probably couldn't even hear him, he thought.

'Sally,' he called after a time. 'Sally, you've got to listen to me.'

She turned her head towards him and there were tears in her eyes. 'Do you know what he did?' she asked, almost as if she were talking to herself. 'He smashed a beer bottle on my . . . on my . . . between my legs; and he brandished his . . . you know what . . . He brandished it – his thing – above my face. He kept hitting me with it and pushing it against my face, and in my hair, and everywhere.' She started crying. 'It was disgusting! It was really horrible. I can't stand it. I wish it hadn't happened! Oh God, I wish it hadn't happened!' She flung herself face down on the sofa and her whole body shook with sobs.

Carson was not quite sure what to do. He waited for a time, not daring to move but, after a while, when her sobbing did not subside, he stood up and crossed the room uncertainly, half-expecting her to leap to her feet and run for the door. But she didn't move.

He crouched on the floor beside her and placed his hand gingerly on her back. She flinched, but she did not try to move away.

'I'm so frightened,' she whispered, burying her face in the sofa. 'For the last three nights, I've dreamt about him. I didn't have dreams about him any more. And now, suddenly, it's all come back!'

'That's because you've been talking about it to me.'

She sat up and looked at him. 'I suppose so,' she said, sniffing, but she did not look convinced.

Carson sat down beside her and put an arm around her shoulder. 'Look, Sally,' he said, 'you've been delving around in memories you've tried to bury for years. Of course you are bound to dream about it – you may dream about it a lot, for a time, while it's all coming out.'

'I don't want to dream about it! I don't want to think about it ever again!'

'I can imagine how awful it is for you, but you must realize that it's necessary, that it's vital even. It's very healthy.'

'You don't understand,' she sobbed. 'I dreamt the most awful things – really awful, horrible things! And I dreamt things I'd completely forgotten until now.'

'That means you're getting it out of your system at last. That's good, don't you see? You're getting rid of it. You're bringing it to the surface and throwing it out.'

She took a handkerchief out of her bag and blew her nose; then sat hunched with her head in her hands. 'I wish,' she said, suddenly sitting up and turning to him, 'that I knew he was dead. I won't ever feel safe until I'm certain he's dead.' To her godfather's surprise she suddenly put her arms around him, gently laying her bowed head like a wilting flower on his shoulder. Giving a sigh into the lapel of his jacket, she whispered, 'I wish that someone would kill him for me.'

Carson did not know what to reply so he rocked her silently in his arms.

'I'm sorry,' she said at last, 'but I had to tell someone. You've been so kind to me. I had to tell you what I feel.'

'That's OK. That's what I'm here for. I'm sure it's very healthy to tell someone what you feel.'

'In my dream,' she murmured, 'I killed him. I stuck a knife through his heart.'

'I don't know much about dreams,' Carson said

quietly, 'but I believe one does a lot of things in dreams that one wouldn't do in real life.'

They sat there for a time, their arms around each other, then Sally said, 'I'm hungry. Do you mind if we go and eat?'

'Of course not. I booked a table at the Maritime Bar, so let's go.' Carson stood up and gave her his hand. 'Come on. A darned good dinner is what you need. Do you want to drive yourself there, or do you want to come in my car?'

She hesitated for a second then said, 'I think I'll take my car, if you don't mind. It'll be easier for me to go home afterwards, apart from anything else.'

He laughed uncomfortably. 'You still don't trust me, do you? OK. I'll meet you there.' She froze. 'What's the matter? Have I said something wrong?'

'I've changed my mind,' Sally replied. 'I'll come with you in your car. I'd forgotten about going into the restaurant by myself.'

He felt totally exasperated suddenly. He was about to tell her to make up her mind when he noticed the expression on her face and decided to hold his tongue. Jesus, she was fucked up, he thought. How the hell did she survive?

He assumed she was going to make a fuss about going in the elevator with him, and he was right. 'OK, OK,' he said. 'I'll walk downstairs with you. I don't mind. It's walking up that I object to.'

She was fidgety in the car and insisted on keeping her window wound down, but they reached the restaurant without incident and, once there, she began to relax. To Carson's relief, the subject of Paris was not raised once. Instead they talked about politics, about his job, about all manner of different things, and Sally once again became the vivacious, pretty girl who had so amused him in the Laurentians in her teens.

'Do you still go up to the mountains as much as you used to?' he asked her.

'Not quite as much, since I don't have those wonderful long school holidays any more; but I go most weekends during the summer. Mum still moves up there for three months in summer because she can't stand the heat here in Montreal, and Dad drives back and forth almost every day while she's there. I always join them for a couple of weeks in July or August.'

'You were such a wonderful swimmer. I'll always remember you skimming about that lake like a dragonfly on the water. It made me and your father laugh so much. You went like a bat out of hell. You never slowed down.'

'I was scared of the catfish. That's why I swam so fast. The catfish and the pike – I was scared of them both.'

'Come on, Sally! You never saw a pike in the lake, did you?'

'Not when I was swimming, but Dad used to catch one occasionally, so I knew they were there.'

'Did he? Well, I'm darned. He never caught anything but perch when I was around.'

'He caught pike, too, sometimes, I swear. The only good thing about it was that we never had to eat them because Dad said they tasted of nothing but mud. He made us eat every perch he ever caught, though. Mum and I used to get so sick of eating perch.'

'Do you still have crayfish in that stream?'

'Sure. There are just as many crayfish as there always were.' She smiled. 'Whenever I think of crayfish, I think of Bobby. Do you remember my cousin, Bobby?'

'Of course I remember Bobby. Funny you should mention him. I saw him again the other day and boy, has he changed! I hardly recognized him. Not the slender lad he used to be.'

'Yeah, he's changed a lot. He's losing his hair, too, did you notice? Anyway, Bobby used to catch crayfish in the stream and chase me with them; and one summer he found this family of grass snakes under a rock, and he started catching frogs and feeding them to the snakes. He used to throw the poor frogs right up in the air so they fell down splat on the dirt track. Then these snakes would slither out from under their rock and gobble them up. It was really revolting.'

'Jesus, Sally! Do you have to tell me about it while I'm eating?'

'Didn't you do things like that when you were a kid? I thought all boys did.'

'I certainly did not! You obviously knew the wrong boys.'

'I did, yes. Both my cousins were like that. I still tease them about it. They were such revolting brats, Bobby and Charlie. They were two of a kind – and now they're both so smart and pompous you'd hardly know they'd ever been kids.'

Carson suddenly felt he was listening to a child. It was as if, he thought, she had somehow been frozen in time, blocked by her Paris experience and unable to grow up. It was difficult to believe that she was anything like twenty-six.

During the course of dinner, his attitude towards her changed. He felt he had taken on the task of turning her into an adult. He wanted to cure her of her nightmare and change the child into a woman. She was pretty, of course, and he'd always found it difficult to resist a pretty girl.

When they had finished dinner, he drove her back to Westmount Square and saw her to her car. 'You're one hell of a pretty girl,' he said, kissing her on the cheek. 'I've really enjoyed tonight. I'd like to take you out again sometime, if you're ever in the mood.'

'I'd like that, too,' Sally replied. 'It's been fun. I'm really grateful, Carson. You've been so kind.'

'Do you feel safe going home on your own, or do you want me to follow you in my car?'

'No, I'm OK, thanks.'

'Right. Well, try not to have any nightmares tonight. You can always ring me if you're scared. You know that, don't you? Even if it's the middle of the night, you can always ring me.'

'Well, I hope I won't have to, but it's nice to know.' She blew him a kiss and waved goodbye out of her car window as she drove off.

## Chapter Twelve

Carson found it difficult to put Sally out of his mind. He knew it would be easy to scare her off, so he forced himself to wait until she called. A week went by without her making a sign of life and he was beginning to feel faintly irritated by her silence when she finally rang.

'I'm feeling scared,' she said. 'Do you mind if I come and see you?'

'I'd be delighted,' Carson replied, giving no indication of his surprise (it was ten-thirty in the evening and he had given up hoping to hear from her that night). 'Do you want me to come and fetch you?'

'It's OK, thanks. My car is outside. I'll be with you in about twenty minutes, if that's all right.'

'Sure. See you in a few minutes.'

Carson took a moment to answer the doorbell when Sally arrived, and his telephone started ringing just as he was letting her in. He raced to answer it, leaving her to follow him into the living-room where she hovered uncertainly as her godfather fired questions at whoever was on the other end of the line. After a time, Carson demanded to speak to various other people and, sensing that he was going to stay on the telephone for some time, Sally finally helped herself to a drink and sat down. She had never seen Carson this excited before: it sounded from what he was saying as if there had been a huge explosion somewhere in Montreal.

When he had finished speaking on the phone, Carson turned to her and apologized. 'A bad fire has broken out in a nightclub on Union Avenue. It sounds as if it may have been a bomb. There are hundreds of people trapped in there. They're all jumping out of windows and falling off the fire-escape. It's complete bedlam, apparently. I'm going to have to return to the office, I'm afraid. Do you want to stay here? You can always sleep in the spare room if you get tired.'

'Can I come with you?'

'You'd be better off staying here. You'll be perfectly safe and, for all I know, this may go on all night.'

'Please, Carson. I promise I won't get in the way. I'll sit in a corner. I won't say a word to anyone. I don't want to stay on my own.'

He was about to refuse but she tugged at his arm and pleaded with him until he relented.

'OK, but nobody's going to have time to look after you. You'll be exhausted tomorrow. I may have to stay there for hours.'

'I don't care. I want to come. Please let me come.'

'Have it your own way,' he said. 'Only don't say I didn't warn you. Come on, let's go. I have work to do.'


Sally sat for hours on a hard chair in the corner of the newsroom watching telex machines spitting out yards of paper, and journalists smoking cigarette after cigarette and drinking instant coffee out of paper cups. The telephones rang incessantly. People ran from telex machine to telex machine, grabbed a handful of paper here and there and, ripping it off, either raced to a phone, or to a typewriter, looking as if the world had caved in.

'Holy shit!' she heard someone saying. 'There were so many of them fighting to get down the fire-escape that the railing broke and they've been falling off it like flies.'

'There are fifty ambulances on the scene, according to the police,' a man called across the room. 'They say there were three or four hundred people in there and, so far, they've only got about half of them out.'

A while later someone else shouted, 'The police say the club's owners have been the victims of an extortion attempt and that's probably the reason for the bombing.'

'That's not what I heard,' someone else said. 'Some of the kids they got out say three guys were ejected earlier and came back with Molotov cocktails.'

There was one man, Sally noticed, who seemed completely untroubled. He had his electric typewriter beside his elbow, his feet on the desk in front of him, his glasses pushed back on his head and an unlit cigarette dangling from the corner of his mouth. He leaned back in his chair with his eyes half-closed, occasionally springing to life to the extent of leaning sideways and bashing out a few words on the typewriter. There must, Sally realized, be something special about what he was doing because from time to time throughout the evening the other journalists would stumble over, one at a time, to stand behind him and peer with fascination at what he had written. Then, nodding sagely, they would wander back to their own desks, light another cigarette and start hitting their own typewriters again.

Carson's main base seemed to be in another room but he came in and out regularly to speak to one individual or another. Whenever he walked past the character with his feet on the desk, he would simply put a hand on his shoulder and give it a friendly squeeze.

Once, a man who until then had been frenetically rushing in and out of the room, stuck a cup of coffee in Sally's hand, saying, 'Here, have this – I haven't time to drink it.' Other than that, no-one seemed to notice she was there.

Around one-thirty in the morning, Carson came to talk to her for a moment. 'I'm sorry about this. I did warn you it might go on for hours. Do you want me to call a taxi and send you home?'

'No!' Sally replied with such vehemence that Carson stared at her for a moment.

'Oh, yes,' he said, remembering suddenly. 'I'd forgotten. I was distracted by all this.'

'Have they got them all out yet?' Sally asked.

'Nobody knows, but I don't think so. They're still taking casualties up to the Montreal General and the Royal Vic. There are at least thirty dead so far, and over fifty injured. It's an absolute shambles. It's pushed Trudeau's announcement of the General Election completely out of the news.'

He looked exhausted, Sally thought, as she watched him walk away to speak to someone else. She shut her eyes, leaning her head back against the wall, and dozed fitfully in her chair. She was aware of the continual clackety-clack of machines all around her but in her dreams these sounds converted into the noise of a train rattling down the tracks. She was running along the roof of the train, trying to escape something that was chasing her, jumping from carriage to carriage, when she saw that they were approaching a tunnel. She knew she would be knocked off if she stayed standing up, so she flung herself on her face just as they plunged into the dark. She realized immediately that the thing she was fleeing was already there, in the tunnel, somewhere ahead of her. She clung desperately to the roof, trying to worm her way backwards on her stomach when, to her horror, a disembodied hand came out of the dark and grabbed her by the shoulder. She jerked with fright and let out a cry, then opened her eyes to see Carson looking down at her. 'Come on, Sally,' he said, gently shaking her shoulder. 'Wake up. I'm going to take you home now.'

'Do you want to come back to my place?' he said once they were in the car. 'You said you were feeling creepy earlier. You can have the spare room if you feel safer in my apartment than in yours.'

'I think I should go home.'

'I'm too tired to argue, Sally, and too tired to discuss why you felt frightened earlier. As I've said, if you want to stay at my place, you can. If you'd prefer me to sleep on the sofa at your place, I will. At this moment I don't care where I sleep. All I care about is getting there quickly.'

'If you take me back to Westmount Square, I can collect my car and drive myself home.'

'Fine. That suits me.'

Her car was parked right outside his building. As he stopped to let her out, she said, 'Thank you for letting me come tonight. I'm sorry if I was a nuisance.'

'That's OK,' Carson replied. 'I'm sorry that I didn't have time to talk to you. I'll give you a ring just as soon as this business has died down and then you can tell me what was spooking you.'

# Chapter Thirteen

Sally had another nightmare in the early hours of the morning. She tried to scream in her sleep but no sound would come out. She woke up, shaking, to hear herself making tiny, whimpering noises. She looked at her watch. It was six o'clock. She had had exactly three hours' sleep.

She decided to have a shower and dress rather than try to go back to sleep at the risk of having another nightmare. Once dressed, she turned on the radio and made toast and coffee while listening to the news. It was almost exclusively about the fire and, following the most obvious train of thought, it made her wonder if Carson was awake.

In the pale light of morning, she felt embarrassed about the previous night. Why had she felt so frightened on her own suddenly? Why had she bothered him with her nonsense? How could she have begged him to take her with him to Radio Canada International when he was so preoccupied with work and when she was bound to be in the way?

The effect on Sally of finally managing to tell someone what had happened to her had been to open a door that had hitherto remained bolted. It was, she reflected, as if someone had discovered and turned on a tap inside her mind. Now that she had told Carson as much as she remembered, she found herself remembering more and more. She wanted to discuss it with him day in, day out. She felt an overwhelming need to talk about it – but only with him, not with anyone else. By the simple fact that it was he who had finally succeeded in opening the floodgate, Carson had made himself (however unwittingly) a necessary part of her cure. She was becoming dependent on him, she suddenly realized. She was doing the classic thing. Although she was loath to admit it, she was, to all intents and purposes, falling in love with her shrink.

Carson, when he awoke, felt he had been a bit rough with Sally the previous evening, but he was too busy during the day to give her a call. He was irritated at having to spend the whole of his Saturday at the office but, given the events of the previous evening, he knew he had no choice. Not only was there bound to be an investigation into the causes of the fire in which thirty-seven had been killed and a further fifty-four injured, but there was also the Prime Minister's election call, which had come during the early part of the evening, several hours before the fire, and which had been largely overshadowed by the nightclub tragedy. Trudeau's announcement had come unexpectedly, just after six, when he had gone on television to address the people in a wide-ranging speech which required greater analysis than Carson had yet been able to give it.

The opening game in the first ice-hockey series ever to be played between Canada and the Soviet Union was to take place that night in Montreal, too, and Trudeau was to perform the ceremonial faceoff inaugurating the eight-game match.

Carson had been looking forward to that historic occasion for days and he was determined to be home in time to watch it on television. He raced back to his apartment, grabbed something to eat and switched on his television just in time to see the Prime Minister dropping the first puck. No fool, he, to manage to appear before the largest television audience in Canadian history, thought Carson – and by then he was too engrossed in the game to give Sally a thought.

Once the game was over, it occurred to him that he ought to phone her but, having had so little sleep the previous night, he felt too exhausted to want to speak to anyone. He'd call her tomorrow, he told himself. She'd have to wait until then.

*  *  *

At four in the morning, he was woken by the telephone ringing. He reached out and fumbled with the switch on his bedside lamp, turning it on and glancing at his watch before answering the phone. His heart sank when he saw the time.

It never occurred to him that it could be anything other than a call from the newsroom, so it took him a moment to recognize Sally's voice on the other end of the line.

'There's a man on the fire-escape,' she said in a terrified whisper. 'I can hear him. What shall I do?'

'Is the fire-escape at the back of the building?'

'Yes.'

'Where's your car?'

'Outside the front door.'

'Grab a coat and go and get into your car – he won't be able to get down the fire-escape and round to the front before you do. Drive over here. I'll call the police and come over immediately. If your car has gone, I'll come back here. If not, I'll break in. Now, get going, but don't panic. I'll be there right away.'

Carson telephoned the police, then threw a coat over his pyjamas, picked up his car keys and ran. Ignoring the speed limit, he drove as fast as he could to boulevard Saint-Joseph, thankful that there were few other cars about at this time of night. As he shot through the deserted streets, a police car sprang into action at the sight of him speeding, and chased him, siren wailing and lights flashing, to Sally's door. Barely able to hide his irritation, Carson showed them his press card and told them briefly about Sally's call, as he raced up the stairs with the cops at his heels.

When they reached the landing outside her apartment, they found two more policemen, who had arrived before them, in the process of questioning a middle-aged French-Canadian in jeans.

'She's gone,' said one of the cops, as he watched

101

Carson ring Sally's doorbell. 'She'd gone by the time we arrived.'

The man in jeans, it transpired, was the tenant of the apartment above Sally's. He had forgotten his keys and, finding himself locked out at four in the morning, had decided to climb up the fire-escape and break in through his own kitchen window.

It was fifteen minutes before the police, who had taken the man's identification, felt they had been given an adequate explanation of both his and Carson's movements. After that, armed with their notes and having lectured Carson on the trouble he would find himself in if he was ever caught speeding again, they departed, leaving the man in jeans to go to bed and Carson to drive back to Westmount Square.

Carson was worried. He hoped Sally would have had the sense to park right outside his apartment block, where he could find her easily. He thought she could be counted on to stay in her car until he turned up; but she was quite capable, if she was frightened, of driving around aimlessly for hours rather than staying in one place. It was absurd, given her frail psychology, for her to be living on her own, he reflected; and it was totally insane for her to be living in that particular part of town.

She was nowhere to be seen when he reached Westmount Square. He sat in his car and waited for a time, thinking she might eventually drive past. After ten or fifteen minutes he parked his car and went up to his apartment to see if she was waiting for him there. There was no sign of her, but he could hear his telephone ringing. Unlocking the door, he ran to the living-room to pick it up.

It was Brock Hamilton on the phone. 'Sally's here,' he said. 'We've been trying to get you to let you know. I gather she rang you earlier. Why she didn't ring us, God only knows. Anyway, I'm sorry she bothered you. She wants to have a word with you and apologize herself. Poor kid, she's in a bit of a state. Are *you* all right? Did you find the guy? I suppose he'd gone by the time the police arrived, had he?'

'Nope. He was there. He was the guy who lives upstairs. He'd forgotten his keys and was trying to break in through his kitchen window.'

'Jesus, Carson, and you were hauled out of bed for that? I'm sorry, pal. I really am sorry. So will Sally be when she hears.'

'For Christ's sake, Brock, it couldn't matter less. As long as she's safe . . . And it could have been dangerous. She wasn't to know.'

'Well, I'm grateful to you, Carson. We're all darned grateful. Next time call us, though, will you? I don't know why you had to be dragged half across town in the middle of the night.'

Realizing that Sally would not want her parents to know that she had confided in him, Carson tried to distract Brock by turning the incident into a joke. 'You know me, Brock: always flattered to be rung up by pretty girls in the night. Still, old thing,' he added, suddenly becoming serious, 'I don't think she should be living down that end of town. I want to talk to her about it sometime, if you've no objection. I'm going to do my darnedest to get her to move back to Westmount, if that's OK with you.'

'Sure is! If you succeed, Louise and I will be more than thankful – and maybe Louise's hair'll stop turning grey. She says it's all the worry – that and my bad temper. Anyway, here's Sally. Don't let her keep you long. It's time we let you get back to bed.'

'Carson?' Sally sounded shaky. 'Are you OK?'

'Sure. It was nothing. It was just the guy upstairs. He'd locked himself out.'

'Monsieur Prud'homme, you mean?'

'Yup. "Prud'homme", that's what he said his name was. "Pierre-Marie Prud'homme".'

'Oh my God, Carson, I'm sorry! How dumb of me! Why didn't he tell me who he was? He could have shouted to me . . .'

'He assumed you were asleep.'

'I should have asked him, shouldn't I? I should have shone a flashlight out of the window and looked to see who it was. I'm sorry. I was so scared, I didn't think.'

'Don't be silly! It could easily have been something. You were quite right to ring me. Anyway, you get to bed now. I won't be around tomorrow – I'm spending the day in Como, with the Hendersons – but I'll give you a ring at your office on Monday, when I've had time to see how my day is working out.'

## Chapter Fourteen

Sally had a particularly distressing case to deal with that Monday: an elderly widow who was being regularly and seriously knocked about by her drunken, middle-aged son. It was the first time Sally had come across a tale of this kind and she was appalled to discover how passionately the woman loved her son, in spite of years of abuse suffered at his hands.

'You cannot allow him to go on living with you,' Sally told her. 'If you are unable to make him leave, we can help you. There's no need to feel frightened. The law is on your side in this type of situation. We can force him to move out.'

'Oh, I couldn't do that,' replied the woman. 'He's got nowhere else to go. He doesn't have a job, you see, so how would he survive?'

'Perhaps, if you weren't housing him and paying for everything he needed, he'd make an effort to find himself a job. From what you say, it sounds to me as if he hasn't really tried.'

'But who would look after him? Who would cook for him? Who would wash and iron his clothes?'

'Don't you think, at forty-five, he should do those things for himself?'

'He wouldn't know how,' said the woman sadly. 'I've always done it for him, you see.'

'Well, perhaps you haven't helped him. Why should you, at your age, be going out to work in order to support him? He'd soon learn how to look after himself if he didn't have you to do everything for him – and you shouldn't give him money if all he does with it is spend it on drink.'

'But it's his only pleasure. He has nothing much to live for. I mean, for a man with no family and no job, there's not very much for them to do, is there?'

'If he didn't drink, he might not be so violent.'

'He doesn't mean to hurt me. It's just ... He gets depressed, you know, and I guess he kind of accidentally takes it out on me because I'm the person that's around. But he doesn't mean it,' she added fiercely. 'I wouldn't want you to get the wrong impression. He's always sorry afterwards. He loves me, you know. He loves me just as much as I love him.'

It was hopeless, Sally thought. It made her wonder whether men always hurt the women they loved, and whether women expected, or even wanted, to be hurt by their men. The longer she worked in this job, the more she had doubts about whether love and violence were not simply two aspects of the same thing.

She wished Carson would ring. She wanted to ask him whether he had ever been violent with women. (She couldn't imagine him hurting a fly, but then she couldn't imagine him going to whores – as he'd so charmingly put it – or doing most of the things he claimed to have done.) She felt depressed and frightened. She needed to be reassured. She wanted to know that there was at least one man who did not behave the way she feared they all did.

Carson had been too busy to give his god-daughter a thought until late in the afternoon. Sally began to think he had forgotten his promise to ring her and felt a surge of relief when he finally called.

'I'm glad you rang,' she said. 'I want to ask your advice about a case that I've been dealing with today.'

'Save it for tonight,' her godfather replied. 'I'd like to take you out for dinner, if you're free.'

Sally was pleased, though she tried not to make it too obvious. She wanted to see him more than she cared to admit.

'I'm not likely to be through here until eight-thirty or nine,' Carson said. 'I'll come and pick you up at your apartment when I've finished here. OK?'

'Fine,' Sally replied. 'It'll give me a chance to show off. You'll be amazed by the place – it's full of arches and pillars, and plaster heads of girls.'

'Really?'

'Yes, it's fantastic. You won't believe it. All the houses around here are gorgeous inside.'

'You astound me. I look forward to seeing it. I must rush, I'm afraid. I'll try to be with you by nine.'

'I'm dreadfully sorry about last night,' Sally said the minute Carson walked through the door. 'I didn't want to talk about it in the office, with everyone listening, but I've been feeling terrible about it all day. I felt so angry with myself afterwards. I don't know how I could have been so dumb.'

'It doesn't matter,' said Carson. 'I wasn't particularly in the mood to deal with burglars or whatever, so I'm not complaining that it turned out to be a false alarm.'

'The police rang me at my office this morning. They weren't too amiable about the whole thing. Were they OK with you?'

'Not particularly,' he said, suddenly sounding irritated. 'Although I don't know why the hell they should mind. It's their job, for Christ's sake!'

'Do you want a drink?' she asked, hoping to soothe him. 'I've got some rye. I think I've got some vodka, too, somewhere, if you prefer.'

'No, let's get out of here and go and have a drink somewhere else. Why do you live here, Sally?' (He sounded annoyed, she thought, and with good reason. He must be tired and fed up with her, too.) He looked at her despairingly. 'What the hell made you choose to come and live in this part of Montreal? If you're going to expect me to turn up in the middle of the night, you're going to have to live somewhere nearer

107

Westmount. Why don't you move back to civilization? This is a godawful part of town.'

'Carson! How can you say that? It's a beautiful street! And it's a really interesting area . . . Anyway, have you ever seen houses like this in your part of Montreal? I've never seen an apartment with ceilings like these, have you? Look at those pillars with the girls' heads at the top! Look at the fireplaces, and the doorhandles, and these beautiful floors!'

'OK, OK! So it's an interesting house . . .'

'Remarkable, not just interesting.'

'Fine. Remarkable. But that doesn't make it safe. You don't feel safe here, so why live here?'

'I *have* to. I moved here because I had to confront the French on their own ground. You must be able to understand that.'

'Well, at least that makes some sense of it; but I still think you should move.' He took off his jacket and threw it over the back of a chair. 'May I change my mind and ask you for that drink, after all?'

'Of course. Which do you want? Rye or vodka? That's all I can offer you, I'm afraid.'

'Rye would be fine,' replied Carson, flinging himself into an armchair. 'Come on, Sally. After last night, don't you think you should move back near your parents? It's insane to live here, especially for a girl on her own.'

'I can't,' Sally replied, handing him his drink. 'It's like getting back on to a horse when you've had a bad fall. You have to make yourself do it, or you'll never be able to do it again.'

'But you've done it now, Sally. Haven't you proved your point?'

'Not really.'

'Why not?'

'Because I'm still scared.'

'Then this obviously isn't the answer.'

'Yes, it is.'

'No, it isn't. Listen to me; in the war, when pilots

made crash landings and survived, they were made to go straight up again so they wouldn't lose their nerve. Now, that worked some of the time, but not always. There were guys who were so scared they went straight out and killed themselves. Some of them lost their nerve so badly that they ended up killing whole squadrons. *You've* lost your nerve and this isn't helping. You know it isn't, so let's try something else.'

'Such as?'

'Such as living somewhere civilized.'

'Carson! I'm shocked! I thought you were broad-minded. There's nothing uncivilized about French Montreal. It's not really unsafe here. It's only in my head that it seems so scary.'

'OK, but there's a world of difference between the French and the English and you feel it more than most, or you wouldn't have bothered to move here. Is that why you had that French boyfriend, by the way?'

'Yes, partly.'

'Only partly? Well, what was the rest? Were you in love with him?'

'No.'

'So what was it all about?'

She turned away from him, without answering, and poured herself a drink. Carson watched her walk to a chair. She sat down without looking at him.

'Was he your first boyfriend?' Carson asked.

Sally nodded but said nothing.

'How did you meet him?'

'I saw him in a restaurant and then I bumped into him in the street a few days later and he asked me to have a coffee with him.'

'And you said "Yes"?'

'Kind of . . . I sort of just went along . . . I didn't really know what I was doing.'

'You mean you picked him up, or you let him pick you up? Is that what you're saying?'

'Yes, I suppose so . . . Sort of.'

'Jesus, Sally, you must be out of your mind! After

what happened to you in Paris, what in hell did you think you were doing? Didn't it occur to you that it might be dangerous?'

'Yes, I suppose so . . . But I had to do it. Because of Paris, really. I had to – you know, kind of cancel the past.'

'Well, you don't seem to have succeeded, and that was one hell of a risk to take! Didn't it occur to you that that was the worst way to go about it?'

'I don't know . . .' She looked at him miserably. 'It's impossible to explain . . . Please stop asking me questions. I don't want to talk about it, if you don't mind.'

Carson decided the best course was to be brutal. 'I do mind, as it happens, and I'm going to ask you any damn question I please. How do you expect me to help you if I don't understand what's been going on?'

He watched her huddled over her drink and felt overwhelmed with pity. She looked pathetically fragile. 'You wanted to be loved. Was that it? Or did you just want to find out what sex was all about?'

'I don't know.' Her voice was almost inaudible. She shifted in her chair.

'Did you find out, Sally? Are you sure you were telling me the truth the other day?' She did not answer, so he continued. 'Look, I've told you before that you'd find it difficult to shock me. You can't expect me to take a high-and-mighty attitude because you've been to bed with some guy.'

'But I haven't!' she burst out, with a catch in her throat. 'I didn't go to bed with him. I told you that – not the way you mean, anyway. I haven't been to bed with anyone. That's what's wrong with me. I can't. I'm too scared.' Carson could see that she was on the verge of tears.

He stood up and walked over to her. Removing her drink, he pulled her to her feet. 'Look at me,' he said. 'There's nothing wrong with you, Sally. You had a terrible experience and of course it's left you scared.

Anybody who'd had that happen to them would be scared.' He put his arms around her as he spoke.

'He told me I was frigid. He said that I was a freak!'

'But you hadn't told him what had happened to you, had you?'

'No. I've never told anybody but you.'

'So you couldn't really expect him to understand. Be logical. If you hadn't told him, how was he supposed to know?'

'He thought I was a dyke,' she wailed. 'He kept calling me these awful names and telling me I was a dyke.'

'Well, you can't really blame him. Try and look at it from his point of view. He was bound to think up a reason that made him feel less rejected.' Sally shivered but said nothing. 'Did you go out with him for long?'

'About six months, I suppose.'

'Well, there you are. That's one hell of a long time to hang around getting "no" for an answer.'

They were both silent. Carson could not see Sally's face because it was buried against his shoulder. 'Did he ever try and force you?' Carson asked her after a moment.

'No – unless by "force" you mean endless attempts at persuasion. He was pretty heavy on the persuasion.'

'Did he walk out on you in the end, or was it you who chucked him out?'

'He was the one who left. He shouted all these insults at me, then stormed out. I've never seen him again.'

'That's probably just as well . . . Tell me, did you feel upset that he'd gone? I don't mean upset at what he'd said, but upset that he wasn't around any more?'

'In a way, yes, but not about him exactly. I guess, if I'm honest, I was upset because I hadn't made it – I mean, I hadn't succeeded . . . I felt a failure. But I didn't really miss *him*. It was the idea of having a boyfriend that I missed. I suppose I sort of wanted a lover without being able to face the idea of making love. It's difficult to explain.'

'I'd say you'd explained it pretty well. You want to be loved and you want to know what it's like making love. On the other hand you're scared. You're scared of the physical act – which is hardly surprising under the circumstances. It all seems absolutely normal to me.'

'But it isn't normal! It's freakish! I'm weird. I'm really weird.'

'You're not weird. You're just a special case because of an incident which was in no way your fault. It was an atrocious thing to have happened and somehow we've got to get you over it, that's all.'

'I feel so alone,' she said, starting to cry. 'You can't imagine what an outcast I feel.' He tightened his arms around her. 'I'm stuck,' she sobbed. 'That man destroyed any chance I ever had. Jean-Pierre was right. I'm different from everybody else.'

'Don't be silly. The only unusual thing about you is that you're twenty-six and you still haven't been to bed with anyone. You think you're abnormal because things are pretty free and easy nowadays, and most people of your age have slept around quite a bit. There's nothing intrinsically wrong with you – it's just the way things have happened. If you'd been born in some other age, you wouldn't have seemed the least odd. There must have been plenty of twenty-six-year-old virgins in your grandmother's day, so you don't want to get things out of proportion. The only problem is, what do you do about it now?'

'There isn't anything to be done. It's hopeless. I might as well be dead.'

'For Pete's sake! What a terrible thing to say! You've got your whole life ahead of you. We've just got to get you over this and then you'll be fine.'

'Oh, yes? How? Just tell me how!' She pushed him away angrily and stalked across the room. Standing with her back to him, she pretended to stare out of the window, but he could see her narrow frame shaking as she tried to control her tears.

There was a poignancy and desolation about the

way she leant her head against the window-frame. He felt unbearably hurt for her, and furious with the man who had caused all this grief.

As he watched her in silence, he felt a sudden urge to protect her. There she stood, with her back to him: a slight figure by the window, looking as vulnerable and damaged as a butterfly with a crumpled wing. Taking a step which would have surprised even himself a moment earlier, he walked over to her, saying, 'Sally, why don't you come and live with me? I promise I won't hurt you. I won't touch you at all if you don't want me to.'

She didn't move. She didn't say anything. It was as if she were holding her breath.

'You can have the spare room, if you want. I won't pester you. I won't bother you at all. You can come and go as you please. It just means I'll always be there if you need me.'

He waited, not daring to touch her, unable to say any more. Suddenly she gave a sigh and lifted her head. Neither of them moved. She continued to look out at the street as he waited for her to reply. Finally, turning away from the window, she stood looking at him as if uncertain what to do next. There was a strange light in her eyes – an almost ecstatic brilliance – with a surface ripple of hesitation, like a sudden gust blowing across a pond.

Carson smiled at her reassuringly. To his relief, she smiled back.

'Would you consider marrying me, Carson?' she asked to his astonishment. 'I'd love to live with you, but I think it might be easier for me if we were married.'

'To be perfectly honest, it's not a thought that had crossed my mind.' Carson was completely taken aback at the suggestion but he did not wish to ruin his chances of helping her by telling her this. 'Let's try living together first,' he suggested. 'You never know, you might hate it. If it works and you're happy, we can think about marriage in due course.'

'OK,' she replied doubtfully, 'but I'm not sure that it'll work as well. For some reason I feel I'd be less freaky if I were married.'

'Well, let's see how it goes and if we decide we want to marry, it's easily arranged. Better than marrying and then discovering it was all a mistake.'

'Yes, I suppose so . . . Can I move in tonight?'

Carson was astounded by the ease with which she had accepted his suggestion. 'Sure,' he said. 'Why don't you pack what you need for tonight and we can do the rest tomorrow. I'd like to go and eat now, wouldn't you?'

Over dinner, Sally seemed as excited as a young girl who has just accepted a marriage proposal. Carson was perplexed as to what to think. He was unable to work out from the things she said whether she saw this simply as a social arrangement or whether she was envisaging a physical relationship. The indications seemed to be that she was hoping it would be more than platonic, but Carson realized that Sally herself probably did not know what she really wanted; and all of her remarks were open to more than one interpretation.

Carson had himself by this time been infected with the spirit of indecision. He was very unclear in his own mind exactly what he hoped for, or wanted from, this arrangement. He had acted impulsively, largely moved by pity; but no doubt also by a steadily increasing affection for his godchild. None the less, it would be untrue to say that the idea of making love to her had never crossed his mind. Had she not been his godchild, had she not been so much younger than he was, and had she not had that appalling experience, he would certainly have tried to seduce her before this; but, given these three facts, he had never allowed himself to dwell on the possibility and, though he had frequently felt a fleeting desire for her, he had always, until now, managed to brush it aside. Or so he liked to tell himself.

Thinking about it over dinner, he knew that under other circumstances her comparative youth would in no way have discouraged him. On the contrary, young women were far more attractive to him than women of his own age; and he had never in the past had the slightest hesitation about having an affair with someone much younger than himself. So what was it exactly that made Sally seem so untouchable? Not just the fact that she was so frightened, surely? Not simply that she was so vulnerable, or that she was his god-daughter and that if he hurt her he would have to answer to her parents as well as to her?

No, it was more than this, although all these things weighed. It was something to do with the fact that she seemed such a child. It wasn't even, he decided, the fact that she was still a virgin. (Although he'd never been particularly excited by the idea of deflowering virgins, she wouldn't be the first one he'd made love to and it wasn't an idea that put him off any more than it turned him on. He couldn't, to be honest, see what all the fuss was about. On the whole he considered virginity something that people were happier without.)

What was it, then, about Sally? He couldn't for the life of him put his finger on it. Was it that her innocent, little-girl ingenuity seemed to lay her so wide open to being hurt? Was it that he felt he was dealing with a child who was so young that he simply could not think of her in those terms? Or was it, he wondered, in an attempt to be honest with himself, that he wanted to be the one who succeeded where everyone else had failed?

He was unable, or unwilling, to answer his own questions, but he was convinced that whoever she finally gave herself to would possess her as few men have ever possessed a woman.

'What are we going to tell my parents?' Sally asked him on the way back to his apartment after dinner.

'Tell them the truth. What else do you want to tell them?'

'Don't you think they'll be shocked?'

'Why should they be? Good grief, Sally, we're both adults! It's hardly as if you were eighteen. Anyway, they didn't make a fuss about your French boyfriend, did they?'

'No, but that was different.'

'It was different, sure, but they may not have been thrilled about it, for all that. To be honest, I don't think they were crazy about him, from what they said to me, but they didn't make a fuss, did they, so why should they now?'

'Because it's you. I mean, you're my godfather; and, anyway, you're so old.'

Carson laughed. 'They may think I'm a bit old for you, and they'd be right.' He glanced at her, hoping to tell from her profile whether they were discussing him as a lover or as someone with whom she was simply intending to share an apartment. He was unable to tell anything from her expression, so he continued, 'At least they know who I am and that I'll take care of you. As a matter of fact, I think they'll be relieved.'

'Will you tell them for me, please? I don't think I'm brave enough to do it.'

'Of course, if that's what you want. Maybe we should tell them together? No? Fine, well, I'll drop in for a drink with them on my way home from work tomorrow.'

He glanced at her again. She was gnawing at the knuckle of one of her fingers. 'There's nothing to worry about,' Carson said reassuringly. 'They won't mind, I promise. I think you'll find they're pleased.'

Back at his apartment, Carson raised the subject again, hoping to find out precisely what Sally had in mind. 'You'd better tell me exactly what you want me to say to your parents. Shall I say you're going to stay in the spare room, or do you want me to say that you are sharing my life in a more serious fashion?'

'I don't know.'

'Well, we should tell them the truth, but I don't know

116

myself quite what you want from me. I've told you the spare room is yours and that I won't ever bother you. If you decide you want to join me in my bed – tonight, or any other time – I'd be more than delighted; but I have no intention of trying to persuade you to do anything you don't want to do.'

'I'd like to sleep in the spare room. To begin with, anyway . . . Maybe it'll be different later, when I'm used to living here . . .'

'Fine.' Carson successfully hid his disappointment. 'Let's put your stuff in there; and then I think we should both pack it in for the night. You know where the bathroom is. Give me a shout when you're through. What time do you want to be woken, by the way?'

'Seven-thirty, but I've packed my alarm clock so don't worry about me.'

'Sure?'

'Quite sure.'

'OK. Let me find you some keys, so you can come and go without worrying about me.'

As soon as he had given her his spare keys, he took himself to his room. Before shutting his door, he called, 'I'll probably be gone before you wake tomorrow. You'll be all right, won't you? Help yourself to anything you want for breakfast. And don't expect me home too early. Remember I'm calling in on your parents on the way back. Try to get a decent sleep tonight, for once, will you?'

'You too. And, Carson . . . sorry again about last night.'

As they closed their doors, they were both half-aware that they were about to embark on a serious, if somewhat unconventional, relationship.

# Chapter Fifteen

Sally's parents reacted precisely as Carson had expected they would. Brock was delighted, Louise was both worried and annoyed. When Carson first told them, he made it perfectly clear that it was an apartment-sharing arrangement and that he and Sally were not sharing a bed.

'She has her own room. She'll lead her own life,' he said to them both.

'It seems an odd arrangement,' muttered Brock, 'but if you're both happy with it, who are we to disagree?'

'Hey, wait a minute!' interrupted Louise. 'What makes you think I agree?'

'For heaven's sake,' snapped her husband, 'she's old enough to decide for herself.'

'I realize it's a little odd,' remarked Carson, hoping Louise was not going to start a scene, 'but she clearly didn't feel safe living where she was; and anyway, she shouldn't be living on her own. This may not be the ideal arrangement, and it may not last, but it seems to me preferable to leaving her in the French part of town on her own.'

Louise gave a dismissive snort but said nothing, saving her breath until she had a chance to talk to Carson on his own. Brock had bullied Carson into agreeing to stay on for dinner and had then rung his daughter suggesting she should join them.

'I'll drive over and fetch you,' he said to Sally when she agreed. 'I'll leave right away.' He turned to his wife and said, 'Get Carson to help you lay the table or something. It's getting late and I'm hungry. I want to eat when I get back.'

The minute Brock left, Louise launched her attack.

'You should be ashamed of yourself, Carson! You know how fond I am of you, but this is crazy! You just can't keep your hands off them, can you? When are you going to grow up?'

'Louise, I swear . . . !'

'I know you, Carson! The younger the better . . . Oh, come on, don't pretend with me! Who do you think you're trying to fool? She's my daughter, let me remind you, and you're going to leave her alone. I mean it. You so much as lay a finger on her—'

'For God's sake, Louise, you can't really think . . . ! I'm trying to help her. I'm just providing her with a safe roof over her head – somewhere where she won't be afraid any more.'

'I'm warning you. Just lay off her, Carson.'

'Listen to me, will you? I'm not going to touch her—' Louise tried to interrupt him but he brushed her objections aside. 'I know, but this is different. Sure, if she were an easy lay, and if she weren't your daughter, I might consider it – I'm no saint; you know that – but I wouldn't dream of hurting Sally. I haven't touched her and I'm not intending to, I promise. I haven't so much as given her a kiss.'

Louise was not reassured, but there was little she could do about it. She tried to persuade her husband, after Sally and Carson had left, that it was his responsibility to put an end to the whole thing.

'Don't be so darned possessive about her!' Brock exclaimed. 'You should be glad it's Carson and not someone we don't know.'

'He's too old for her, Brock. I've told you that before. He's a lady-killer. He hasn't changed. She'll only end up getting hurt.'

'Carson is not going to hurt her. He wants to look after her. She needs someone like him – someone older who makes her feel safe. Come on, honey, give him a chance. You can't want her to go on living on her own, terrified every time she hears someone fart on the stairs!'

Unable to make any impression on either Carson or Brock, Louise had lunch with her daughter before admitting defeat.

'I'm only sharing an apartment with him, Mum. I've got my own room and he doesn't bother me – not at all. Anyway, I like him. He's fun to be with. And he's really kind to me. If I did have an affair with him, I don't know why you should mind.'

'It would be very unseemly. He's old enough to be your father.'

'So? There's nothing wrong with that. I feel safer with older men.'

'He's a womanizer, honey. He was so unfaithful to Gail you wouldn't believe . . . He's the worst kind of man for you. Believe me, I know what he's like.'

'Well, I'm not having an affair with him, so I don't know what you're fussing about. Anyway, I'm old enough to make up my own mind.'

Louise was obliged to admit that Sally had never looked happier. She seemed to have gained a self-confidence that had been noticeably lacking until then. Studying the untrammelled contours of her daughter's face, Louise noticed that Sally's prettiness had acquired another dimension and realized, with fore-boding, that her daughter thought she was in love.

Sally was nervous at first. She slunk about the apartment like a cat that is unhappy at being moved to a new home. Carson frequently had the impression that she was about to bolt.

'Do you want to bring some more of your things here?' he asked her one evening. 'You might feel more comfortable if you had some of your own pictures and books around the place.'

'Maybe,' she replied with little conviction. 'Would you mind if I changed my room around a bit?'

'Of course not. Do what you like with it. It's your room. Do you want to get it redecorated? I'll pay for it if you want to have it redone.'

'No, it's very pretty. I'm not crazy about those hunting prints, that's all.'

'Nor am I. Let's get rid of them. Do you have any pictures you want to put up instead?'

'I have a couple of landscapes that I bought in a sale last year, and a water-colour that I found in a junk shop off Saint-Denis. They're not worth anything, but they're pretty – or, at any rate, I like them. And I have a Fox that I'm fond of. You didn't see it. It's in my bedroom – my old bedroom, I mean. It's quite a good one. I think you'd like it. Dad gave it to me when I graduated and I'm used to having it around.'

'Fine. Why don't we go to Saint-Joseph tomorrow evening and see if there's anything else you want to bring back? Is there any furniture you want? I don't mind. I'm not especially attached to anything that's here. We can get rid of it and start again, if you want.'

'Would you mind if I brought that little desk that was in my living-room? I'd like to have that, too, if it's really OK with you.'

'Sure. Bring anything you want. I mean it. As far as I'm concerned, you can change the whole apartment. I haven't had time to do much with it since I moved in – and anyway, interior decorating isn't really my scene – so I'd be delighted if you want to take over and organize the whole place.'

He encouraged her to change everything. He wanted her to feel at home. She began to enjoy it, and it gave her something to do at weekends and in the evenings when Carson (as often happened) had to go somewhere without her, or was held up at work.

They gradually settled down to a workable routine. They agreed to take turns doing the cooking, though Carson (who was the better cook) tended to monopolize the kitchen when he was around. Sally did all the shopping, and Carson was happy to leave that to her, though he was faintly worried when he realized she still did most of it in the east end of town.

Carson paid for everything and insisted on giving her a generous household allowance. Sally felt uneasy about this at first. She repeatedly asked him to allow her to pay him something towards the bills, but he would not hear of it.

'For Pete's sake,' he would say whenever the subject came up, 'it makes no difference to me. I'll tell you when it begins to bug me, I promise. In the meantime, you keep your dough. Buy yourself some clothes or something. Have yourself a ball.'

She did just that. For a few weeks, she bought lots of new clothes; and books, and records, and bits and pieces she thought would look pretty in her new home.

A couple of months passed before Carson brought up a subject he had avoided until then. 'Shouldn't you get rid of that apartment of yours? You never use it. You haven't been back there once. It's crazy to go on paying rent on it.'

'I've been thinking about that, but I don't think I want to get rid of it yet. I like to feel I can go back there if I want.'

'But you never go back there. Wouldn't you rather have that money to spend on yourself?'

'What if you get tired of me living here? I have to have somewhere to go.'

'I won't get tired of you living here. I like it. I'm enjoying it, aren't you?'

'Yes.'

'Then get rid of that place, baby. You don't need it any more.'

As the months passed, Louise was forced to accept the situation. She assumed that Carson was sleeping with her daughter but was unable to deny that, whatever was going on, he was clearly making Sally happy.

'What did I tell you?' her husband asked her. 'It's the best thing that ever happened to her. I haven't seen her so relaxed since she was a kid.' (What he meant was

122

'since Paris' but these days he and Louise avoided all mention of that episode.)

'She's happy with him. You're right; but I'm worried about it, even so. If he's serious, he should marry her and stop fooling around.'

'What's the hurry?' asked Brock. 'They may well marry in due course. Give them time.'

# Chapter Sixteen

For some months, Carson and Sally continued to sleep in separate rooms. Carson made no attempt whatever to change the *status quo*, though he found it increasingly difficult to regard Sally with a physically indifferent eye. He spent less and less time at home, coming home late whenever possible in order to avoid being confronted with an insoluble problem. He was unable to avoid tripping over Sally in the mornings, however, since they both left for work at much the same time; and he found the sight of her wandering around in a nightdress more disturbing than he cared to admit.

They spent a fair amount of time together during the first couple of weeks; but, after that, Carson made sure that they saw as little of each other as possible. He came home late most nights, and even at weekends they tended to go their separate ways.

They both felt uneasy at the prospect of joint activities, in any case, fearing that their relationship might be misconstrued if they were seen together all the time. Sally was worried at the thought of putting her godfather in an awkward position, and Carson told himself that Sally must be left to lead her own life. He had offered her a home, he reflected, knowing that she might never wish it to be more than a safe haven in which to live. He had only himself to blame if he found it tricky; but he felt frustrated, none the less. As the weeks passed, he found it more and more difficult to ignore her physical attractions, and living in close proximity with her only increased his desire.

His chance came unexpectedly, after weeks of hoping that things might suddenly change. He had been asleep for several hours when he was woken by Sally's screams. He raced to her room and flung open the door.

'What on earth's the matter?' he demanded, switching on the light.

Sally was sitting up in bed, clutching her knees and making an odd, gasping noise. She was shaking. Her eyes looked huge and she was drenched in sweat.

'He was going to strangle me,' she whispered. 'He had his hands around my throat. He was kneeling on my arms and strangling me and he was . . . I couldn't breathe. I was choking. He was going to kill me . . . He . . .' She tried to say something else, but her words were inaudible through her tears.

Carson went over to the bed and picked her up in his arms. 'It was a nightmare, baby. It wasn't real. It was only a dream.' He rocked her in his arms, leaning his head against hers. 'He's three thousand miles away, Sally. You must try and forget it. As I've said to you before, if he's still alive, he's bound to be locked up. They'll have caught him long ago.'

'He might be out of prison by now even if they ever caught him.'

'If he is, he's certainly not going to be looking for you. He'll have forgotten who you are by now. It won't happen again. I give you my word.'

'I can't stand it . . . I can't stand it . . .' she sobbed, drenching his chest with her tears.

'It's OK, babe,' Carson kept repeating. 'It's all over. No-one's going to hurt you. It was just a bad dream.'

He felt at a loss as to how to reassure her. 'You need a brandy,' he said when at last she stopped crying. 'Why don't you take a shower while I get it? You'll feel better after a shower and a drink.'

While she was in the bathroom, Carson came to a decision. He was convinced there was only one way to demolish her demon and that was to tackle it head on. Somebody was going to have to fuck her, he thought crudely: it was the only solution – and if anyone was going to do it, it might as well be him.

'Sally,' he said as she emerged from the shower in a clean nightgown, looking fresh and angelic, 'come and sit down. I want to talk to you.' He handed her a brandy and waited while she settled herself on the sofa. 'Go on, drink up. It'll do you good.'

Sitting down beside her, he let her sip her drink in silence. Then, gently removing the glass and placing it on the table, he took her two hands in his and looked her straight in the eye. 'You may not like what I'm going to say to you, but somebody has got to say it; and, since there's nobody else around, it's going to have to be me.'

She shifted uncomfortably, but Carson continued to grip her hands tightly. 'First, I think you should reconsider your views about analysis—' Sally tried to intervene but he cut her short. 'Don't interrupt! As I say, I think you should reconsider your position – I'm not a great believer in shrinks myself, but I honestly believe your case requires one . . .' She tried to free her hands, tugging them away in agitation.

'Calm down,' Carson said. 'Just calm down and listen. You know I wouldn't suggest it if I weren't sure about it in my own mind. We all know there are some quacks out there, but there are bound to be some good ones, too, and provided we find the right one they might be able to help you.'

Sally tried to stand up but Carson prevented her.

'I'd be happy to find out who the best person is for this sort of thing – yes, of course it has to be a woman! – and I'll pay for it for as many years as it takes to—' he was going to say 'to make you better' but corrected himself at the last minute '—as many years as it takes for you to get rid of this nightmare.'

'I tried that before.'

'I know. Your father told me. Anyway, I don't want you to answer me now. I want you to think about it for a day or two.'

'I've thought about it often.'

'I'm sure you have, but I want you to think about it again.'

'OK, but I can tell you, it won't work.'

'Well, let's see. Let's talk about it in a few days' time, OK?'

'OK.'

'Good girl.' He patted her on the head, then took her two hands in his again. 'And now to my other point.' He took a deep breath. He was not sure how to broach the subject, but he knew he had to try. Squeezing her hands tightly, he said, 'You're never really going to be free until you overcome your terror of sex.' He felt her freeze. 'In your mind, it's inseparable from violence and even death. That's why you're so scared of it.' She tried again to free her hands, but he hung on to them, saying, 'I'm not going to attack you. Don't look so frightened. I just want you to listen until I've said what I have to say.'

'I don't want to talk about it.'

'But I do, and I'm going to, so you'll just have to listen. You need to find out what sex is all about. I'm not talking about vicious abuse but about real, loving, gentle sex. If you want, I will show you ... Stop pulling away – I'm not going to force you. I've told you all along, I'm never going to force you; I'm simply telling you it's what you need.'

'How do you know what I need?' Sally snapped.

'It's obvious, Sally. It's so obvious there's no point in discussing it. You know yourself, or you would never have picked up that French-Canadian boy ... Don't start denying it. You more or less said so yourself; and anyway, what did you think you were going to do with him? Why did you pick him up in the first place?'

'I wanted a friend. I just wanted a friend.'

'Come on, be honest. You wanted to go to bed with somebody – anybody. OK, you wanted to go to bed with him, if you like. The point is that you wanted to go to bed. You wanted someone to make love to you. You wanted to know what it was like, didn't you?'

Sally refused to answer, but he was determined to make her admit it. 'Didn't you, Sally? Isn't that what you wanted? Nobody's going to criticize you for it. It's the most natural thing in the world. Why do you find it so difficult to accept? What do you think is so awful about it?'

He let go of her hands and put his arms around her, pulling her towards him. 'Listen, babe, you've got a problem and you know it. Why won't you let anyone help? Here I am, a respectable guy who really cares for you and who's only trying to help. You know I'm not going to hurt you. I'm very, very fond of you. I care about you. I want to help you; and I'd love to make love to you. So where's the harm? Why not try?'

'How do I know you won't hurt me? You might turn out to be the same. All men may be the same, for all I know.'

'Jesus, Sally, don't you know me better than that? Bring a carving knife to bed with you if you want. Would that make you feel safe? I'm prepared to take the chance. You can stab me in the guts if you don't like it.'

She laughed, and Carson relaxed his hold. 'Well, at least you've recovered your sense of humour,' he remarked. 'Do you realize how frustrating it is for me to live with you and never be allowed to touch you? Now, what do you say? Do you want to try, or not?'

'Maybe,' Sally said pensively, 'if you let me finish my brandy first – and if you'll really let me bring a knife with me.'

That first attempt was not a success. Sally was paralysed with fear, and Carson found the knife discouraging. However, being a patient man, he persevered. He showed Sally all the tenderness of which he was capable until finally, one night, the knife was removed from his line of vision and was thereafter allowed by Sally to lie hidden under the bed.

Even then, their love-making remained incomplete, restricted to caresses and kisses and declarations of affection. This, thought Carson, was going to be the most complicated and long-drawn-out seduction he had ever undertaken; the most difficult, he was convinced, ever attempted by any man.

Because it was such a challenge, it became a kind of game to him; a game, it has to be said, that he was determined to win. The thought of his eventual achievement became a goal so irresistible that he was just about able to smother his immediate desires.

He was aware, however, that it was a game that could go desperately wrong. One false move on his part and it would be over. Sally certainly wasn't going to give anyone a second chance. He was so anxious not to frighten her that he forced himself to take a passive role, assuming that if she felt she was the dominating partner she would lose her fear of being overpowered and abused.

As a result, it became an entirely new activity from his point of view: more like being fondled by a beautiful child, he decided, than anything remotely to do with sex. Sometimes it seemed a pleasant form of relaxation, sometimes excruciatingly frustrating to have her lovely body clambering all over him. He supposed she hadn't the faintest idea how provocative she was being, or how near to madness she sometimes drove him.

Sally was intrigued, but she remained wary none the less. Unconsciously, she was testing him to see whether he was truly safe. She was also, equally unconsciously, settling an old score: repaying torture with torture and hitting back at the masculine sex.

Carson, of course, had a safety-valve about which Sally knew nothing. When desperate, he knew plenty of Montreal women eager to provide solace. He soon established a satisfactory routine for himself whereby, most nights, he came home physically satisfied and quite able to contend with his god-daughter's curious game. Sally never queried his increasingly late home-comings which seemed to her the inevitable result of his job.

But the Square Milers, like those with social aspirations in any other city, live in a hive of intrigue and gossip where little passes unremarked; and this apparently congenital tendency among the socially competitive to mind each other's business is made all the easier in North America once the winter sets in. However silently lovers may flit to each other's doors at dead of night, the snow – which deadens their footfalls – holds the prints of their footsteps, frozen indelibly, long after, for all to see. Worse still for anyone attempting to move about surreptitiously under cover of night, if you look out on snow under a clear, nocturnal, Northern sky, the world appears floodlit; stars without number glitter across the heavens; the earth is bleached by the moon's pale light; the snow glistens frostily; the streets look dazzling; and lovers stand out darkly in that brilliant, white world.

Inevitably, Carson Mackenzie's activities were noted. He was frequently spotted trudging across Redpath Place late at night. Everyone knew, of course, the lady on whom he was calling. She was one of the richest and most popular members of their social élite. No-one thought anything of it. They were eminently suited. But tongues went on wagging nevertheless.

It was not long before they found out who all Carson's mistresses were, and the details of his philandering became a favourite topic of conversation at cocktail parties all over Westmount.

Brock Hamilton tried hard to keep it from his wife; but she found out, as he knew she was bound to do.

'What did I tell you?' Louise demanded. 'I'm going to kill him for this!'

She telephoned Carson at work and insisted on meeting him for lunch. Seeing that something was troubling her, Carson ordered two large Martinis before allowing her to speak her mind. He was not expecting the violent onslaught that Louise had been preparing and nearly choked on his drink when he heard her first words.

'You're a bastard, Carson! You inveigled Sally into living with you when you knew what she was like – I mean, you know she's never played around and she's fragile – and then you go and screw half of Westmount! Don't you try and deny it! I know all about it! Everybody knows! You're having an affair with Martha, aren't you? And with Kathy, from what I hear. And with Audrey! You've been two-timing my daughter all over town! I can't believe it! After all those promises! It's got to stop, Carson! You promised you wouldn't lay a finger on Sally and then, look what happened! You promised you wouldn't hurt her and then you rush straight into Martha's bed. You couldn't be faithful if you tried, not to Sally, not to anyone! There isn't a female in this town that you haven't laid at some point! Why did you have to have Sally as well? Why couldn't you leave her alone?'

'Hey, wait a minute!' Carson interrupted her. 'You're making some wrong assumptions here! That little girl of yours . . . I haven't done anything to her.' He saw Louise's expression and tried to choose his words carefully. 'I swear to God, Louise, I haven't touched her. As far as I know, she's still a virgin.'

'Do you really expect me to believe that?'

'You can believe what you like – but I'm telling you, it's the truth.'

'She's in love with you, Carson. You know she is. It's written all over her. Are you trying to tell me you've been living all these months with a young and attractive girl who you know is head over heels in love with you, and you haven't touched her? Come on, Carson, who are you trying to fool?'

'Well . . .' Carson was not sure how much he should tell her. 'I've touched her, sure, but nothing more.'

'You bet you've touched her! You couldn't keep your hands off her if you tried! I know you! I remember what it was like for Gail . . . So what do you think this is going to do to Sally when she finds out? Had you thought of that? Have you ever spared a second to think about what it'll do to her?'

'For heaven's sake, Louise, so I've touched her, OK? I've kissed her and I've held her, but that's all, I swear. I've never . . . She doesn't want . . . Hell, Louise, you know what I'm talking about. Try and imagine what it's like for a minute. There I am, sharing my apartment with this really lovely young girl. She's sweet, and pretty, and funny and affectionate; and she's running all over the place in her nightdress, or just wrapped in a towel. She even gets into bed with me, but she won't fuck. I'm not going to try to force her, for Christ's sake! So what the hell am I supposed to do? Live like a goddam monk?'

'Are you telling me the truth?'

'Of course I am. That girl needs professional help. She needs analysis. I've been trying to persuade her – I've told her I'll pay for it – but she's terrified of the whole idea. She's got a real block about it. I'd like to help, but I don't know how. Maybe you know. Maybe you should talk to her.'

'I will,' said Louise. 'You're darned right I will! And if I find you've been lying, Carson, you can start praying now! I'll make you pay for the rest of your life! You'll never be able to set foot in Westmount again! I'll ruin you! I'll—'

'OK, OK, I get the general idea. I'm not lying, as it happens, so you can cheer up. But,' he could not resist adding, 'if you can persuade your daughter to give me her beautiful body, you'd be doing me a favour.'

'You! That's all you can think about!'

Carson laughed. 'You're right. It's becoming something of an obsession . . .' Seeing her expression, he

132

realized he'd gone too far. 'Calm down, for Pete's sake. It was meant to be a joke.'

It was not a joke, however, and he knew it. He had somehow, stupidly, managed to fall in love with an exasperating, screwed-up, cute, demented kid.

Louise was determined to find out the truth. She hadn't intended to tell Sally about Carson: it just slipped out by mistake. Well, it was Sally's fault for being so hoity-toity. Who did she think she was, anyway? What on earth did she have to get on her high horse about?

She felt bad about it, all the same. Sally's face . . . Well, she didn't want to think about her face. She should know, anyway. She had to know. She'd have to find out sometime what he was like; and if it was true that she hadn't been having an affair with him, why should she mind? Maybe it would save her from getting further involved with him. Maybe it was the best thing she could have done, telling Sally like that. She didn't want her daughter involved with a guy who was going to play around. She didn't want her having an affair with Carson. She never had.

Carson did not often misjudge people, but he totally misjudged Louise on that occasion. It never occurred to him that she might tell Sally about his trivial dallying. He did not think she was capable of such a thing, so he was totally unprepared for a drama when he went back to his apartment that night.

'You've been with Audrey Beaumont, haven't you?' Sally asked the minute he walked in. She was sitting huddled on the living-room floor, white as a sheet and clutching a drink.

'What?'

'Is that why you're always so late? Do you see her every night?'

'Sally, what is this?'

'I know about her. You don't have to pretend. And I know about Martha Mitchell and Kathy Henderson as well. When do you manage to see them? Do you see them in the daytime, or after work?'

He walked over and stood looking down at her. 'Who told you all this?' he asked.

'Mum.'

'Your mother told you?'

'Yes, Mum told me; and I'm glad she did. Why didn't you tell me?'

'I didn't want to hurt you.'

'Well, you have,' she said; then repeated to herself in a whisper, 'You have! You have!' He pulled her to her feet and tried to take her in his arms. 'Don't touch me!' she shouted, trying to push him away.

'Sally,' he said, for once ignoring her wishes and taking her in his arms, 'let me explain.'

She gave a snort of derision, hearing those time-honoured words. 'There's nothing to explain,' she said.

'Oh, yes there is!' Carson contradicted her. 'There's one hell of a lot that needs explaining around here.' He dragged her to a sofa and sat down, pulling her onto his lap. She wriggled furiously, but he had no intention of allowing her to escape.

He waited until she stopped struggling. 'You don't have the faintest idea,' he said, 'what it feels like to live with you and not be allowed to make love to you. You *know* what I feel about you, but maybe you don't know what it feels like for me physically. It's torture having you in bed with me and not being allowed to do anything. I want to make love to you – you must know how much I want to make love to you; but you won't ever let me. It's driving me crazy. You come to my room every night; you do everything on earth to get me excited; but you never let me make love to you. Can you imagine what that feels like? Can you imagine what you're putting me through?'

Sally said nothing, so he continued. 'I've been as patient as I know how. I've put up with agonizing frustration for months. I'm in love with you, goddamm it, and I want to make love to you more than I've ever wanted to make love to anyone. So what am I supposed to do? You know I'll never force you. I gave you my word – and I'm not about to break it. But, be reasonable, Sally. I'm not made of stone.'

Sally looked shamefaced. 'I didn't realize,' she said.

'Oh, but you did! You're not the complete innocent you like to make out you are. You may not want to admit it, and I don't know how conscious it is, but I'm telling you, babe, somewhere in there you know darned well what you are doing. You're punishing me for that guy in Paris – and I don't blame you! Not one little bit. You have every right to want to pay men back. You don't think I'd have stood it if I wasn't aware of that, do you?'

'I didn't mean to—'

'Don't fool yourself. You meant it. You wanted to see if I'd go back on my word. That's what it's all about, isn't it?' Sally nodded. 'Yeah, well, I figured that one out. You wanted to see whether I could be trusted or whether I'd suddenly turn into a monster. Fair enough. That's understandable. But, hell's bells, how long does it take to prove something to you? I mean, we've been together nearly six months. How much longer do you need?'

'I don't know,' she said miserably.

'For Christ's sake!' Carson exploded. 'And you expect me not to screw around? You've got one hell of a nerve, Sally! Jesus, you've got a nerve!'

'Don't get mad at me,' Sally whimpered. 'Please don't get mad at me.'

'I'm not mad at you! I'm mad at myself! Can't you understand that? I want you. I'm crazy about you. You're driving me insane! One thing I can tell you and that's for sure: whether you like it or not, until you let me make love to you – assuming you ever do, of course – I'm going to screw any woman I can lay my hands on; otherwise I'll probably . . . go completely insane!' (He had been about to say, 'Otherwise, I'll probably

135

end up strangling you,' but thought better of it just in time.)

Sally said nothing for a while. She sat on his lap, as limp as a rag doll, her head hanging down like a snowdrop dangling on its stem. Suddenly she came to life and looked at him. 'If I let you make love to me, would you stop going to bed with other women?'

'Yes, as long as we're not talking about a one-night-only affair. I mean, one night would be great – don't misunderstand me – but it might not keep me going for the rest of my life.' He laughed, hoping that he might succeed in making her smile.

She did not smile, however.

'OK. You can make love to me,' she said in a resigned voice. (Did she mean it? He wasn't sure.)

'You don't look too thrilled at the prospect.'

'I don't know till I've tried, do I? I want you to do it right now.'

'Right now?'

'Yes.'

'Are you sure?'

'Yes.'

'Wow! I'm in luck!' He was trying to sound light-hearted, but it fell flat. Sally looked more tense than he had ever seen her. 'Don't forget the carving knife's still under the bed,' he tried. 'You can still chop me to pieces, you know. It's an extremely sharp knife.' He looked at her face. It was completely expressionless. 'Come on, baby,' he said, kissing her on the forehead, 'can't you give me just one little smile before we go to bed?'

# Chapter Seventeen

And so, at last, Carson reached his goal; but it was not quite the triumphant achievement he had envisaged. It was almost as if Sally thought their roles had to be reversed so totally that she felt unable to take any part whatever and, from being the active partner, became passivity itself.

At first Carson made allowances; then it became another challenge. Eventually he stopped worrying about it, and for a while found it oddly exciting making love to this limp doll.

But the excitement soon wore off, leaving him discouraged and perplexed. Sally did not seem unhappy, nor did she seem frightened. He reassured himself with the thought that it had taken her ten or eleven years to reach this point so that he could hardly expect her to become an enthusiast overnight. Time, he kept telling himself; things would improve with time.

Nevertheless, as the months went by, he began to feel increasingly despondent.

'Don't you like it?' he asked Sally one night.

'It's OK.'

'Just OK? Nothing more?'

'It's OK,' she repeated. 'It's fine.'

'You're not still frightened, are you?'

'No.'

'Not at all?'

'I don't think so.'

'You don't sound too sure.'

'I would be frightened with anyone else, but I don't feel scared with you.'

'Well, that's something, I suppose.'

He looked at her lying there and felt irritated suddenly. Her head was turned sideways so that he could only see her profile; her eyes were closed as if she were trying to forget where she was; and her arms lay inactively by her side. (He often had the impression, when making love to her, that her limbs were completely detached from her body.) 'It's meant to be fun, Sally,' Carson exclaimed in exasperation. 'You're meant to be having fun!'

Opening her eyes, she turned her head and looked at him. 'Yes, I know,' she replied. 'I'm sorry. I think it's something to do with not being married. Do you remember I told you I thought it wouldn't work unless we were married? I can't explain it exactly, but I feel as if I'm being used.'

'You think I'm just using you?' Carson was astonished.

'I know it doesn't seem like that to you, but it feels like that to me. I can't see any difference between me and those other women you had. I suppose I feel insecure about you. I worry that you might go off and leave me. I don't think I could survive without you, now, so I guess I need to know it's for real. I need to know it's permanent.'

'And you think you'd feel differently if we were married?'

'Yes, of course.'

'Why on earth didn't you tell me this before?'

'I thought you knew.'

Carson was silent for a while. Sally closed her eyes again, but he could sense that she was waiting for him to reply.

'OK. If that's what you want,' he said, after giving it some thought. 'We'd better tell my kids – we'll have to go and see them. We can tell your parents after we've told them. I bet they'll be happy about it!' (He had his doubts about Louise, but he was not going to tell Sally that.)

'What about your friends?'

138

'They'll be pleased as punch. You can bet your bottom dollar. Everyone will be thrilled.'

He was right. Everyone was delighted. It was an entirely suitable joining of two well-established families; and if Sally seemed a little young for Carson, the Square Mile had had time to become accustomed to the idea that they were a couple.

Carson's friends were particularly pleased. They'd noticed how fond he was of Sally. He must be very happy, they told each other, because he hadn't strayed for months – and that, for Carson Mackenzie, was quite something, they all knew. They'd felt sorry for him when Gail died. He'd been so lonely for a while; and although his children were grown-up and off his hands, it'd be nice for them to know their father was happy at last.

Sally needed to settle down, too, they all told each other. Think of the worry she'd caused poor Brock and Louise when she had that French boyfriend and went off to live in the east end of town. It was high time that she married; there was no doubt about it. It was clearly a very good thing for them both.

Even Louise was delighted. She wanted to see Sally married; and she was as aware as the rest of Westmount that Carson had finally given up womanizing. Maybe Sally was what he had needed all along. He certainly seemed to have changed. She was the first to admit that.

Louise felt that everything had slipped into place, now that they were actually getting married and Carson had stopped fooling around. She realized, with a slight pang, that it was because she had once been in love with Carson herself that she had found the whole idea of him and Sally so difficult to accept.

During the months that followed, Carson went along with Louise's determined efforts to make sure that her daughter's wedding would be remembered for years. He was not enthusiastic. He did not want a big wedding; but he could see that Louise had made up her mind. Anyway, as far as he could tell, Sally seemed to like the idea. He supposed that if she needed to be married in order to feel safe, the more spectacular the public declaration of intent, the more secure she would feel. That's what it was all about, he told himself: a public announcement of one's private intention. Anyway, what the hell, if it made her happy? He was nuts about the kid, and he wanted her to have fun.

Similarly, when things between him and Sally remained as before, he consoled himself with the thought that this would change once they were married. Although he did not understand it, he believed Sally when she insisted that it would be completely different once they were wed.

## Chapter Eighteen

The Carson Mackenzies were a popular couple, and in many ways it could be said that their marriage was a success. They were devoted to one another; Sally seemed less insecure now she was married, and everyone agreed that she kept Carson young. Carson had no wish to start another family, and this was a great relief to Sally, who renounced the thought of motherhood without a moment's regret.

Carson wanted her to give up her job, but Sally felt a moral obligation to continue to help women who were being mistreated. 'You don't need to work,' Carson kept saying to her. 'I earn enough to keep both of us comfortably; and I have plenty of family money, besides.'

'That's not the point,' she replied. 'Somebody has to help women in trouble and if people like me don't do it, I can't imagine who will. Anyway, I'd be bored if I didn't work.'

'But you get too involved. It makes you depressed — and no wonder! All you ever see is the worst side of life. Don't you think it's time you started having some fun?'

'You sound just like Mum and Dad! You don't want to know what really goes on out there, do you? You seem to think that if a country is not at war, life is as cosy and safe for everyone as it is for you. It's not like that, Carson. Life is full of horrible people doing atrocious things to each other. It's full of madmen and maniacs and people being hurt.'

It took Carson four years to persuade her to do something different for two afternoons a week, and he only achieved that by developing her interest in art. 'You're good at it, Sally. You have an eye for new talent. Why don't you go and learn about it properly and put it to use? You could enrol for an art course, or study history of art, or decorative arts, or something like that.'

Sally was tempted. 'I'll think about it,' she said.

In the end she agreed to spend two afternoons a week working for a friend of theirs who was a picture dealer, but she continued to work for battered women the rest of the time.

Through her marriage to Carson, Sally had been obliged to take up a lifestyle which did not interest her and with which she would not have bothered had it not been for wanting to please her spouse. They entertained extensively. They were seen in all the right places; and their names appeared regularly in the social columns of the *Gazette*.

Although she would have preferred a less gregarious existence, Sally believed herself to be happy, and Carson thought she seemed content. He had, by this time, resigned himself to the fact that she was never going to be much fun in bed. It was not, he told himself, that she was totally frigid; but it was clear that she did not enjoy it in the way that most people did. She tried her best, however. That much was apparent. He could not complain. She was very pretty, she was affectionate and funny, she fitted in with his lifestyle; and it was obvious to everyone that she loved him, just as he clearly loved her.

In desperation, Carson occasionally made love to other women but he was a great deal more circumspect about these liaisons than he had been in the past. He made sure that what he did on trips out of town could not possibly reach any Montreal ears.

He and Sally had worked out a *modus vivendi* which was acceptable to both of them and in this fashion kept each other happy for the better part of ten years. Carson was nearing retirement when, totally unexpectedly, Sally at last understood the power of sex.

\*     \*     \*

The Scott-Williams were giving an enormous party. Everybody who was anybody was going to be there. As always, Sally managed not to be ready. No-one ever expected them to be on time – they never were – so Carson poured himself a large drink and sat sipping it and watching television while his wife spent another hour trying on different garments and fiddling with her hair.

'Come on, baby, get a move on!' he shouted eventually.

'OK,' she replied, 'I'm ready. Let's go.'

They drove in silence, Carson thinking how beautiful she looked. Years later he still remembered what she was wearing that night.

A maid opened the door and took their coats. There were people milling about on the landing above and a sudden burst of laughter carried towards them as they followed the maid upstairs. They were shown into a room packed with the amiable, heavy-drinking faces of their friends; but Sally did not see any of them. She saw only one.

An atoll. An iceberg. An arctic floe. The room slipped as she was thrown into the howling wastes of her past. Carson saw her sway and, putting out his hand to save her, caught his breath as he noticed the expression in her eyes.

'What's the matter?' he asked, but she did not answer. She clutched at his arm, and beads of moisture glistened on her brow. 'What's the matter?' he repeated; but it was obvious she did not hear.

His eyes were blue, she thought. How on earth could she have forgotten? And he still had that thick, well-cut, light-coloured hair.

A geological fault – a huge rift – had opened beneath her. She stood mesmerized, like an animal caught at night in the headlights of a car.

They stared at one another. Neither moved. But Sally had recognized her complementary. It was as if a long-disused mineshaft had suddenly collapsed inside her and she was plunged headlong to lie buried under an incalculable weight of fear.

Carson was still holding her arm as their host and hostess came to greet them. 'My, Sally, you're cold!' said Jamie Scott-Williams. 'Let me fetch you a drink. I want to hear about this exhibition of Seyrauds I hear you are organizing. Is it true that they're all from his European trip?'

Sally did not hear him. She was staring over his shoulder. 'Who is he?' she whispered. 'Who is that man over there?'

Jamie turned to look at the assembled company. 'Do you mean Philippe Marignac?' he asked. 'Haven't you met each other? I thought everybody'd met him. You know him, don't you, Carson?'

'No, but I've heard a lot about him. Isn't he the guy Sue Macintosh was telling us about the other day – the one who's teaching at the University of Montreal?'

'That's right. He's a friend of hers. Anyway, if you haven't met him, let me introduce you.'

'Come on, babe,' said Carson, taking Sally's arm as their host forced his way between the guests, trying to lead the way.

His eyes never wavered as he saw her approaching. He said, 'Good-evening,' in English and held out his hand. Ignoring this gesture, Sally plunged her hands deep in her pockets, leaving Carson to talk to him as she turned to move away.

She walked slowly, as though attached to him by a heavy chain. She felt him pulling her backwards as she tried to move away. It was like her worst nightmares when she dreamt she was being chased and tried to run only to discover she was unable to move. She knew she must get away from him, but her movements had become leaden. She dragged herself across the room as though he had hooked a grappling-iron through her heart.

She could do no more than nod to the many friends who tried to talk to her. She was in a desert where every other human being seemed totally illusory: a mere shimmering of heat on the horizon; a mirage in the sands. Again and again she told herself it was not possible. It could not be her Paris attacker. But it was. This time the nightmare was real.

Is it possible to know the hour or the day? Do we ever understand the contours of the heart? From the litter of dusty canvases, can we recognize our own souls? Are we simply bequeathed a fate which it is impossible to alter? Has there ever really been such a thing as free will? Are we not just the bondsmen of barren intercourse and wasted ideals, trying to hack our way out of the labyrinthine alleys of the mind?

Twice during the evening the Frenchman approached Sally. The first time she fled to the kitchen, assuming no-one would find her there. But Carson, who had been watching her with increasing anxiety, saw her leave the room and followed her. Entering the kitchen behind her, he took her in his arms. 'What on earth is the matter?' he asked. 'You're shivering. Don't you feel well?'

'It's him,' Sally said in a voice that seemed to Carson to have dropped an octave suddenly. 'I know it's him.'

'Who?'

'That man. That French guy. That's the man that . . . that . . . abducted me in Paris.'

'Philippe Marignac?' Carson sounded incredulous.

'It's him, Carson. I'm almost sure it's him.'

'Sweetheart, don't be ridiculous. How can it possibly be him?'

'It just is. I recognize him. I'm practically certain it's him.'

'Come on, honey, you've made a mistake. Anyway, you always said you couldn't remember his face.'

145

'But I do now,' Sally rasped in a voice that Carson barely recognized. 'I sure do now.'

'You must be wrong, baby, but there's no sense in discussing it here. Do you want me to take you home?'

'No,' replied Sally with deathly resignation. 'What's the point? He's found me. I always knew he would.'

'Come on, sugar. I promise you, you've made a mistake. Maybe he's the same height, or the same colouring; or maybe it's because he's French. That's it, for sure.' Carson was ready to grasp at any straw. 'I bet you, it's just because he's a real Frenchman from France.' Seeing her expression, he felt he had to justify this remark. 'Association of ideas,' he muttered feebly. 'It's natural. It often happens.'

'It's no use, Carson. I know and you don't.'

'Come and talk to him – that is, if you're sure you don't want to go home? No? Well, come on then. I'll come with you. I promise I won't leave your side.' He kissed her on the forehead. 'You'll see that it can't be him.'

Carson was embarrassed by the grilling Sally gave Philippe Marignac. She asked him every question she could dream up about his early life. To her husband's relief, the Frenchman did not appear to mind. He answered readily; and his responses must, thought Carson, put Sally's fears to rest.

He had grown up, he explained to them, in Martinique where his father had held some military post. They returned to France rarely and, when they did, it was never to Paris. They had no relations in the capital and no reason to go there. His grandparents lived in the Midi, and it was there that they went when they were on leave.

He had been to university in Paris, it was true, but that was in 1957. He'd moved on to Harvard by 1962. He never went back to France because his grandparents were dead and, since his parents still lived in Martinique, he preferred to spend his holidays there with them. He had never felt the slightest attachment to France, he explained; and he had no reason to visit the country of his birth.

'How come you went to University in Paris, in that case?' Sally would not let it rest.

'I'd done all my schooling in French,' he replied, 'so it seemed the natural place to go.' He was looking at her fixedly and there was a strange glint in his eyes.

Carson had never before seen his wife employ such an aggressive style of questioning, and he suddenly wondered whether this was how she dealt with the men she encountered through her work. After an awkward half-hour, he decided he had better take her home. 'It's time we thought about leaving,' he remarked, apparently addressing himself to the Frenchman. 'I'm sorry to interrupt you both but we really must be making tracks.'

As they were saying goodbye to their hosts, one of Carson's cousins came up to them. 'Do you mind,' he asked Sally, 'if I have a few words with Carson in private? It won't take a minute. Jamie says you're going to Ottawa tomorrow, Carson; is that right?'

'Yes, but only for the day.'

'Well, there's something confidential I want to discuss with you before you go.'

He and Carson left the room and walked across the landing to the study opposite. As Sally saw them shut the door, she sensed Philippe Marignac approaching. Whirling round, she dropped her evening bag in her haste to leave the room. As she bent to pick it up, she could see two feet coming towards her. She wanted to run, but it was too late: by the time she had picked up her bag, he had already reached her side.

'Why do you keep running away from me?' he asked. 'I want to talk to you.'

She stood up, gripping her bag, unable to take her eyes from his. They were blue, she kept repeating to herself. She must always have known they were blue –

clear, intelligent, rational blue; and they were plunged into hers, holding her to him so strongly that she was unable to look away. She felt he knew her. He knew everything about her. He had always known her. There was nowhere she could hide.

He held her mesmerically, his eyes exploring hers. She felt him tramping the darkest alleyways of her past.

'You've asked me a lot of questions,' he murmured. 'Now I'd like you to tell me about you.'

She stared at him, paralysed. He was wrapping his presence around her, enclosing her in the twilight realms of her fears. She delved desperately for a response, for anything she could give him. She knew she must offer him something to make him go away.

As people in debt attempt to ward off disaster by searching their houses for anything of value they can sell, so Sally scoured her subconscious for any payment that might satisfy him, any treasure with which to bribe him, any threat with which to blackmail him; but she had known from the first moment that these efforts were in vain. She had nothing to offer him and her search proved disastrous; for from the crepuscular corners of an unpunctual life she had dredged up all her stores of incalculable pain.

'You haven't answered me,' he said. 'Is there so much to tell? But I see your husband coming back. Perhaps you will tell me the next time we meet.'

He bowed over her hand, as she knew the educated French still tended to do. The touch of his fingers repelled her; but destruction, like a lizard, was already sliding through her veins.

Hope is always stillborn to those who live in fear. The only cure for them is to render impotent the object of their terror. Sally had hoped that marriage would do this for her but, in her heart of hearts, she had always known that Carson – for all his tireless efforts and painstaking care of her – was totally powerless against her night. She loved her husband dearly but, when all was said and done, his emollient solicitude had served no other purpose than to stem the flow of blood from an amputated heart.

She was filled with self-revulsion; but just as people are attracted to horror and can stare with fascination at fatal accidents or at lethally poisonous snakes, Sally was drawn with infinite longing into the whirlpools of her fear. It was almost as if she had attended her own death in Paris, long ago, and her ghost could not take form until the murderer returned.

Over the years she had turned inwards, seeking resolutions she never found; and, by this time, too much self-examination had crippled her ability to love. In a sense, the amoral nature of her love – which was inevitably entirely self-seeking – had, with time, obliterated the earlier annotations of her soul. She had made ceaseless efforts to cure herself and had relied on Carson to save her; but, that hope dashed, a moral lassitude had overcome her long ago.

'I hope you feel better,' said Carson as soon as they were in the car. 'That was some going-over you gave the poor guy! What the hell he can have thought, God only knows!'

'It's him, Carson. Whether you believe it or not, I know it's him.'

'Come off it, babe! Forget it. He wasn't even in Paris at the time. You've been fine for years. Don't go back to all that now.'

Sally was silent. What was the point of trying to explain? It was too late, in any case: she knew she was about to walk unerringly to her doom.

149

# Chapter Nineteen

The telephone rang peremptorily at noon the following day. Sally knew before she picked it up that it could only be him.

'I'd like to see you,' he said. He had no accent at all. 'I'll be there in fifteen minutes.'

'No,' she gasped. 'I don't want to see you. Carson—'

'Your husband is in Ottawa. I've just checked. He won't be back till late tonight.'

'He didn't go,' she lied. 'He's here. He didn't go.'

'Why lie?' he asked. 'I've just telephoned Ottawa to make sure. He's been there for two hours. I'll be with you in fifteen minutes.' He hung up and the line went dead.

How did he know where Carson was? How did he know where she lived? How had he got hold of her number, if it came to that? She wasn't in the book. But it was easy, she supposed. He could have asked anyone last night.

Sally paced her apartment. She knew she should leave. She wanted to run away but somehow lacked the resolve. Her life had always seemed to her like a syllogism without a premise and now she thought she had discovered the missing piece, she had to find out whether it was he. She was sure, but she wasn't sure; and she would not rest until she knew.

She opened the door to him with barely a second's hesitation. A sigh of recognition escaped her as she stepped back to let him in.

'You wanted to see me. Otherwise you'd have left,' he said as he entered the hall and closed the door. Taking off his coat, he flung it on a chair, then picked her up gently and cradled her in his arms.

She did not resist. She made no noise as he carried her to her room.

Slowly, deliberately, he began to remove her clothes. 'Don't be hypocritical,' he said in reply to her unconvincing protestations. 'You know perfectly well that from the moment you saw me, you had only this in mind.'

'You're wrong. You don't understand. It was something else. It was—'

'I understand,' he interrupted. 'You need me. I'll find out why when we're in bed.'

The various shades of neurasthenia are as difficult to discern as a horizon in mid-Atlantic when one cannot distinguish sky from sea. In the penumbra of her subconscious Sally had always sought her attacker, not so much as someone against whom she sought vengeance but rather as someone to whom she felt she belonged. On one level, she was permanently terrified that he would find her and attack her again, fooling herself that, if she met him, she would kill him and finally have her revenge. But at some deeper level which she had never recognized, his violence had become synonymous with passion so that she believed her own passion could only be expressed with him. In one of those curious distortions that occur between the conscious suppressing of intolerable memories and the unconscious repression of frustrated sexual desire, Sally had almost begun to think of him as if he had once been her lover, and of herself as if she were a devoted concubine waiting patiently for his return. Believing that, after all these years of waiting, it was he who now stood before her, she gave herself up to this stranger with stylized gestures of submission and tiny, self-sacrificing cries.

Was it perhaps that, over the years, she had come to believe he was her only true lover? Was it the need to relive her nightmare in order to obliterate her fear? Was it simply that she was attracted to the very thing she loathed? Or was it – as she believed – that she wanted him to give himself away?

She wanted proof, she told herself. She wanted more than just the suspicion. She knew there must be something she would recognize, and she needed incontestable proof.

He had plunged his claws in her, for all that. He owned her. She belonged to him. She was his from the moment she saw him. In her mind, he had come to claim her, as she had always known he would. The eagle had swooped when she was defenceless and had permanently embedded his talons in her heart – or so she thought as, through the distorting glass of memory, she attempted to reconstruct the past.

He pinned her to the wall, to the floor, to the bed. The violence of his love-making matched the violence of her need. He bit her, kissed her, caressed her; he claimed the body that was his. He sought out each crevasse and hidden secret with his mouth and hands and tongue. He cradled her in his arms and carried her from room to room. He stood her against the wall and made her the prisoner of his embrace; then turned her around abruptly so she was facing the other way. He took her standing, lying, kneeling. He knew what she desired.

Only later, when it was over and she lay, damp and exhausted, beside him, did she emerge from the blackout of passion to think again about who he was.

She was deeply disturbed by the fact that she thought she recognized his face. Yet his voice was not the one she had carried with her all those years. He hadn't said anything in French, of course, but still . . . He hadn't said anything sweetly; he hadn't used endearments, or whispered to her about love. He hadn't knelt on her arms, rammed her stomach, or flayed her with his belt. He hadn't brandished broken bottles or hit her in the groin. For all the violence of his love-making, he had not hurt her in the least. She was puzzled. She wasn't sure. It was possible that she had made a mistake.

He turned his head and caught her studying him. He studied her calmly in return. Scanning her face, he correctly read her unspoken query.

'I have discovered the key to your sexuality, that's all,' he said quietly. 'Now I want to find out *why* it is the key. Let's get dressed and get out of here. I want to talk to you somewhere else.'

They made the bed and tidied up. She did not want to leave a trace. Then he took her to his apartment and tried to fathom her dark world. They talked for hours, but it led nowhere. She was not prepared to tell him anything. She was pretty sure he was not her attacker, but still not sure enough for that. Either he knew everything, as she half suspected, or he would simply have to guess. The fact that she was inexorably tied to him physically in no way removed her fear that he might be the psychopath of the past. She did not mention that she had ever been to Paris. She told him nothing of her life. If he was the person she was seeking then it was he who must give himself away. She expected him to answer all her questions but saw no reason why she should answer his.

Philippe Marignac was both baffled and intrigued. During their love-making Sally had displayed a highly charged and erotic sensuality, combining an extraordinary violence of passion with an almost oriental desire to please. He suspected that she had been hurt but he was unable to make her admit it; and the reason he thought this was because she appeared to be expecting – virtually begging – to be badly hurt again.

He asked her endless questions, watched her reactions, and waited patiently for answers which were not forthcoming. He used all the force of his intelligence to press against her wounds. Like a diagnostician seeking an explanation, he wanted her to tell him when it hurt.

But if one is to believe that character is largely formed by experience, then one must also believe that personality is influenced by landscape and climate. Sally was the child of blizzards and frozen rivers; but also of summer lakes and blazing suns. Reflecting the climate, her mood could fluctuate from sub-zero temperatures to ferocious heat; but, like the city she inhabited, she was sometimes locked in by ice.

At the moment she was in turmoil, like the St Lawrence in the spring. She could feel her defences cracking but, like an ocean liner forcing its way through the ice to the open sea, she continued to press against her fate as if she believed it to be her only hope of escape.

The Frenchman sensed something highly dangerous in her which he was at a loss to explain. Her exterior seemed weak, but he was convinced she possessed an element of astounding strength. A strength perverted, none the less: he could not fail to notice there was something wrong. From the fragmented world of her passions he picked out collusion, betrayal, taboos.

He returned to physical exploration when the verbal one ran dry. Somewhere here must lie the answer, he assumed, but he had no idea how to find it amid this explosion of desire.

A slim, white haunch, a rounded buttock, a glimmer of shoulder, rumpled hair; were these, as they seemed, offered in atonement (and, if so, for what?) or were they signs of iniquity disguised by beauty like the pure and irresistible voice of the siren serenading the mariner to his death?

Whatever she was, he had to have her. He had searched for years for this slender-throated creature of the translucent regard and opalescent thigh. Now that he had found her, he intended to keep her. He wanted her desperately. He wanted her all for him.

It was an extremely potent mixture, this mutual investigation through a mutual sense of danger and desire; but, whereas Philippe hoped to find happiness, Sally looked only for respite. In her occluded world she had long ceased to distinguish truth from false-hood – myrtle, hemlock or nectar: they were all the same to her. What she wanted was the key to herself which she believed this man to hold.

Beneath his glancing fingertips he felt the shock waves of desire. A blind obsession overtook him. He wanted this creature for his own. Thrown completely out of time and context by the violence of their emotions, they both suddenly ceased to wonder who or what the other was. She could have been a whore from the city's docklands, or a witch among the skyscrapers, for all he cared; and if, to Sally, he seemed (at least, at times) to be some appallingly seductive apparition of death, it was a death she could not resist: it was a death she desperately wanted to die.

There is always, in this search for unity, the desolation of impending loss; and for Sally, each moment of ecstasy was marred by the sense of encroaching loneliness that separation brings. Hour after hour, they clung to each other as if to stave off an approaching end; and each time they completed the cycle, their search for fusion had begun again.

'I must go home,' Sally said eventually. 'Carson will be back in less than an hour.'

'Does it matter?'

'Yes, it does. He mustn't know. I couldn't bear him to be hurt.'

'Will you ring me later tonight?'

'I can't. You must know that I can't.'

'You can if you want to, and you will. You can call me any time during the night.'

# Chapter Twenty

Philippe was right. Sally needed to hear his voice. She wanted to speak to him so urgently that she could not wait until the next day. At one in the morning, while Carson was sleeping, she dressed; then tiptoed downstairs and, ignoring the night porter's stare, walked out into the street.

It was the first time she had ever gone out alone at night without fear. Now that she had confronted the thing she most dreaded she felt jubilantly free. At last, she knew where the danger was and so no longer imagined it to be everywhere. The result of this certainty was that fear – her malevolent companion of twenty years – had entirely deserted her. It was as if she had been shadowed for years by an enemy agent who had been called off the job permanently now that his controller had her fixed in his sights.

The city was sleeping peacefully, its skyscrapers standing sentinel. Accompanied by the sound of her own footsteps, Sally made her way to a public telephone. It never occurred to her to worry about what Carson might think if he woke to find her gone.

She had always been frightened by Atwater Avenue and Saint Catherine Street, particularly at night; but on this occasion she moved fearlessly, thinking only of Philippe.

He was not asleep. He was waiting impatiently for her call. 'Where are you?' he asked.

'In a phone booth. I couldn't ring from the apartment.'

'Come here,' he said. 'I need you.'

'Don't be absurd, Philippe. I can't. It's the middle of the night. I left Carson sleeping, but he may have woken by now, for all I know.'

'Let's not waste time arguing about it. Just get in your car and come.'

She had never had much autonomy, and what little she possessed had now entirely vanished. She walked back to Westmount Square and climbed into her car. Sparing barely a thought for her husband, she drove through the silent city, relentlessly impelled to seek her lover's arms.

She returned at four in the morning to find Carson still asleep. Undressing quietly in the bathroom, she slipped on her nightdress, crept back to the bedroom, and slid carefully between the sheets beside her sleeping spouse. He murmured and turned over, but he did not wake. Unaware that she had been absent, he could not know that she had set the pattern for their future nights.

Sally knew, though, and so did Philippe. In the space of a few hours they had become that two-headed beast that true lovers sometimes are – a monster belching forth such flames of passion that no earthly creature could have severed it in two.

Yet no-one noticed that Sally's life had changed. In spite of the incessant risks she took, her husband remained ignorant of her activities and state of mind. She continued her uxorial and social duties with the same apparent application as before; but she now belonged elsewhere. She moved in an entirely different world. When she had first met Carson, she had believed him to be the St George to her dragon; but he had proved, she reflected sadly, to be an ineffectual knight at arms.

Never a day went by without her somehow managing to see Philippe. If they were unable to meet during daylight hours, they met at dead of night.

The most potent aspect of this obsession was Sally's sudden loss of all her fears. If Carson remained blind to all the rest, he should, she felt, have noticed that.

Carson had noticed it – he could hardly have missed

it – but he was struck by the effect rather than by the cause. His wife, for no obvious reason, always seemed to be in a hurry; and she had taken on a great many activities which did not require his presence. At long last, she had become independent, he concluded with relief.

Sally had only one fear nowadays, and that was the new and overwhelming one of not seeing Philippe for any length of time. (It was not the fear of 'losing' him – there was no possibility of that – but she felt she could only function for a very few hours without his physical presence.) All her previous fears had vanished to be replaced by this.

She met him at any time and in any place that he desired. She went alone into restaurants to wait for him – and they were always restaurants in the remotest parts of town.

Within a couple of weeks of meeting they realized that the French sector was the solution. Philippe took an apartment on rue Beaudry which he reserved for them alone. He kept his apartment on Peel Street, which remained his only address as far as the rest of Montreal was concerned; but because he had to be seen to be living there, he, like Sally, found himself driving around the city a good deal at night.

Time and again Sally waited until Carson had been gently snoring for an hour or more, then crept out of bed, slipped on her clothes and drove to that other, more dangerous, bed. During their lunch-hours, in the early evenings, on Saturday afternoons, at dead of night: every moment that they could steal, they spent together there.

Sally's world was that apartment, and that apartment all her world. Philippe filled it with the French furniture that his parents had shipped to him from Martinique and that he had, until then, left in storage because his Peel Street apartment was not large enough to hold it all; and he had it decorated in a style as remote from North America as the Equator from the

Poles: all gilt-framed mirrors, tapestried *Voltaires,* and escritoires with spindly legs.

Sally loved it. She felt at home there, though it bore no resemblance to any world she had ever known. It was as if she had stepped into the French provinces to discover that this was where she had always belonged. Behind heavy brocade curtains and *passementerie* cords and tassels she prowled, savage as a leopard, totally transformed. Subsumed into the anarchic, demonstrative, deeply passionate world that is France, she roamed naked among the *petit point,* brass candlesticks, coloured crystal and pot-pourri.

Philippe was besotted with her. He found her maddeningly seductive with her impenetrable secretiveness, her inexplicable masochism, her sinuous beauty, and her dream-drenched face. He wanted to disinter her mystery; he wanted to know what went on beneath that cloud of Botticelli hair.

'You're like the lady with the unicorn, or a Renaissance damsel: you're like Botticelli's *Primavera*,' he whispered to her one afternoon.

She looked up at him with a smile, resting onyx elbow on marble knee. Her lips were parted as if about to say something, her eyes dreamily blurred. He waited expectantly; but suddenly she lowered her lids and sighed, withholding whatever it was she had been about to say.

These exasperating glimmers of things she might have told him; the poignancy of her childlike arms and lamenting, quattrocento head; the mysterious and sometimes tragic manner in which she sighed: it was intolerable! He would destroy them both if he could not find a way inside her mind.

He knew that pleading was not the answer, but there were times when he would have crawled to her on bended knee. He wanted to grovel, he wanted to beg; he wanted to bury his head in her lap. He wanted to feel her palms pressing against his brow, and have her run her fingers up and down his spine.

One afternoon, in desperation, he plunged his face in the tangled masses of her hair. He wanted to force her to give up her secrets and feel her dissolving in his arms. But no, he couldn't crack it; there was something there he could not grasp. He could have wept as he watched her dressing, knowing that she would soon be gone, taking her secrets with her, the kernel of her personality still intact.

'What is it about you?' he asked her as she was leaving. 'There's something you're not telling me. I want to know. I have to know.'

Dragging her across the room to a chair, he forced her to sit down. 'Come on, tell me,' he said, standing in front of her and keeping a hand on her shoulder so she could not rise. He waited. Her lids were lowered, her grey eyes hidden; but he could see she was struggling with herself.

'There's nothing to tell,' she said finally. 'It's just the way I am.'

'There is something,' he insisted. 'What way are you? What does that mean? Tell me what it means.'

Her hands fluttered. 'I want you to hurt me,' she whispered. 'I don't know why, but I like being hurt.'

'I am aware of that,' Philippe replied. 'But why? Why should I hurt you? I love you. I haven't the slightest wish to hurt you.' He thought for a moment, then asked, 'Does Carson hurt you?'

'No, but I'm not in love with Carson. Maybe that's why.' She looked up at him with a troubled expression. 'Are you sure you weren't in Paris in 1962?'

'I was at Harvard. I've already told you. What's that got to do with all this, anyway?'

'Nothing,' she said. 'I just wondered.' He noticed that her eyes had clouded over, just as they always did when they were making love.

Philippe felt suddenly irritated. 'What the hell is this Paris obsession? Why are you so interested? Have you ever been there? What is Paris to you?'

'It's somewhere I've always wanted to visit,' she remarked untruthfully. 'I'd like to go there sometime, that's all.' She was trying to sound casual, but he heard the anxiety in her voice.

'Then why do you want to know if I was there in 1962? What's special about that year?'

She lowered her eyes without replying. The answer must be here, he thought, watching her fingers plucking at her skirt.

'I asked you a question,' he said. 'I want to know what was special about 1962.'

'Nothing.' He put his hand under her chin, forcing her to look up. 'Nothing,' she repeated. 'I just like the date, I suppose. I don't know.'

'There's something you're not telling me. I've got to know or I think I'll go mad.'

'There's nothing,' she exclaimed fretfully. 'Leave me alone! I've got to go. Carson was aiming to leave the office early, and if he gets home before me, he'll wonder where I am.'

'To hell with Carson! You're not leaving until you've told me what all this is about.'

'I don't know what you're talking about. You're imagining things. There isn't anything to tell.'

'You're lying,' he said. She was agitated and he knew it. 'I know you're lying. If I have to keep you here for a week, I'm going to make you tell me the truth.'

She pushed his hand away and stood up, shaking. 'I've got to go,' she repeated, walking towards the door.

'Oh, no you don't!' He grabbed her arm.

'Stop it! I'm fed up with your questions. You're being extremely boring and I want to go.'

He was stung. 'Maybe you'll find me less boring,' he remarked, 'if I do what you want. Let's see how you really like being hurt. I'm going to beat the truth out of you if that's the only way you can be made to talk.'

Gripping her arm tightly, he dragged her back to the chair.

161

'Don't!' she pleaded as he sat down and flung her, struggling, across his knee.

'Then tell me why you want to know if I was in Paris in 1962.'

'I can't. There isn't anything to tell.'

Holding her with one arm, he used his free hand to undo his belt. Pulling up her skirt, he brought the belt down hard. She jerked violently but made no sound.

'Tell me,' he repeated. He waited in silence for a moment, then brought his belt down again.

Within no time he was beating her with all the pent-up frustration he had felt for weeks. 'Will you tell me?' he exploded. 'Godammit! Come on, tell me! I'm going to keep this up until you talk.'

She whimpered. He waited a second, his arm poised in mid-air.

'Did you say something?' he enquired.

She remained silent and again his belt came down with a resounding crack.

'Please . . .' she whispered.

He laid down his belt. 'Please what?' he asked.

'Please stop.'

'If you want me to stop, you must answer me.'

'I can't.' He picked up his belt and lashed her again.

'I love you,' she moaned.

'Yes?' He brought the belt down again. 'And what else?'

'I need you. I love you. I can't live without you.'

'Paris,' he said. 'You're going to tell me about Paris.'

'I don't know anything about Paris,' she gasped. 'I don't know why I ever mentioned it.'

Finally, exasperated, he carried her to bed and made love to her more violently than he had ever done before.

He studied her face as she lay where he had flung her on the bed, and for a moment he understood precisely why men kill.

'I love you,' she said in a whisper, as he wound his fingers through her hair.

'Then tell me the truth.'

'The truth is that I love you,' she insisted. 'There's nothing more to tell.'

'You're lying,' he said as his hands closed round her throat. She said nothing as she felt them tighten, but he saw her expression change.

His eyes held hers for one blinding moment, then she felt his hands relax. Jerking her head backwards, he stared at her in desperation before engulfing her in the rage he felt at the knowledge that there was part of her he did not possess.

As the afternoon sun grew cooler and the sounds of activity gradually subsided in the street outside, they explored the dangerous quicksands of each other's torment and became again that monster of passion, twisting and coiling with the deadly ferocity and savage contortions of demonic love.

Untamed and unrepentant, she sobbed in her lover's arms as he tried every form of erotic torture in an attempt to make her talk. But for all the intensity, all the languid beauty, all the shifting moods of that afternoon, Philippe remained unsatisfied because the doors he had thought to open he was unable to force apart. The light was fading outside the shutters when, defeated and enraged, he crushed out his carnal longings in brutal, throbbing thrusts while the post-meridian shadows crept in silence up the bed.

# Chapter Twenty-One

Covered in lash marks and love bites, Sally hobbled home at dusk. Feigning illness, she took herself to bed in the spare room before Carson returned from work. She could think of no other way of hiding her bruises from him and, exhausted, was asleep by the time he came home.

Carson was concerned, took her temperature, told her it was sub-normal and offered to make her some tea. She accepted gratefully, saying she was cold, and grasped the opportunity to slip a bed-jacket over her nightdress while he was out of the room. By the time he reappeared with a tray she was sitting up in bed, having successfully hidden every inch of her body except her face and hands.

'Do you want to stay in here?' Carson asked her gently as he placed the tray on her knees.

'I think it's better. I must be going down with flu and you're more likely to catch it if we sleep in the same room.'

He was touched by her thoughtfulness and kissed her on the brow before withdrawing to the living-room to pour himself a drink. At regular intervals throughout the evening he popped his head round the door to ask her whether she needed anything and to reassure himself that she was all right. Sally was profoundly irritated by his concern, not because she felt guilty (she did not feel the slightest guilt) but because, quite simply, she wished he would leave her alone so that she might sleep.

Meanwhile, Philippe had returned to his Peel Street apartment, intending to make up for a lost afternoon;

but in spite of his efforts to catch up on work, he could not put the previous few hours out of his mind. To his horror he had discovered that he enjoyed hurting Sally as much as she apparently liked being hurt.

He found it impossible to concentrate. Instead of seeing the pile of papers awaiting his attention, he saw the soft afternoon light caress the curve of her spine; and the slight down, barely visible, on a pale, love-bruised thigh.

Turning his attention to a batch of publishers' catalogues that had just arrived from France, he tried to decide which books were worth ordering for his students, and which he needed for his own research; but the jargon of the blurb writers seemed specifically designed to cause him pain. Words, so misused or over-employed that in normal circumstances they would have made him cringe, shot out from the pages as if purposely chosen by a malicious fate determined not to allow him to forget. 'Powerful and sensitive', 'a new interpretation', 'devastating events', he read as, in his mind's eye, he saw the inaccessible mysteriousness of that other-world face; *'un défi'*, *'un exercice de style'*, and on the instant all her nervous beauty hovered before him: her coltish movements, her hesitation; her enigmatic sighs and compliant limbs.

He was unable to rid himself of the agonizing pleasure he had felt as he did appalling things to her in the semi-darkness of their shuttered room. The indescribable exhilaration of it had left him in a state of such excitement that he knew this was something he would repeat again and again. A volcanic sense of power had overcome him as, pleading with him to stop, begging him to go on, crying in his arms, melting at his touch, she slowly dissolved and – fragile, nude, exhausted – lay sprawled in maddening perfection among the tangled sheets of his ravaged bed.

An hour passed with little to show for it: he was unable to take in a single fact. He tried to read about the effects of the French Revolution in the Caribbean, hoping, in the process, to dispel the wave of ashen degradation that was sweeping over him as a result of his appalling self-discovery; but he could not slough off the memory of her body flinching at the impact of leather belt on satin skin. He ran his hand absently over his desk, wondering how all this would end. It was a dangerous game that they had embarked upon, and it was she who had dragged him there.

Why? And why the endless questions about Paris? What was it about Paris and about 1962? She must have a reason: the subject came up far too often to be treated as unimportant. She must have been there, although she had always denied it; and, if she had, surely someone must know? He would ask every person with whom she was acquainted. He would start frequenting the Westmount parties; he'd become part of the English social scene. If necessary, he'd ask her parents, or even Carson. He was determined to find out the truth.

His gaze slid vacantly over the carpet, across a bookshelf and back to his desk. He toyed with the idea of telephoning her, but decided against it. Carson was bound to be at home. Walking over to the window, he looked out and saw that it had begun to rain. Puddles glistened in the light cast by the streetlamps; the tyres of passing cars sprayed water from the gutters and the occasional pedestrian splashed by with coat collar turned up and umbrella dejectedly clutched in a damp hand. He could not work. It was hopeless. He might as well make something to eat, then go to bed.

One thing he could do, he decided, with a sudden burst of energy, was to pick up his address book and start telephoning anyone that Sally knew. He must make an effort to become friends with her family, become part of her social world.

From that evening, Philippe developed an interest in the English inhabitants of that curiously divided town. The 'French from France', he soon discovered, were as treasured in Westmount as the French Canadians were unwelcome so it did not take him long to become an accepted part of their group. He was an exotic outsider of the sort that the Square Milers liked to cultivate and so had no difficulty in becoming the hostesses' darling: the essential educated, handsome, supposedly un-attached and 'available' man (if not exactly 'eligible' when thinking in terms of one's daughters, certainly a welcome addition to any dinner party and the object of many a married woman's romantic fantasies and optimistic coquettishness).

He did the social rounds and waited patiently until, one evening, his neighbour at dinner brought up Sally's name in connection with a local sculptor she was helping to promote. Looking faintly bored, Philippe nonchalantly enquired, 'She spent some time in Paris when she was younger, didn't she?'

'Did she?' the person asked. 'I don't remember her ever going to Paris.'

He tried again with various people, but always without success, until he was introduced to a close friend of the Hamiltons at a drinks party. With the minimum of cunning, Philippe steered the conver-sation towards a discussion of Sally's parents; then, having listened to a lengthy dissertation on Brock's famous hospitality, Louise's talent for organization, and the pros and cons of the Hamiltons' move from Pine Avenue to Rosemount Crescent, Philippe snatched the opportunity to ask a question while his companion paused to light a large cigar. 'That daugh-ter of theirs was talking to me about Paris,' said Philippe. 'It's odd. She seems to have an obsession with the place.'

'She's never talked about it to me,' said Donald Henderson. 'She had a bad time there, I believe,' (Philippe was listening attentively although he made a show of brushing an imaginary speck of dust from his lapel) 'but for some reason it's always been something of a taboo subject with Louise and Brock.'

'I didn't realize she'd ever been there.'

'Well, it was years ago and she didn't stay there long. She ended up in hospital – she'd only been there a few days – and she came home as soon as she was better, so she can't have seen much of the place. It must have been very disappointing for her because she'd been so keen to go there. I remember that she had quite a tussle with her parents beforehand because they wanted her to go to some summer school outside Lausanne.'

'What bad luck! Was she seriously ill?'

'I seem to recall that the story Louise put about at the time was that her daughter had nearly died of a nosebleed. But they've never talked about it much and, as I say, Sally has never mentioned it to me, so I'm not too sure what really happened.'

Philippe changed the subject, not wishing to appear unduly interested, and made a mental note to check this information with the Hamiltons before confronting Sally with her repeated lies. To his immense frustration, he had to wait another couple of weeks before a suitable occasion offered and throughout that time he was still seeing Sally at some point every day. He was sorely tempted to have it out with her immediately, but restrained himself with the thought that he must be sure of his facts before tackling her on the subject. However, because he felt frustrated by the wait, and angry with Sally for withholding the truth, he was far rougher with her physically than he would otherwise have been.

He talked to the Hamiltons whenever the opportunity arose, but there always seemed to be other people about, and he knew it would be unwise to try and raise the subject until he could somehow corner them on their own. He thought of inviting them out to dinner, but felt he did not know them well enough to do so. He tried to think up an excuse to pick Brock's brains on legal matters, but could think of no adequate reason to consult a lawyer. At last, hearing Brock blasting off about some new rule that the University

Club had just brought in, he hit upon what seemed to him to be a simple and satisfactory scheme.

They were at the opening of an art exhibition and Sally and Carson had just left. 'That reminds me,' Philippe said to Brock, 'speaking of clubs, could you recommend a tennis club that I could join?'

'Sure,' replied Brock. 'How good are you?'

'Reasonable. I've played a lot – but not since I moved here. I miss it and I need the exercise.'

'Maybe we should see if we can get you into the Hillside Club. I don't know what their rules are regarding non-residents, but I can easily find out. I'll tell you what, why don't you have a game with me there one evening next week? It'll give you a chance to look at the place and, if you like it, we can see about it then.'

They fixed a date and Philippe withheld his questions for another week.

# Chapter Twenty-Two

They were evenly matched and had an excellent game. Philippe won, but only because he was younger and therefore able to cover the court with greater rapidity than Brock.

'That was a great game,' exclaimed Brock as they made their way to the men's changing rooms. 'But boy, do I need a shower and a drink! It's too hot to play tennis at this time of year. I'll give you another game in September, but I think I'm going to pack it in until then.' Flinging a towel over his shoulder, he headed for the showers, turning back to shout, 'See you in the bar when you're ready.'

'Carson Mackenzie is a good friend of yours, isn't he?' asked Philippe as they settled back with their drinks.

'Sure is. We've been pals since we were kids.'

'He's an interesting guy,' said Philippe. 'He must be very good at his job. He's far more aware of what's going on in international politics than anyone else I've met here.'

'Yeah, well, so he should be! It was his job for about twenty-five years – and he's lived in a lot of places and seen a lot of things. I was worried he'd be bored when he came back to Montreal, but he took to it again like a duck to water. You'd think he never left.'

'He speaks excellent French, with hardly a trace of an accent. I heard him interviewing a French politician the other day, and you could hardly have told he wasn't French.'

'He spent a lot of time in Paris during his London posting. He even had an apartment there for a time. He just loved the place.'

'Was that before he married your daughter? She's never been to Paris, has she?'

'Only for a few weeks once, when she was in her teens – and at that time Carson's first wife was still alive. He and Sally didn't really get to know each other until years after that.'

'I didn't realize your daughter had been to Paris.'

'Well, she wasn't there for long and she spent practically the whole time in hospital, poor kid.'

'What was wrong with her?'

'We never really found out.' Brock put down his drink and shifted his weight in his chair.

'Nothing too serious, I hope?' Philippe was desperate to make him talk.

'She had a nosebleed, a bad nosebleed.' Brock picked up his glass again and gave an unhappy laugh. 'Ridiculous!' he muttered. 'It doesn't sound serious, does it? But believe it or not, she damn near died.'

'How terrible! I had no idea one could die from nosebleeds. You must have been worried sick.'

'We were, I can tell you.' Brock took a gulp of his Martini. 'It was the worst thing we've ever been through. We didn't know anything about it until she'd been in hospital for about a week. There we were, on holiday, travelling round the States, and suddenly we get this news that our daughter is dying the other side of the world.'

'Why didn't they let you know sooner? What hospital was it?'

'A terrible dump called the Bichat. You've never seen anywhere like it. Their excuse was that she was unconscious when they found her, so they couldn't ask her; but those damned French doctors probably never even tried. It was the Canadian Embassy that tracked us down in the end.'

'She must have lost a lot of blood, if she was unconscious. What a dreadful thing to have happened! How old was she at the time?'

'Sixteen. She was only sixteen. It was something

171

else, I can tell you. We thought she'd be dead by the time we got there. And then she didn't recognize us. That was the final straw. You should have seen her: she was lying there, in this barbaric hospital, white as a sheet, with tubes coming out of both arms, and she didn't damn well recognize us! Louise has never got over it. Can you imagine what it feels like when your own daughter doesn't recognize you? I thought it was over then. I really thought that was it.' Brock studied his empty glass for a second, then looked at Philippe and exclaimed, 'Hey, you need another drink! Come on, that's empty.' He shouted at the barman to bring them another round.

Philippe was determined to keep the conversation going. Knowing that Brock became more loquacious the more he drank, he waited for their refills before asking, 'Is your daughter prone to nosebleeds?'

'Never had one before – or since, as far as I know. To be honest, I think she was beaten up.'

'Beaten up?'

'Yeah, some guy beat her up, I'm sure. That's what the hospital thought, although Sally never admitted it.'

'Surely she would have told you?'

'She wouldn't talk about it. The doctor said she was suffering from partial amnesia, but he thought it looked as if she'd been beaten up.'

'Surely she'd remember if someone had punched her on the nose?'

'It was more than just being punched on the nose, let me tell you. Oh boy, it sure was more than that! I mean, that kid was covered in bruises, and cuts, and strangulation marks. Some guy must have had a real go at her. She was bleeding from her stomach . . .' He stopped suddenly. 'Anyway,' he added angrily, 'who's ever heard of someone dying of a nosebleed?'

'My God!' Philippe had a sudden image of Sally encouraging another man to do the things she encouraged him to do. He felt sick, but it was a sickness not born entirely of shock. A sense of revulsion swept over him: revulsion at what had happened to her, revulsion at her taste for it, revulsion at himself for being drawn into her game, and, worse still, a sickening realization that he was becoming more and more violent with her – that he could end up doing the same. What had come over him? What had she done to him? What had she done to the other man to make him behave in such a way? Had *he* been besotted with her, driven mad by her, bewitched into violence, too? She had told him again and again that Carson was the only other man with whom she had ever made love. She had seemed so innocent, so inexperienced. It had never crossed his mind to doubt her, fool that he was. What an actress she must be! What an astounding talent for deception she must possess! A terrible nausea overcame him as he realized she had done it all with someone else.

'I shouldn't have told you,' said Brock, interrupting Philippe's thoughts. 'Hardly anyone knows about it. I don't know why I told you. Once in a while, I just have to get it off my chest. Sally won't talk about it. Never has. Louise pretends it was just a nosebleed. Most of the time I go along with that, but I guess it's more difficult for me . . . I wanted to get the bastard but I never did.'

'You should have gone to the police.'

'I did, believe me. I wasted days with the French cops. They couldn't do anything. With no proof, no statement, no accusation . . . Sally always denied it. The doctor said she'd blocked it out.'

Of course she had denied it, Philippe thought. She would hardly have admitted it when she had consciously provoked it. The fact that she denied it was proof positive, as far as he was concerned, that she had encouraged this other man to be violent with her, since she would obviously have shouted it from the rooftops if it had been an unsolicited attack.

'Carson must know, presumably?' Philippe was having trouble marshalling his thoughts.

173

'He knows because I told him. I told him at the time; and again before he married her – but Sally has never mentioned it to him, as far as I know.'

Philippe was unable to think of anything else to say. They finished their drinks in silence. As they rose to leave, Brock put his hand on Philippe's shoulder. 'Keep it to yourself,' he said. Then, changing the subject abruptly, 'Let's have another game when the weather cools down. I'll see what I can do to get you in here. I'll be in touch in a day or two.'

Philippe nodded. 'Thanks,' he said. 'I'd be pleased to join: it's exactly what I've been looking for. And thanks for the game. I really enjoyed it. We must do it again sometime.' He paused, eager to leave but not wishing to seem discourteous. 'Thanks for the drinks, too,' he added lamely.

'That's OK. You must come and have dinner sometime.'

On that note, they parted and went in search of their cars.

# Chapter Twenty-Three

Philippe drove home in a towering rage. What a harlot! What a liar! She was so convincing in her role of hesitant child that no-one, he felt, could have failed to believe her.

If she'd done it with one, how many others might she have slept with – slept with and played with, playing her dangerous games? *'Putain de merde!'* he exclaimed angrily. If she'd started at sixteen, she must have been through legions of men by now.

He was so overcome by jealousy that he was hardly able to drive. He thought he would suffocate, such were his feelings of desperation and rage. Pulling in sharply to the side of the road, he braked violently and sat for a moment, thumping his head on the wheel. He could bloody well kill her, he thought, as he set off again and, jaw clenched, foot on the accelerator, sped angrily for home.

Once there, he flung himself on his bed and tried to collect his thoughts. He was supposed to be seeing her in about four hours' time. He'd have to tell her he couldn't make it. He would not be able to answer for his actions if he saw her now. Although he was desperate to confront her with the truth, he was sane enough to realize he ought to wait until he had calmed down. In any case, a couple of hours were not enough for what he wanted to do. He wanted to take her away somewhere where there was no-one else around and where he could keep her to himself for as long as he liked. If he had to lock her up for a week and torture her, he intended to make her talk this time.

He continued to lie on his bed, staring vacantly at the ceiling. It was covered with cracks, like the lines on the palm of a hand. How odd, he thought, that he had never noticed it before.

Eventually he rose and went to the kitchen to look for something to eat. He must remain calm, he kept telling himself. He could not avoid telephoning her: he had to cancel tonight's assignation; but he must somehow make himself sound totally calm. He did not want her to have an inkling that he had found out anything about her past.

He made himself a sandwich and considered the situation. This time, come hell or high water, he would make her tell him everything there was to tell – but to do so he might need several days on his own with her.

Having made himself a coffee, he carried it to the living-room but, after one sip, lost interest in it and put it down. He leant back in his chair, staring at the telephone. He knew that Carson was likely to be at home. Too bad, he decided; he'd have to take the chance. To hell with Carson, anyway. He picked up the phone and dialled.

To his relief, it was Sally who answered.

'I can't make it tonight,' he said in reply to her 'Hello'.

'Hello?' she repeated in a strained voice.

'Is Carson there?' Philippe asked.

'I think you have the wrong number,' Sally said coolly before hanging up.

Carson must have been in the room, Philippe thought. Well, she'd call him back, although possibly not for some hours. He might as well get plastered in the meantime, although he doubted whether any amount of alcohol could assuage his pain. He wished there were a way to obliterate the startling image of Sally, at sixteen, making sado-masochistic love with another man.

He drank half a bottle of Scotch, but instead of feeling drunk, he felt increasingly sober. How had she found someone to do these things with her, if she had only been there a few days? It can't have been the first time she'd done such a thing; it was obvious that no complete innocent would be up to that in a foreign language and an unknown town. She was only sixteen, for God's sake! How old had she been when she started all this, and how many men had she dragged into her net over the years?

She must have been truly beautiful in her teens: a little slip of a girl with a Renaissance air. How good was her French, he suddenly wondered. How had she explained to the man what she wanted him to do? If *he* ever made love to her again he'd make her say everything in French. He wanted to hear what she said and how she said it. He would become the other man, or men. He'd expunge them from her mind; he'd force all her memories out and force himself forever in. It was unendurable. Why hadn't he met her when she was sixteen, instead of becoming embroiled with an incurably faithless woman who had strung him along for years and then married someone else?

He thought of the time he had wasted trying to recover from that blow; the endless search for a complete innocent who would be his and his alone. Was there no woman on earth who was monogamous? Were they all lying, cheating, nymphomaniac tramps?

He began drinking straight from the bottle, but it might have been water for all the solace it provided. How much did one have to drink, for God's sake, to lose consciousness entirely? He longed to wipe out all he knew. He sought oblivion. He wanted to be totally, mindlessly drunk.

He snatched up the phone the moment it rang.

'Philippe?' Sally's voice sounded anxious.

'Yes.'

'Carson was there when you rang.'

'So I gathered. Where are you?'

'In a phone booth across from the Forum. Why can't you make tonight?'

'Because it's intolerable, all this clock-watching and

177

---

sneaking about at dead of night. I don't want to see you, if it's only for a short time. I want to take you away somewhere for a few days: somewhere where there are no other people around, and where we don't have to worry about time.'

'But I can't get away. You know that I can't.'

'Why not? Most of the women in this town seem to manage it. They all go away during the summer. Why can't you?'

'I don't have children, so I don't have the same excuse. Anyway, I've never done it, so it would look odd if I started now.'

'You and Carson have a house in Knowlton, don't you? Why can't we go there?'

'The locals all know us. It would be bound to get back.'

'What about your parents' house? Couldn't you go there for a few days? You could say you were finding the heat too much and that you needed a break.'

'My mother's already there. She went up last week. Anyway, there are too many people from Westmount with houses around there.'

'OK, so where don't you people go? The Ottawa River? Prince Edward Island? The Gaspé? There must be somewhere we can go where we'll be on our own.'

'I don't know. They go most places. There aren't many Anglos around Oka but there are plenty in Como, and it's so near. And the Gaspé is worse – we have lots of friends with houses there. It'd be better to go to Ontario or New England, although even there we could be unlucky and bump into someone we knew.'

'What about the French villages?'

'Well, they're all French in this province; but I suppose if one went much further north it might be safe. I mean, you wouldn't meet anyone you knew in Chicoutimi, I shouldn't think.'

'Where's that?'

'Way north. About two hundred kilometres north of Quebec, I should guess. It's a town, not a village, so it

178

should be easy to pass unnoticed. I've never been there but I'm told it's not a place one needs to visit – it's supposed to be a complete dump.'

'Great! Well, this isn't getting us very far. I'll do some research – but I want you to promise that you'll come away with me when I've found somewhere for us to stay.'

'Will you see me tonight if I say "yes"?'

'No. I'm not going to see you until we go away.'

'Philippe!' Sally wailed. 'I can't wait that long. It might be weeks . . .'

'It won't be, I can promise you.' His voice sounded unexpectedly menacing.

'Why can't we meet before then?'

'Because I have decided that we shall not.'

'Why?'

'I will explain that to you when we go away.'

'What if I can't wait?'

'You haven't much choice. I shall not go near our apartment on Beaudry again – not until we've been away together, at any rate.'

'Suppose I decide to come and see you on Peel Street?'

'I wouldn't advise it.' Sally was surprised at the tone in which he said this. 'Don't provoke me, Sally,' he said, his voice dropping. 'Don't even think about coming here. I'll bloody well kill you if you do.'

Sally froze. She could not breathe. The night had turned as black as pitch. As the darkness closed in on her, she broke out in a cold sweat and imagined she was back in Paris, struggling on an attic bed. She closed her eyes and felt herself hanging onto the window-bar with all her might, then realized with a start that it was the telephone receiver that she was gripping in a panic-stricken hand.

She stood in silence, listening to him breathing on the other end of the line. She had been right at the beginning. It *was* him, after all.

'I repeat. Don't even try it,' he said again after a time.

'I'll ring you in a day or two when I've found somewhere for us to go.'

What should she do? Should she call the police? Should she tell Carson? No-one would believe her. She had no proof.

She gulped. He was going to kill her. It was him. It had to be him.

There was one way to find out, she thought.

'Say something to me in French,' she whispered. 'I want to hear you say something in French.'

The half-bottle of Scotch suddenly took effect. That was it! Of course! He should have thought of it before! All this time, she had been pretending to herself that he was that other man. Having felt painfully sober, he became on the instant exceedingly drunk. She didn't love him in the slightest. She was still in love with someone else. In his torment, he suddenly hated them both.

'Say something in French,' she insisted. 'I want you to talk to me in French.'

'*Salope!*' he exclaimed in fury. '*Laisse-moi tranquille! Fous-moi la paix!*'

For a second Sally stood paralysed, staring out at the street, then she carefully replaced the receiver without saying another word.

She ran towards Westmount Square through a night that had sprung claws. The sky was filled with menace and the moon seemed to leer: it hung, evil and curved – a thin slice like a sabre, ready to strike. Sally was sure she could feel someone's eyes on her back. She glanced behind her. There was no-one. Not a soul to be seen.

She shouldn't have told him where she was. What if he tried to intercept her before she reached her apartment? Could he do it in the time? Even if he'd run to his car the moment she'd hung up, surely he couldn't drive here quickly enough to catch her before she reached her front door? But last time he'd caught her, hadn't he? Just when she'd thought she'd lost him.

He'd pulled her into a car. He was after her, and she knew it. She had no hope of escape.

Should she keep to Saint Catherine? She could go along de Maisonneuve, but there was less light there and the grounds of the convent would be an obvious place for him to hide. She wished she had the courage to use the tunnel linking Alexis Nihon to Westmount Square, but she had never been brave enough to use it even in the daytime: she'd have telephoned from there if she'd been able to face the place at night.

Sensing danger, she flattened herself against a wall: but it was only a cat in the shadows. She watched it slink out of sight. Following its example, she darted from doorway to doorway, trying to keep out of the light. She was within sight of her building when she heard a car approaching. She stopped and held her breath. It was coming nearer. She must chance it and run.

Those last few yards seemed like miles. As she flung herself against the doors, she heard the noise of the car's engine fading and realized with relief that it must have driven past. He would turn round, though; she knew he'd come back.

The porter was not at his desk. Had he gone out? Was he sick? In her terror, she suddenly wondered whether he had been murdered. Supposing Philippe had arrived before her and the porter had let him in? Philippe would have killed him, she was certain. Maybe he was lying in wait for her. He knew she never went in elevators, so he'd be somewhere on the stairs. She'd better use the elevator this time. It must be both safer and quicker than walking up four flights of stairs.

As soon as the elevator started moving, she realized her mistake. There was no-one else about at this time of night. She should never have entered the building; and she was crazy to have taken the elevator: he could stop it on another floor. They'd be on their own. She'd be trapped. He could kill her and leave without anyone seeing a thing.

She pressed frantically on the button marked '5', keeping her finger on it and willing the elevator not to stop at the other floors. With pounding heart, she watched the numbers lighting up on the panel above her head as the elevator flashed past the third and fourth floors. It hadn't stopped. She felt a surge of relief as it jolted noisily to a halt at the fifth floor.

Her relief was short-lived. She let out a scream as the door opened and a hand grabbed her arm and pulled her out.

'Where the hell have you been?' asked Carson. She swayed, then fainted and fell.

'For Christ's sake,' muttered Carson, as he picked her up and carried her into their apartment.

# Chapter Twenty-Four

'What in God's name have you been up to?' Carson demanded as she came round. 'It's two in the morning, for Christ's sake. Where the hell have you been?'

Sally flung her arms around him in relief and clung to him tightly for a moment before she was able to reply. 'I had to get some air,' she said finally. 'It's suffocating in here. I couldn't sleep. It's so hot.'

'With this air-conditioning? Come off it! It's far cooler in here than it is outside.' He glared at her angrily, but she said nothing, so he continued. 'Since when have you been brave enough to go out by yourself in the middle of the night, anyway? And since when have you started taking the elevator on your own? You must have been with someone else.'

Sally had long since stopped expecting Carson to wake up when she went out at night. Being unprepared for a confrontation, she could think of no reply. She stared at him helplessly, then burst into tears.

Carson remained unmoved. 'I'm waiting for an explanation,' he said. 'You've been gone for a good half-hour, and I want to know why.'

'I walked to Atwater and back. I couldn't sleep. I've already told you. I couldn't breathe. I had to get out.'

'I want the truth, Sally. This isn't the first time. You did the same last night. You were gone for nearly three hours.' (Had it been anyone but Sally he would have supposed she must be having an affair but, in her case, this seemed unlikely. He was baffled as to what to think.)

She wondered what Carson would do if she told him the truth. She was so relieved that it had not been Philippe waiting for her outside the elevator that she

183

was tempted to tell him everything. What if he threw her out, though? What if he didn't believe that Philippe intended to kill her? He might be so angry that he walked out on her and never came back. It wasn't something she could chance: it simply wasn't worth the risk. She knew Philippe would kill her if Carson left her on her own.

'For Christ's sake!' Carson exclaimed. 'I don't want to have to sit here all night. Let's have the truth. Then, perhaps, you'll allow me to get to bed.'

'I've been tracking him,' Sally blurted out. 'I'm going to get him before he gets me.'

'Tracking who?' Carson thought for a moment that he must have misheard.

'The rapist. You know. The guy who abducted me. That Frenchman. Philippe Marignac.'

'Good God, Sally, what on earth are you talking about?'

'He wants to kill me. I'm so scared, Carson.'

Her husband stared at her in astonishment. All this time, when he had thought she was so much better, she'd been heading for a nervous breakdown.

Overcome with pity, he took her two hands in his. It was obvious to him suddenly. He had let her do too much, left her too much on her own, and now she had finally cracked. What on earth should he do? He was at a loss as to how to respond.

'I think,' he said finally, 'that you should see a doctor.'

'You don't believe me, do you? I knew you wouldn't. That's why I didn't want to tell you.'

'My dear, nobody is going to kill you. You're not well, that's all. You need a rest. You need to get away.'

'You're not going to send me away! He'll find me and kill me if you do.'

'Don't be ridiculous, Sally. No-one wants to kill you. What on earth are we to do with you? Maybe you should spend the summer in the Laurentians with your mother. I'll call Dr Humphries in the morning and see what he can suggest. He'll want to take a look at you, I expect. I'll come with you if he does. Then we'll really have to talk to your parents; but, in the meantime, I think we'd both better try and get some sleep.'

On reflection, Sally was relieved that Carson had taken it the way he had. The more doctors and concerned relations she had around her, the less vulnerable she would be if Philippe tried to attack.

'Don't go wandering out again, whatever you do,' Carson said to her once they were in bed.

'Nothing would induce me to go out again,' Sally replied with such obvious sincerity that Carson was reassured. He put his arms around her and kissed her, then almost immediately fell asleep.

Sally listened with envy to her husband's steady breathing, and wished that there were some way she could make him understand. She felt like someone who has been told they are about to be hanged. What did those who are condemned do, she wondered, to stay the executioner's hand? Did one protest one's innocence? Did one try to convince the hangman that he had picked the wrong person and was making a terrible mistake? That wouldn't work with Philippe, she felt sure. He knew her, just as she knew him. She would have to kill him. It was the only solution if she herself was to survive. Wasn't that why she had become embroiled with him in the first place? She had wanted proof and, now he had furnished it, she must act before it was too late.

The more she thought about it, however, the clearer it became to her that she was totally incapable of murdering anyone in cold blood. She simply could not do it; and, in any case, she wouldn't have the faintest idea how to set about it even if she could bring herself to try. She had been fooling herself all these years. She was incapable of killing him – except, perhaps, if he tried to kill her; but even then, how would she do it? Guns were out of the question: she hadn't the faintest idea how to get hold of one; and she probably wouldn't know how to load it or even aim it correctly, if it came to that. Poison was no good: you can't poison someone when they're trying to strangle you. As far as she could see, there wasn't any choice. From now on, she'd have to go everywhere armed with a knife.

She wondered why, if he wanted to kill her, he hadn't done it before. Why had he gone to all the trouble of making her fall in love with him first? (She might have asked herself how he had succeeded in this, but she had always lived with the belief that her life was in the hands of a pre-ordained fate and, having a victim's mentality, remained convinced that there was no possibility of being able to control her own destiny.)

As she mentally reviewed the events of the previous months, she thought she recognized a pattern in the Frenchman's behaviour, and believed she was finally beginning to understand the workings of his psychopathic mind.

At the beginning of their affair, he had carefully avoided hurting her, although he had often played at being rough; but as their relationship developed, he had become increasingly violent until, recently, it seemed to her to have ceased to be a game. He had continued to speak to her as if he loved her, though. This was the first time he had ever sounded as if he hated and despised her. He was seldom violent with words and, when he was, she never felt they were directed against her: on the contrary, he always spoke to her sweetly, as he had in Paris all those years ago (until, that is, he had cracked so unexpectedly at the end).

It occurred to her that he must have wanted her to be willing. That was clearly the explanation of his odd behaviour in Paris. He had wanted to pretend to himself that she was in love with him so that it would not seem like rape. Having failed dismally, he'd eventually lost his temper and chucked her out.

It was so obvious that she wondered why she had not thought of it before. This was simply a repetition of those early events. For some reason he needed to feel that she loved him. Like a cat with a mouse, he couldn't just kill her: he had to play with her first; and now, suddenly, he had had enough. He had used the same words he had used in Paris; he'd called her a '*salope*', and shouted, '*Fous-moi la paix.*'

He had last used those words when he was about to let her go. Was this why he did not want to see her? Had he decided to let her go? And if so, why? Had she done something to provoke it? Had she said anything to make him believe she did not love him any more? Of course, there might be a part of him that did not want to be a murderer: one had to consider that. Perhaps he was trying to save the situation before it was too late.

Sally's thoughts churned round interminably as she searched for an escape, but wherever her ideas led her, she kept returning to the same point: if he could only kill someone who loved him, she must convince him that she no longer cared for him; then he might lose interest, as he had done last time, and not wish to see her again. She must telephone him in the morning and tell him she didn't love him any more. She would say that she had never loved him; that she had been pretending; that she was really in love with someone else. Then she could go to the Laurentians and stay with her mother while he calmed down.

What if he tried to follow her, though? Would her mother be a sufficient deterrent? Would the thought of a possible witness be enough to keep him away?

He hadn't attempted to follow her last time, though, had he? Once he had tired of her, he'd let her go. There was no reason to suppose he'd behave any differently this time. He'd presumably lose his temper and shout horrible things in French at her down the telephone; and then, surely, that would be an end to it – or would it? She wasn't sure.

Her mother would see him off, anyway. Louise

would never allow anyone to hurt her. Sally knew she was strong enough to deal with Philippe.

She longed to tell her mother the whole story. She was sure Louise would somehow manage to make it all right; in fact, she couldn't imagine why she hadn't told her before.

It was seven in the morning when at last Sally fell asleep. Carson woke as she was dozing off, and lay watching her in silence for a while. The longer she slept, the better, he thought. It would give him a chance to telephone Dr Humphries without his wife overhearing what he said. Making every effort not to disturb her, he rose and collected up his clothes, then tiptoed to the kitchen to make himself breakfast and listen to the news.

Sally was vaguely aware of him moving about the room. She opened her eyes briefly; but Carson, seeing she was awake, said, 'Go back to sleep, babe. There's no need to get up yet. I won't go out, I promise. I'll take the day off from work.'

He kissed her forehead, then left the room and quietly closed the door.

Sally fell asleep again, and, some hours later, plunged into a startlingly vivid dream.

She dreamt she was a small girl, running about in the Provençal hills. She could see nothing in any direction except red earth, and rocks and scrub. She was clambering about alone in that perennially cheerful landscape. There was not another soul, not so much as an animal, to be seen.

The mistral was rising. Dust-laden and already strong, it thudded across the countryside with that throbbing, mesmeric rhythm that maddens both beast and man. Suddenly she heard her mother sobbing; and her name echoing round the hills. The sobbing became louder and took on the rhythm of the wind. Soon, it was the wind that was howling, the wind that was calling her name. She ran wildly to keep up with it; for her mother had become the wind.

There were snakes and scorpions everywhere. She had to keep jumping over them. Then she saw her mother ahead of her: there was water pouring down her face, and her face had turned to stone.

In her dream, Sally was thirsty. She wanted to run to her mother. She wanted to drink her mother's tears; but her father was standing between them, among the olive trees, shouting at her to keep away. He seemed enormous. She could not find a way around him. He started to chase her, and she knew he would beat her if she did not run away.

On the instant, she was crawling: scrambling frantically through the undergrowth, trying to reach the clump of mimosa she could see, far below her, at the foot of the slope. She knew her mother was there, somewhere, waiting for her, hidden among the mimosa; but she did not know how to reach her because there was a strange man blocking the way. He had laid out a picnic on the path and seemed to want Sally to join him, but she didn't like the look of him and started slithering back up the hill through the undergrowth, trying to remain unseen while she crawled away.

She was running and running, and the mistral was pounding, when suddenly, from nowhere, her father again appeared. He had grown in the meantime. He was the size of a giant. 'Where the hell have you been?' he roared . . .

She woke up with a start, instantly on the defensive. She had heard those words before. She seemed to have been hearing them all her life.

She sat up abruptly, trying to adjust to her surroundings. Suddenly, and quite clearly, she remembered that childhood day.

She had been on holiday with her parents. They had rented a farmhouse in Provence for the Easter holidays and, although it was early spring, the sun had been so warm, until that morning, that it seemed as if summer had begun. But then the wind had started to rise: a cold, dry wind with a steady beat. Sally was excited by its savage rhythm. She wanted to run with it. She wanted to dance. But it was precisely its intense and unremitting tempo that her parents could not stand.

The moment the mistral started, her father had, for no apparent reason, worked himself into a terrible rage; and Louise had developed a migraine which sent her, moaning, to her bed. Sally thought she would be doing her parents a favour by keeping out of their way and, since they had repeatedly told her never to go down to the rocky shore by herself, decided to play on the uncultivated slopes behind the house.

She scrambled about in the undergrowth for a time, chasing a lizard, until she remembered her father's warnings about scorpions and snakes. Frightened at the thought, she picked up her heels and ran back to the path. She kept her eyes on the ground and, soon forgetting about snakes and scorpions, started playing games with her shadow. It seemed to be much smaller than usual, whereas she wanted it to be tall; and it fell on the ground just in front of her, which seemed to her all wrong. She thought shadows were supposed to trail along behind you. She tried jumping over it, running ahead fast, then taking a sudden leap to the side, in an effort to unglue it from her feet. Nothing worked. She tried everything. She turned her back on it in disgust, expecting it to rush round in front of her. To her delight, it stayed behind her, and she thought she had tricked it.

She started to walk round in a small circle, hoping that it would follow close to her heels; but though she moved slowly and very quietly in an attempt not to give the game away, it was not to be fooled; and by the time she was facing uphill again, it had somehow sneaked its way back in front of her. She was furious with it and decided to run so fast that it wouldn't be able to keep up.

Taking a deep breath, she ran as fast as she could. She darted about like a butterfly, dashing from one side of the path to the other in her determination to free herself from her irritating companion, but the shadow was determined to stay with her. Annoyed, she made one last attempt at jumping over it but, when this did not work, grew bored with the game and gave up.

Feeling out of breath and thirsty, she scanned the slope ahead for somewhere out of the wind where she could sit down. To her right, further up the hill, she noticed a group of olive trees. Forced to abandon the path once more, she looked carefully where she placed her feet as she made her way, with childlike determination, across the scrubland towards the trees.

As she drew near, she thought she heard the faint sound of trickling water. Then she saw it, as enticing as an oasis in the desert: a tiny trickle coming out of a thin pipe that had been hammered into the rocky outcrop, just beyond the trees. Immediately beneath this, someone had attempted to hack the rock into something resembling a basin, and into this roughly hewn hollow a dribble of water feebly fell.

At the sight, Sally began to run. Circumnavigating the trees without sparing them a glance, she reached the rocks and stretched out her hands to catch the trickle of water as it fell.

It was cold. She splashed her face with it, then drank some. Still feeling hot from her exertions, she put her head under the dribbling pipe and wet her hair. Cold water dripped on the back of her head and down her cheeks, then fell in tiny droplets into the rocky hollow below. Feeling refreshed, she stood up and shook the water from her hair.

Hearing a sound, she turned to see a man walking towards her from the direction of the trees. The moment she saw him, the thought occurred to her that this land might be private and the spring might well belong to him. Would he be angry with her for trespassing? She suddenly felt afraid.

The man said nothing, but he did not appear to wish to chase her away. He approached unhurriedly and did not look agitated, which Sally assumed he would if he were cross. He was wearing blue trousers; a grubby jacket; heavy, lace-up shoes and a battered, felt hat. He had a large bundle slung over his shoulder, which seemed, amongst other things, to contain his lunch (Sally could see a wine bottle sticking out of it, and part of a large baguette). He was only a few yards from her so she smiled uncertainly and mumbled, '*Bonjour.*'

He grinned at her: a simple, idiotic grin. Two of his teeth were missing, and his eyes were close together and very small. Sally didn't like him. He looked dirty, and she hated the uneven stubble on his chin. She did not want him to come any nearer. She made a few steps sideways to avoid the rocks and began cautiously backing away.

He dropped his bundle and took another step towards her, still grinning stupidly and scratching his ear. Then, to her astonishment, he pulled down his trousers and waggled a flaccid penis at her, saying, as he did so, something she did not understand.

Sally did not wait to find out any more. She raced through the stunted undergrowth and back towards the path. Glancing over her shoulder when she reached it, she saw he had pulled up his trousers and was starting to follow her, albeit not very fast. Assuming that any adult must be able to run faster than she could, Sally plunged into the undergrowth on the far side of the track and bent down as she ran between the bushes looking for somewhere to hide.

In the land of the *maquis*, a five-year-old child soon disappears from sight; but Sally was too young to realize this and ran for a long time before she thought she was safe. Even then, she hid in the undergrowth for nearly an hour, listening out for the sound of footsteps and peering in all directions to make sure he was not there.

At last, still very frightened, she started creeping

back through the undergrowth in the direction of the house. She kept well away from paths, and darted from one shrub to the next, as she made her way cautiously down the hill.

Her parents, in the meantime, were frantically worried at her long absence. Leaving Louise at home, in case Sally returned, Brock had set off in a panic to scour the hills. As Sally came in sight of the house, she heard her mother, who was standing in the doorway, hysterically and repeatedly calling her name.

The moment Sally saw Louise, she knew she was safe. She raced down the hill and flung herself into her mother's arms noticing, as she did so, the overwhelming smell of mimosa that surrounded the house.

Louise ran towards her and, with tears in her eyes, picked Sally up and held her tightly, murmuring, 'Thank God! Your father and I were so worried. We were afraid you were lost.'

Putting her down, she took Sally's hand and hung on to it as they walked back towards the house. 'Please don't go off on your own again,' she said. 'You must never go out of sight of the house. You could so easily get lost.'

'I'm really sorry, Mum. I didn't mean to. I was scared, too,' Sally replied, squeezing her mother's hand.

She wanted to tell her mother about the man who had frightened her but felt embarrassed about the incident which she thought of as 'very rude' and therefore difficult to discuss. Like many children in these circumstances, she felt it somehow reflected on her and that she might be blamed for something which seemed to her disgusting and which she sensed, in a vague way, might displease her mother. In any case, a small child's vocabulary being limited, particularly when it comes to expressing emotions, she did not possess the words to describe what she felt.

Trying to change the subject, she asked, 'What's that smell, Mum? It's lovely. What is it?'

'It's mimosa. Do you see that great clump of trees over there – the ones with the tiny, yellow flowers? It's coming from them. That's why the house always smells so wonderful. We're surrounded by it. I always think it's so pretty with the sea in the background. I hope you'll be able to remember it when you're older. It's such a very lovely sight.'

Sally stood holding her mother's hand and looking out across the Mediterranean where a couple of sailing boats were battling in an unusually gusty wind. In the foreground, the mimosa was being buffeted as the mistral continued to pound across the countryside; and beyond this, the land fell away sharply, tumbling down to the rocky coastline where Sally and her parents often took picnics, though the water was not yet warm enough for them to want to swim. There were crabs down there, and small squids, and all manner of interesting things. There were sea urchins, too; Sally, who liked paddling in rock pools, had soon learned to be careful where she put her feet.

She watched the wind blowing the mimosa trees. Their delicate trunks bowed gracefully at each gust, and it seemed to her that they were waving their pale branches and tiny flowers at her in gold and silver salutation, as if to welcome her home.

Suddenly remembering her mother's migraine, she looked up at her and asked, 'Is your headache better?' but before Louise could answer, there was a shout from behind them, and they looked round to see Brock storming angrily down the hill.

Sally could see at a glance that he was still in a terrible rage. She clung to her mother, who put her arm round her and whispered, 'Don't be frightened, sweetheart. He's not really mad at you. It's just that he was terribly worried.'

'Where the hell have you been?' Brock shouted at her, as he approached them . . .

It all came back to her with hideous clarity. She must

194

have been about five-and-a-half at the time. How odd that she should have forgotten all about it until now. Perhaps her memory had been jolted when Carson greeted her, at two in the morning, with the same words her father had used that day.

She remembered how Brock had yelled at her, demanding to know where the hell she'd been and why she'd been gone so long. In order to make him understand, she had attempted to tell him about the man. (She realized now, of course, that she had described the creature poorly, but she still felt her father should have tried to understand.)

She had told him that she'd been chased by 'a funny man who pulled his pants down and was all bare underneath'. This information had made her father even angrier. 'There's nothing the least funny about a man pulling his pants down!' he had roared. 'Anything might have happened! Goddamit, Sally, how many times have you been told not to talk to strange men? Do you ever listen to anything you're told? I'm going to make sure you never want to go off on your own again as long as you live. I'm going to give you such a hiding that you'll never forget.'

He had, too. He'd spanked her exceedingly hard with the back of a hairbrush; although, ironically, almost as if to spite him, once they had returned to Canada, she had forgotten the entire incident: flasher, spanking, the lot. She'd never thought of it again until this moment, though she remembered, now, that she had been very upset and hurt by his reaction at the time. He had wounded her pride as well as hurting her physically, and had managed to instil in her a deep sense of guilt and shame about the whole affair.

For the rest of their holiday, she had felt nervous of her father and had avoided him as much as possible. She had made a hiding-place for herself in what she thought of as her 'mimosa forest'; and whenever her father was in a bad mood, she vanished into that secret and magical world. There, drenched in its wonderful smell, she played in peace and knew she was safe.

She told her mother about this hiding-place but made her swear never to tell Brock. Louise kept the secret and, by mutual agreement, whistled out of the window to warn Sally whenever Brock enquired as to his daughter's whereabouts. Sally knew the whistle meant she must come immediately (she did not wish to risk another bout of paternal rage) but on one or two happy occasions when Brock had gone to the local town to pick up the mail, her mother joined her in her 'forest' and played whatever games of imagination Sally suggested until Brock's return.

She had felt safe in her mimosa hide-out; she wished she had it still.

# Chapter Twenty-Five

Sally rose and put on a dressing-gown, then glanced at her watch. It was three in the afternoon, for heaven's sake! She'd been asleep for eight hours.

Carson stood up, looking concerned, as she entered the room. 'That was what you needed,' he said. 'Do you feel better now you've had a good sleep?'

'Yeah, except I had this unpleasant dream about something that happened to me when I was a kid. I was chased by a repulsive old flasher – it really happened, only I had forgotten all about it until now.'

'When was this?'

'It was the first time Mum and Dad took me to the South of France. I must have been about five. I was drinking water from a spring in the rocks, and this kind of peasant character came up behind me and pulled his pants down and sort of waved his thing around. I was terrified. I ran away and hid for hours. It seems ridiculous now but it was really scary at the time.'

'Did he do anything else?'

'He said something in French, but I didn't understand.'

'Did he touch you?'

'No, but he was only a few yards away, and I'm sure he would have done if I'd stuck around.'

'Did you tell your parents?'

'I told Dad, and he was furious. He was really mad at me. He spanked me so hard you wouldn't believe. I hated him for ages afterwards. I was really scared of him for a while, too.'

She was silent for a moment, but Carson could see she had not said everything she wanted to say. Her head was tilted sideways, as if she were listening to sounds only audible to her, and there was an air of perplexed contemplation in her overcast eyes. Suddenly, she gave a sigh and lifted her head. 'It's strange,' she said, almost as if she were talking to herself, 'I thought, when Philippe attacked me in Paris, that it was the first time I'd ever seen an adult man's sexual equipment, but I realize now that I had seen it before – although it wasn't quite the same, I suppose.'

Carson could think of nothing to say. 'What you need is something to eat,' he suggested. 'It's three-fifteen. You must be famished. I'll make you some lunch while you're getting dressed.'

Carson waited as long as possible before telling Sally about the appointments he had made. She was likely to be upset, he knew, so he decided not to broach the subject until she had finished eating and he had helped her wash the dishes and put them away.

'Do you want a coffee?' she asked him, when they had finished tidying the kitchen.

'I'd love one, if you're making one – but let's have it in the living-room. Give me a shout when it's ready, and I'll carry it through.'

He waited until they were both sitting in the living-room; then sipped his coffee in silence for a few moments before taking the plunge. 'Well,' he finally said breezily, 'I spoke to Dr Humphries, and he wants to see us both at six. He wants to give you a general check-up, and then we'll see where we go from there.'

'What did you tell him?' Sally asked.

'I just said you weren't sleeping properly, and that you thought someone . . . Well, to be honest, I told him a bit about what had happened, in Paris, and said you seemed convinced that the guy was here, in Montreal.' Seeing her expression, he added, 'I had to tell him. He can't be expected to help, if he doesn't know.'

'He can't help. You should have spoken to the police, not to Dr Humphries,' Sally snapped, rising abruptly from her chair.

'Come on, babe. Finish your coffee, for Pete's sake. We don't have to be there for over an hour, so don't start getting into one of your states.'

She sat down again. 'What on earth good is a general check-up? It's Philippe who needs to see a doctor, not me.'

'Maybe, but let's start by making sure you're OK. Humphries is a perfectly sensible man. It can't do any harm.'

'And then what?'

'He has some friend he'd like you to see who he thinks might be able to help. I've already spoken to the guy, and he sounds just what we need.'

'What do you mean, "just what we need"? I bet *I* don't need him. Who is he?'

'He's a psychologist who's made a lifetime's study of rape trauma and of clinical criminology. If you could bring yourself to describe what happened, he'd doubtless be able to bring some light to bear on the man's behaviour, as well as helping you.'

'That hardly solves the immediate problem, does it?'

'What do you mean?'

'I mean, if he takes too long about it, I may be killed first.'

'Oh, for crying out loud! I've told you again and again, nobody's going to kill you. You really must try and put all that out of your mind. If you give this guy a chance, he may get to the root of your fears, and then you'll understand that you are simply inventing all this.'

'For God's sake!' exclaimed Sally, suddenly losing her temper. 'You still don't believe me, do you? You just want me to sit about, waiting to be killed, while some professor tries to convince me it's all a figment of my imagination. I'm sick of you telling me it isn't true! There's a guy out there who wants to kill me, and you don't bloody well care!'

At this, Carson's patience suddenly deserted him.

'I'm sick of it, too!' he shouted. 'I'm sick of having to

deal with all your crazy ideas. Do you think it's easy for me to live with you, the way you are? I'm doing my best to be understanding and to help you to stop being frightened, and all you do is yell at me. I don't know if I can take much more of it. You should know that, Sally, because I really mean it. There are limits to everyone's patience, and I've just about reached mine.'

'If you really want me to stop being frightened, why don't you go out and kill Philippe Marignac? I bet you'd kill him if it was you he was after!'

'Why are you so goddamn violent? Why does everyone have to kill everyone in your world? What the hell's the matter with you, for Christ's sake? Sometimes I wonder why I ever married you.'

'And I wonder why I ever married you! You're about as much use to me as a hole in the head!'

Carson shrugged his shoulders in exasperation, then turned and walked towards the door. 'Cancel the appointment, if you don't want to go,' he said curtly. 'I'm going out. I can't take any more of this. And don't expect me back for dinner. I need the evening off.'

'Carson!' shrieked Sally, leaping to her feet and rushing after him. 'Don't leave me on my own! You can't leave me! He'll come here and kill me if you do!' She flung herself at him and hung on to both his arms.

'For crying out loud, Sally! How can anyone kill you if you stay here? Just refuse to open the door to anybody, and nobody can get in.'

'He'll pick the lock, or something. I know he'll find a way.'

'Don't be ridiculous! Anyway, there's the porter downstairs.'

'So what? All Philippe has to do is say he's coming to see us, and he'll be told to come on up.'

'No, he won't! You know perfectly well the porter will ring you first to tell you who it is.'

'So? He can give some other person's name, can't he? He could pretend to be one of our friends.'

'Well, refuse to see anyone, in that case. Tell the

porter you don't want anyone coming up, whoever it is.'

Sally tugged at his sleeve, pleading. '*Please* don't go! Carson, please! You don't understand. Supposing he kills the porter, then what would I do?'

'Oh for God's sake!' Carson tried to shake his arms free of her grasp. 'Reassure yourself: if he kills the porter, somebody is bound to notice; and he doesn't have a key to this apartment, so you're perfectly safe.'

'He could have had my key copied.' In her terror, Sally did not think what she was saying.

Carson stared at her. 'Yours?' he asked, after a second. 'How could he do that?'

Sally paused too long before replying. 'Well,' she muttered lamely, 'he could have made a wax copy of it, or something – I don't know.'

'He would have needed your key in order to do that.' Carson was studying her face intently.

'Yeah,' Sally was trying to sound casual. 'But he could easily have looked in my handbag sometime when we were all together – for instance, at the opening of the Pivot exhibition a few weeks back, or when we had dinner with Douglas and Anne last week.'

'You kept your bag with you all the time at the gallery. You wouldn't have found anywhere to put it down if you'd wanted to, anyway; and as for that dinner with the Davisons, you can hardly have forgotten the scene you made when you thought you'd lost your keys. You had left them at your office, if you remember – or, at any rate, that is what you claimed when you produced them again the next day.'

Carson's voice was cold, but Sally barely noticed. A terrifying thought had occurred to her. Of course she remembered that evening – she remembered it all too well. She had panicked for an hour, ruining the dinner for everyone, before she realized she must have left the keys in the rue Beaudry apartment. She knew she'd had them with her when she and Philippe had met

201

there, earlier in the day. She remembered taking them out of her bag while she was looking for a pen.

She had been right. Philippe had returned them to her the following night. They'd been in his possession for over twenty-four hours – plenty of time to have had duplicates cut.

Carson was still staring at her. There was something about her line of reasoning which did not make sense, and he was struck by her expression – it reminded him of the look on her face when she fell screaming out of the elevator during the night. It was all too unreal. Why would she have gone looking for Philippe, if she was so terrified of him? Thinking of her behaviour over the past six months, he was at last granted a lacerating insight into his wife's soul.

'You've been having an affair with him, haven't you? You've been having an affair with Philippe Marignac!'

Sally was caught off guard. 'No, I haven't!' she exclaimed nervously. 'I most certainly have not! What on earth gave you that idea?' But her voice gave her away.

'When you disappeared at night . . . Of course. And all those phone calls when the person hung up . . . All the times you pretended it was a wrong number . . . I should have guessed.'

'I don't know what on earth you're talking about!' Sally cried, but Carson was not listening. He was still murmuring to himself.

'All those evenings when you had to work late, but were never at your office . . . You weren't visiting battered women at all, were you? You were with him!'

'You're out of your mind,' Sally shouted. 'You've really lost it!'

'Is that why you've gone back to doing all your shopping down east? Is that where you meet him? Somewhere down there?'

'Of course not! You're totally crazy! You're the one who needs to see a doctor, not me!'

But Carson knew. He could not prove it. She'd

always deny it, he was sure. But right in the centre of him, with excruciating certainty, he knew.

They stared at one another for a moment. Suddenly Carson could not take any more. This frail little wife of his had finally succeeded in wearing him out. It had snapped, whatever it was. The link of tenderness had gone. All the pity he had ever felt for her had vanished without trace. He wanted out. He wanted to breathe. He wanted a normal, unhampered life.

'Well, my dear,' he said after a moment, 'I did my best to help you. I'm afraid there's nothing more I can do.' He gave a sigh, and stepped backwards. 'You can go on living here, if you want to. I'll look for somewhere else. I really think you should talk to your parents. I'm sure they'd want to help . . . I'd give them a ring, if I were you . . . Anyway, I must be off.' He turned very slowly and made his way unsteadily towards the door.

Once again, Sally tried to prevent him leaving, weeping and imploring him to stay.

'I'm sorry, Sally,' he said. 'I can't help you. I don't feel anything for you any more.'

He did not bother to say goodbye. He simply walked out and shut the door.

He'd left for ever, and she knew it. Philippe was bound to get her now. She bolted the door on the inside, then ran to the kitchen and grabbed a large knife. After a moment's hesitation, she helped herself to a second knife. One for each hand, she thought, taking them with her to the living-room and pouring herself a drink. With the knives beside her, clutching a brandy and soda, she sat on the sofa wondering what to do next. She wanted to get out of there, but how? Supposing Philippe were hanging around downstairs, or out in the street? She must somehow tell him she didn't love him so that he wouldn't be interested in her any more. Then she'd go to her mother in the Laurentians. She'd be safe with Louise. He wouldn't try and follow her there. She'd better ring his number and find out if he was at home: if he was, she'd have time to make a dash for it, once she'd said what she had to say. If he wasn't, then she'd know he was lying in wait for her somewhere and that she must not, under any circumstances, open the door or try to leave.

She checked the bolt on the front door again, then, glancing at the knives as if to reassure herself, she dialled Philippe's number with a trembling hand. She gasped when he answered, having by now convinced herself that he was downstairs. Taking a deep breath, she forced herself to summon up all her courage. She must do it, she thought. She must tell him she didn't love him: it was her only hope.

Philippe had woken late, feeling angry and ill. His first thought was that Sally had hung up on him during the night. She had asked him to speak in French. She was pretending he was someone else. Then she had hung up on him, just like that, without saying a word.

He went over and over the scene in his mind. What the hell was she playing at? He wanted to talk to her urgently. He had to understand what all this was about.

He telephoned her several times during the morning, but each time it was Carson who answered the phone. Why on earth wasn't he at work, Philippe wondered. What the hell was going on?

When Carson answered for the third time, Philippe thought he would explode. He wanted Sally to apologize for hanging up on him. He wanted her to say that nothing Brock had told him was true: that it was pure invention, that there wasn't anyone else, there never had been, he was the only person she had ever loved. He had been through the conversation endlessly in his mind. He wanted her to tell him that she had never been to Paris; that her father always invented wild tales when he was drunk; that Brock would be the first to admit that none of it was true.

Unable to speak to Sally as long as Carson was at home, Philippe decided he'd better use the time to find somewhere for them both to go. He had a French colleague who owned a cottage somewhere very remote; and, on the spur of the moment, Philippe rang him and suggested they meet for lunch.

'I'm going crazy here,' Philippe told Jean-Marc over lunch. 'Do you realize I've never been out of Montreal for more than a day since I arrived here? And then it was only to the Eastern Townships – I've never even been to the Laurentians! I've been stuck in this city for nearly nine months. I'm going to go completely insane if I can't get away, for a short time, somewhere on my own. Can you think of anywhere I could go for a few days where I'd be totally alone?'

Jean-Marc reacted exactly as Philippe had hoped he would. 'You can borrow my cottage for a few days, if you want, but you'll have to do it quickly because I'll be going up there myself in a couple of weeks, and it's not really suitable for more than one person, as you'll see. Being a bachelor, I didn't want anything that required much upkeep. I only go up there when I want to do a bit of fishing and sailing; and I never have anyone to stay.'

They discussed it over coffee, and by the time they left the restaurant, it had all been agreed. Jean-Marc gave Philippe detailed instructions as to how to get there, then took him back to his apartment and gave him a set of keys.

Philippe was elated. Hearing his friend's description of the place, he thought it sounded ideal. It was apparently situated on a privately owned lake, in a remote part of Quebec; and all the surrounding land belonged to Jean-Marc. The nearest hamlet, which was tiny, was 15 kilometres away, so the chances of encountering another human being were infinitesimal, and there was no possibility of running into anyone they knew.

He returned to his own apartment and tried again to

call Sally. He was determined to persuade her to leave right away. To his fury, it was Carson who answered the phone yet again; but he was certain that Sally would ring him as soon as she could, if only to apologize for her strange behaviour during the night.

He spread out a map of the province and set about studying it as a way of passing the time usefully until she was able to phone.

He had to wait until five in the evening. When the telephone rang, he rushed to pick it up. It was a repentant call that he was expecting, so her words came as a shock.

'Philippe?' Her voice sounded high-pitched and strained. 'I want to tell you something . . . I should have told you before.'

'You might start by apologizing for hanging up on me last night! And why the hell hasn't Carson been at work? I've been trying to get you all day.'

He was dangerous, and she knew it. She could hear it in his voice. Her courage began to fail her, yet she knew she must force herself – it was her life that was at stake.

'I don't love you,' she blurted out. 'I never loved you. I was pretending. I was trying to forget someone else.'

The silence that followed was filled with menace.

'Where are you?' Philippe asked eventually. His voice was unnaturally soft. (She wanted him to shout the words he had hurled at her in Paris long ago. Had he done so, she might have clung to the hope that he had decided to let her go; but, to her despair, he sounded dangerously calm.)

'I'm at Dad's office,' she lied instinctively. She must set traps for him, she realized. She must lay a thousand false trails.

'That's in Place Ville-Marie, isn't it? OK, just give me the full address . . . Right, I'll come and collect you right away . . . Because I want to talk to you. We need to talk . . . No, this isn't the sort of discussion to have over the phone. I'll be there in about fifteen minutes, so if you don't want your father to see us together, you'd better wait for me downstairs. Go to the McGill College entrance, and I'll meet you there.'

Good, thought Sally, as she put down the phone. While Philippe set off in the wrong direction, she could race to her car and head out of town. He'd be unlikely to try to follow her: he had no idea where her parents' country house was, and, anyway, she had told him last night that her mother was already there.

Having made up her mind, she did not waste time. She was a sitting duck as long as she stayed here. She grabbed a shoulder-bag into which she put the two knives; but instantly had second thoughts about this and took them out again. She would keep them in her hand until she reached her car.

Clutching the knives firmly, she picked up her car keys, and the keys to her parents' house. There was no time to pack – she had a few old clothes in the Laurentians, and she'd have to make do with them.

Opening the door of her apartment cautiously, she peered nervously outside. Seeing no-one, she shut the door behind her and made a dash for the stairs.

As she reached the landing below, she heard one of the elevators ascending. It was coming up from the lobby as she continued down the stairs. Sailing on up, it passed her and she heard it stop on a higher floor. She froze for a second. It had stopped on her floor, she was sure. She tried to convince herself that he could not have driven to Westmount Square in the few minutes since she had put down the phone; but she felt nervous, none the less. She did not want to go down to the garage by herself. There might be no-one else about. He could find her and kill her down there.

Perhaps she could persuade the porter to accompany her to the garage – or maybe she'd see someone she knew in the lobby whom she could ask: she'd pretend she was locked out of her car.

By the time she reached the main entrance to the building, she was out of breath and her heart was beating fast. The porter looked up casually and said, 'Good evening, Mrs Mackenzie,' as she heard the elevator descending again.

'Good evening,' she replied, as the elevator came to a halt. As she heard its doors open, she whipped round to face it, instinctively brandishing the knives.

Out stepped one of her neighbours – the man from the apartment two doors down on the same floor. He was carrying a heavy suitcase which he lugged towards her, as she stood by the porter's desk.

'Hi!' he said jovially, as Sally tried to hide the knives in her bag. (She knew he had seen them. She must think up some credible explanation.) 'Boy, is that case ever heavy! It weighs a bloody ton! You haven't seen Abigail, have you? She went to the liquor commission to stock up on booze . . . I wish she'd hurry up. I want to load up the car. We're off to the cottage as soon as she gets back. What about you? I hope you and Carson are going to be able to get away soon.'

'Carson says he can't leave the office for another couple of weeks, but I've decided to go and stay with my mother in the Laurentians until he's able to get away.'

'You should do that! It's too hot to hang around Montreal at this time of year. That husband of yours works too hard, you can tell him from me.' He pointed to the knives which were sticking out of Sally's bag and gave a bray of laughter. 'Meanwhile, you're off to kill the fatted calf, are you?'

'You could call it that.' Sally had, by this time, prepared an explanation. 'I'm leaving for the Laurentians right now, as it happens, and my mother is having a barbecue tonight. She has invited a whole heap of friends, and she has this crazy idea that we're going to barbecue duck. She wants to cut them in half and charcoal-grill them, and she asked me to bring some extra knives so we can all help her cut them up.'

'Sounds like hard work to me. It's bad enough carving duck when it's cooked. You need poultry scissors. You'll never do it with knives. Still, I'm sure it'll be a great party.'

'Yeah, I hope so.'

'Well, enjoy yourself, OK? Let's get together when we're all back in the fall.'

'Are you leaving right now, Mrs Mackenzie?' asked the porter, who felt that listening to the residents' conversations was an essential part of his job.

'I am, yes. I'm sorry, I should have told you. It's all been rather sudden – but my husband will be around for quite a while yet.' She knew Carson would not come back here, if he could help it, but she felt disinclined to tell the porter this.

'Well, I hope you enjoy your holiday.' The porter's tone conveyed a barely concealed reprimand which was not lost on Sally.

'Thank you. I'm sure I shall,' she replied, anxious to escape. Philippe could easily have arrived by now, she thought in desperation, and could have driven directly down to the garage from the street.

'I have a huge favour to ask you, Pete,' she said to her neighbour, giving him an ingratiating smile. 'For some reason, I can't unlock my car door. I don't seem to be able to get the key to work. That's why I came up here – to see if I could find someone to help me. You wouldn't be an angel and come down to the garage with me for a moment, would you, and see if you can get it open for me?'

'Sure,' he replied. 'No problem. Let's see what we can do.'

She was relieved to have him with her as they went down to find her car. She had always hated that garage, and this evening, she could not have faced it on her own.

There was no sign of Philippe, and her neighbour did not seem to mind being asked to open a car door which was perfectly simple to unlock. 'You must have been turning it the wrong way,' he said. 'You women, you're all the same when it comes to anything mechanical. I don't know how you all survive. Anyway, have a nice holiday, and see you when you get back.'

'OK. Thanks again. I'm sorry to have been so stupid.' Sally waved goodbye to him as he turned to walk away, then, checking that all the windows were tight shut, she locked the car doors from the inside, placed the knives on the seat beside her, and set off into the summer evening.

Carson left his apartment in a state of total shock and drove in a daze to the nearest bar. He ordered a double Scotch and sipped it dejectedly whilst trying to summon up the energy to telephone Louise. He ought to tell her to come and fetch her daughter – in spite of his anger, he knew Sally was in no fit state to be left on her own. She ought to be locked up, in his opinion, but it would be unwise to say that to Louise, he supposed. Damn Sally, anyway, he thought angrily. If she ruined her life, she had only herself to blame.

He felt uneasy, none the less, and by the time he had finished his drink, his unease had turned to guilt. He wanted to get the hell out as fast as possible, but he wanted to unload the responsibility for Sally on someone else first. He pulled out his address book, looked up the Hamiltons' number in the Laurentians, downed a second double Scotch, then walked to a phone. He'd have to lie – he'd have to tell Louise he was calling from out of town, or she'd insist on him going back to Westmount Square. That was one thing he couldn't face. Although he was worried about her, he had no wish to see Sally ever again. He simply could not cope with her any more and, anyway, at that particular moment, he wanted the consolation of someone else's arms.

'Louise,' said Carson, the moment she answered.

'Hi, Carson. How's things?' Louise asked. 'I bet it's

been hot in Montreal today, hasn't it? It's been scorching up here, but now it has clouded over and it's horribly muggy. I'm afraid we're in for one godawful storm.'

'Yeah, it's been hot as Hades – but, listen, I'm calling you for a reason. I have a huge favour to ask you – I'm afraid it means driving back to Montreal. I want you to go and fetch Sally and take her back up north with you and keep her there for the time being. She needs looking after ... She really needs to talk to someone ...'

'What's wrong? She's not sick, is she?'

'Not the way you mean,' Carson replied, 'but it's too complicated to explain on the phone. The point is that I've had to go out of town for the night and I don't believe Sally should be left on her own.'

'Why? What's the matter with her?'

'She's in pretty bad shape mentally – in fact, she's cracking up completely, if you want my opinion. She's got this idea that someone is out to kill her—'

'Are you serious?' Louise asked, half-suspecting this remark to be one of Carson's less good jokes.

'Dead serious,' Carson replied. 'I want to talk to you and Brock about it as soon as possible, but I honestly think it's better if Sally tells you about it herself first.'

'Are you two getting on all right?' Louise sounded suddenly suspicious.

'We had a row this evening, as it happens, but that's not the problem. I wish it were as simple as that,' Carson sighed. 'I can't help her any more, Louise. I've come to the end of the line. She's a complete nervous wreck, and I can't take it any more.'

'What exactly are you trying to tell me, Carson?' Louise was angry, and she was beginning to shout.

Carson took a deep breath, uncertain how much he should tell her. 'I think she's having a mental breakdown: a serious mental breakdown. She ought to be in a hospital, not running around loose.'

'You're crazy! Sally's not the sort to have a break-down! What's going on with you two? Have you been straying again?'

'Louise, listen to me, will you? It's far more serious than that. She says she was attacked in Paris – you know, when she had that nosebleed – and she's convinced that Philippe Marignac is the guy. She's absolutely adamant that he's the same man that abducted her and beat her up.'

'I've never heard such rubbish! Anyway, she has always said she wasn't attacked. She just had a nosebleed. You know that's what she has always said.'

'She *was* attacked, I promise you. She told me about it years ago. Whatever else she has invented, she certainly didn't invent that.'

'Are you telling me that she's been lying to me and her father all these years?'

'She wasn't lying in the way you mean. She couldn't talk about it because she couldn't handle it at all. She was scared of Brock's reaction, if you want my opinion, so she tried to convince herself it wasn't true.'

'What do you mean, "scared of Brock's reaction"? Why should she have been scared?'

'Well, she told me about some incident when you took her to the South of France when she was about five. Some local flashed at her, apparently, and scared her witless; but when she told Brock, he went berserk – or so she says. She told me he was mad as hell with her, and beat the living daylights out of her, and that she was terrified of him as a result.'

Louise was silent.

'Did that happen, Louise? Can you remember anything like that?'

'Yes . . . Brock had been so worried, you know. I don't think he realized . . . But I don't see what that's got to do with this.'

'Well, I've read a good deal on the subject, over the years, as you can imagine. I thought that if I couldn't persuade Sally to see a shrink, I could at least try and find out as much as I could myself, so that I could help her. Everyone seems to agree that the reaction to any kind of attack of a sexual nature is worse if the incident occurs in adolescence – which, of course, was Sally's case; but I also remember reading somewhere that if a parent reacts badly when a child is molested, it damages the child far more seriously than the actual incident does. Kids are more scared of their parents' reactions, apparently, than they are of all the rest. So if the parent – particularly a father – blames the child for inviting the incident, it causes terrible guilt and fear. Now, Sally only told me about the episode with the flasher this afternoon, so I'm just guessing; but it seems to me that this could explain her determination to deny that she was attacked.' Carson sighed. 'Anyway,' he added after a second, 'whatever the explanation, one thing is certain: I can't deal with her any more. I've reached the end of my rope. That's why I'm asking you to take over. I simply can't cope any more.'

'Why, for God's sake? You can't give up on her now!'

'Look, Louise, you don't know what I've been through. Sally's getting worse by the minute, let me tell you. It's beyond anything I can deal with now.'

'If you knew all this, Carson, why the hell didn't you tell me and Brock? We're her parents, for God's sake! How dare you not tell us?'

'I couldn't. She made me promise not to tell you. She made me swear never to tell anyone. She'd never have trusted me again if I had. Anyway, there's no point in going into all of that now. The real problem is this obsession she has with Philippe Marignac. She's seriously convinced he's the guy who attacked her, and that he's aiming to do it again.'

(Carson was tempted to tell Louise that her beloved daughter had been having an affair with the man. If that wasn't proof of madness, having an affair with the guy you think is trying to kill you . . . But then, he had no way of proving this, and Sally would deny it, he knew.)

'Sally thinks he's going to kill her,' he repeated. 'She won't listen to reason. As I say, she needs professional help.'

'What if she's right? Had you thought of that? Maybe she's not having a breakdown. I mean, if you're so sure that she was really attacked in Paris, then how do you know that Philippe isn't the same guy?'

'Oh, for God's sake, Louise! Don't you start on that, too! It wasn't him, that's perfectly obvious. Apart from anything else, he was at Harvard at the time. Don't think I haven't checked. I've checked everything he ever said. He was brought up in Martinique. His grandparents lived in the South of France. He never went anywhere near Paris except for three years at university, but that was much earlier. He hates the place, anyway.'

'It happened in July, Carson. It was during the summer vacation. He wouldn't have been at Harvard during his vacation, would he? Have you checked what he was doing in July that year?'

Carson gave a sigh of exasperation. 'Yes, I checked. Of course I checked. I told you – I've checked everything. He went back to Martinique.'

'How do you know? Who told you?'

'He always went back there when he was on vacation. I've spoken to several people who knew him at Harvard, and they all say the same.'

'He could have gone to Paris from Martinique, couldn't he? Have you any proof that he didn't do that?'

'Darn it, Louise! I can hardly telephone his parents when I don't even know them. Be reasonable! You can't seriously expect me to ring them up and ask them what their son was doing every minute of his vacation twenty-one years, or whatever it is, ago.'

'So you don't really know.'

'Oh, for crying out loud! Let's not waste any more time arguing about it. Sally is on her own, and she's frightened. She's capable of doing something crazy.

Apart from anything else, she has taken to wandering around Montreal by herself at dead of night.'

'What on earth do you mean?'

'I mean just what I said. She gets dressed and goes out in the middle of the night, looking for Philippe. God knows why, but she does.'

'Are you trying to tell me that Sally goes out on her own at night?'

'That's exactly what I'm telling you.'

'By herself?'

'Yes.'

'Come on, Carson! Sally's never gone out by herself at night in her life.'

'She was out last night and the night before.'

'You're joking! I don't believe it.'

'It's God's own truth, I promise you. She was out last night for half an hour, to my certain knowledge, and for a good three hours the night before that. The first night, I pretended to be asleep when she came back. I thought she must be having an affair and I wanted to see if she did it again; but when she went out again last night, I waited outside the apartment till she came back. She came up in the elevator – you know she never goes in it – and she screamed when the doors opened and fell out in a faint.'

'Carson!' Louise shrieked. 'You shouldn't have let her do it! You should never have let her go out on her own!'

'I didn't – or not intentionally. She waited until I was asleep. Both nights, I just woke up and found her gone.'

'And you've left her on her own? You must be out of your mind!'

'I'm sorry, Louise, but I have a job to do – and, anyway, I keep telling you, I can't take any more. I don't feel great about it, believe me. That's why I'm calling you. *Please* go and fetch her. I won't have a moment's peace until you do.'

'Where are you calling from?'

'I'm on my way to Sherbrooke,' Carson lied. 'I'm booked to speak at a dinner there, and I'm going to be late as it is.'

'Why the hell didn't you ring me before you left?'

'I told you, we had a row. I was too angry to think. Come on, Louise. Do me this favour, please, will you? Go and fetch her and take her back to the Laurentians with you. You can yell at me afterwards, when we know she is safe.'

'My God, I'll have something to say to you when I see you!'

'Yeah, fine, but just get going now, will you? You'd better warn Brock, too. Maybe he could keep an eye on her until you arrive. I'll call you both later to make sure everything's OK.'

Carson felt exhausted. As soon as he had put the phone down on Louise, he picked it up again and dialled the number of a woman he visited from time to time. She lived in the Eastern Townships, and he happened to know that her husband was away.

Having made this call, he returned to the bar for one last, quick drink before driving across the Champlain Bridge, and on east to the place where he intended to stay the night.

Meanwhile, a thousand frightful images fought their way through Louise's mind: her sixteen-year-old daughter lying ashen in that Paris hospital bed; her only child being attacked by a maniac – where? In some seedy back street in Montmartre? In a squalid hotel? In her own room? In some deserted parking-lot somewhere? What had happened? She wanted to know. *Why* had it happened, and with whom?

She had visions of a leprous creature whispering obscenities to her daughter as he squeezed his hands round her adolescent neck: a Marquis de Sade, a Count Dracula, a Vicomte de Valmont in modern dress – some hideous seducer with the devil's charm and a hangman's vile heart; or a wine-sodden tramp in filthy clothes, reeking of garlic and *gitanes*; or perhaps a younger version of Philippe Marignac (a man whose good looks and polished manners might well hide a depraved mind and rotting soul). She wanted to kill him, whoever he was. She wanted to find and kill him. Dear God, how she wished she had known all this before!

She dialled Sally's number the minute Carson put down the phone but, listening to it ringing, she knew that her daughter was not there. She counted to twenty before giving up and telephoning her husband instead.

'Is Sally with you?' she asked Brock, when she was finally put through.

'No,' Brock replied, sounding irritated. 'Why the hell should she be? What's the matter with you guys? Philippe Marignac is here, in my office. He's just walked in looking for her, too.'

'Oh my God!' gasped Louise. 'Well, don't let Sally bump into him! Just listen to this . . .' She told Brock briefly what Carson had told her, adding, 'I've just tried her number and she's definitely not at home. You've got to go out and look for her right away. I'm coming back. I'll leave immediately. You'll be through at the office soon, won't you? OK, I'll drive straight home and meet you and Sally there.'

'How the hell am I supposed to find her?' Brock asked. 'She could be anywhere, for Christ's sake.'

'Ring her friends. See if anyone knows where she is. This is serious, Brock. She needs our help.'

'OK, OK. I'll do what I can, but you'd better get back here fast.'

# Chapter Twenty-Six

Philippe drove to Place Ville-Marie in a state of total fury. He felt angrier than he had ever felt in his life. He had hoped to have this discussion with Sally in some isolated spot, over a period of days; but she had, by her telephone call, unexpectedly brought matters to a head.

He marched into the building by the McGill College entrance, only to find, to his annoyance, that Sally was not waiting downstairs. She was trying to hide from him, he thought. She was purposely trying to make it impossible for him to talk to her. If she believed, for one moment, that she could avoid this conversation by hanging about upstairs, in her father's office, she would soon discover how mistaken she was, he told himself grimly, as the elevator doors opened and he stepped in.

There was no sign of Sally in the McEwen & Hamilton reception, so Philippe told the girl behind the desk that he wished to see Brock. The latter was surprised when told that a Mr Philippe Marignac was demanding to see him, but told his secretary to show the Frenchman in.

'Hi! What a pleasant surprise! What brings you here?' asked Brock jovially, as Philippe walked through the door.

'Your daughter telephoned me, about twenty minutes ago, and asked me to meet her here,' Philippe lied. 'It sounded urgent, so I came right away.'

'She told you to meet her *here*?' Brock sounded incredulous. 'Are you sure?'

'Absolutely.'

'Did she say why?'

'No.'

'Well, I think you must have misunderstood her. I'm not expecting her here.'

Philippe stared at Brock angrily. 'She said she was calling from your office,' he said, his tone implying that he thought Brock knew where she was.

'Well, I'll be darned. Are you sure she wasn't calling from Carson's office? That would make more sense. I bet—'

Brock's next reflection was interrupted by his intercom buzzing.

'Yes?' he said, picking up his receiver. 'OK. Put her through . . . Louise? Yeah . . . What? No. Why the hell should she be? What's the matter with you guys? Philippe Marignac is here, in my office. He's just walked in looking for her, too.'

Philippe listened with interest and tried to guess what Louise was saying at the other end.

'OK, OK,' Brock said finally, giving a sigh. 'I'll do what I can, but you'd better get back here fast.'

Putting down the phone, he turned to Philippe. 'I don't know what the hell's going on round here,' he said. 'Louise is worried because Sally isn't answering her phone. She thinks she's—' Brock broke off in mid-sentence. He wanted to warn Philippe, in case Sally turned up suddenly, yet he did not feel he should tell the Frenchman everything that Louise had just told him. (He did not, for one moment, suspect Philippe of harbouring sinister intentions towards his daughter, but he thought Philippe might be deeply offended if he knew what Sally was saying about him. He might try and sue her for defamation of character . . . Anyone who was accused of being a rapist and potential murderer would be likely to sue, he thought.) 'Louise thinks she's having a nervous breakdown,' Brock finished lamely.

'What makes her think that?'

'Carson rang her just now, apparently, to tell her he thought Sally was cracking up and needed help.'

'She must be with Carson, then,' Philippe said, looking pensive.

'No, she isn't. That's why he rang Louise. He was on his way to Sherbrooke, apparently. He's speaking at some dinner there tonight, and he was worried about leaving Sally on her own.'

Philippe said nothing, but he was interested to learn that Carson had left town.

'I'd better try her number again,' Brock muttered, picking up the phone and dialling. He listened to the ringing tone for a while before shrugging his shoulders, with obvious irritation, and hanging up.

Leaning back in his chair, he clasped his hands behind his head. 'Christ, I really needed this like a hole in the head!' he suddenly exploded. 'I bet it'll turn out to be a complete storm in a teacup! I don't suppose there's anything the matter with her at all. Still, I'd better ring her porter, I guess . . .' He buzzed his secretary. 'Get hold of the guy on the desk in my daughter's building in Westmount Square, will you?' he said to her; and then, a moment later, when she rang him back, 'OK, I need to speak to him. Put me through to him, please.'

Philippe's face remained expressionless, but he was listening attentively.

'This is Mrs Mackenzie's father . . . Mrs Carson Mackenzie, yes. That's right. She's out at the moment, but I want to get a message to her urgently, so when she comes in . . . What . . . ? Are you sure?' Then, after a moment, 'You're sure she wasn't going to Knowlton? They have a house there, you know . . . Did she? To her mother? What time was this? She actually mentioned the Laurentians, did she? OK. Well, thanks for your help . . .'

Brock replaced the receiver and waved his hands about in disbelief. 'Goddammit!' he exploded. 'I should have guessed! That's just the kind of crazy thing she would do! Why the hell didn't she think of telling anyone? I should have told Louise to stay put – I hope to God she hasn't already left!'

He turned to Philippe, saying, 'I'm sorry, but I must try and catch Louise and warn her that Sally is on her way there. I won't be a minute. I really apologize for all this.' He dialled and listened for quite some time before giving up. 'Damn it!' he muttered eventually. 'She must have left.'

He rang for his secretary, who put her head round the door. 'Get hold of the garage in Val-des-Lacs for me, please,' Brock said to her. 'You'll find the number in my card file, under "Dufour" – that's the guy who owns it. Put him through to me as quickly as possible, will you?'

Val-des-Lacs, thought Philippe. He had a feeling that was somewhere up towards Mont Tremblant. He had a map of Quebec in the car, so it wouldn't be difficult to check. He rose, intending to take his leave, but Brock's call to the garage was put through as he stood up.

'Monsieur Dufour? Hi! It's Brock Hamilton here,' shouted Brock, waving at Philippe to wait.

Philippe sat down again. 'I have a favour to ask you,' Brock continued. 'I want to get hold of my wife urgently. She rang me from the cottage about fifteen minutes ago to tell me she was coming back to Montreal, so she should be driving past you any minute . . . What . . . ? Oh, hell and damnation! Yeah . . . I was going to ask you to flag her down . . . I guess there's nothing we can do about it now . . . I suppose so . . . Well, thanks for your help, anyway. Sorry to have bothered you . . . The spare tyre? Oh, yes, I'd forgotten all about it. Yes, I'll be up there at the weekend. I'll collect it from you then. OK, see you on Saturday. Thanks. Bye.'

Replacing the receiver, he turned to Philippe, saying, 'She's driven past already. I've missed her, god-dammit!' He stared at the phone for a moment, then muttered, 'Oh, well, Sally has a key to the place, so I guess she'll be all right.'

'Is there anything I can do to help?' enquired

Philippe, wondering how long it took to drive to Val-des-Lacs.

'I don't think so, thanks. I'm only sorry that Sally bothered you. I can't imagine why she asked you to come here.'

Philippe knew, though. She was a coward. She had made him come here on purpose in order to avoid having to explain. The thought that she had fooled him made him absolutely furious. How dare she behave like this? And how very mistaken of her to try her tricks on him . . . If he was angry when he walked in, he was even angrier now.

'Well, I suppose I'd better get going, in that case,' said Philippe, once again rising to his feet. 'I'm supposed to be helping a friend move out all his gear from his Outremont apartment, and get him unpacked and settled in his new place in St Lambert tonight. I said I'd be there before this. He's going to kill me for being late!' Philippe had thought up this story while Brock was on the telephone. He wanted to cover his tracks in case anyone thought of checking on him later that evening; and he didn't want Brock suspecting for one moment that he might follow Sally to Val-des-Lacs.

'OK, Philippe; well, so long. I'm sorry you were dragged here for nothing. Darned irritating, this whole business: a complete waste of everybody's time. Anyway, I'll be in touch next week sometime, when we've sorted ourselves out; then maybe we can have lunch together, or something.'

'Sure, let's do that,' said Philippe, eager to leave.

He walked out of the office casually, in an effort to look unhurried; hid his impatience until he had left the building, and then raced to his car. Pulling out the road map of the province, he found Val-des-Lacs without difficulty, and set off in the direction of the Laurentian *autoroute* without wasting further time. If he hurried, he might catch Monsieur Dufour . . . There'd be bound to be a telephone there somewhere, anyway. He could look up the Hamiltons in the local phone book: presumably, there wouldn't be many people with that name around there. In any case, it was only a village ... Probably everyone would know them. Someone would point him in the right direction once he was there, he felt sure.

Most people had already left for their summer abodes and were scattered about the province on various rivers and lakes. There were few cars on the road, so Philippe was soon clear of the city and heading north fast.

He kept a wary eye out for traffic cops as he hurtled up the *autoroute*, determined, if he were caught speeding, to use his Frenchness for all it was worth. It seemed odd to him, on reflection, that these English Canadians, in spite of all their difficulties with the *Québécois*, still preferred to live in this French, Catholic province rather than in Protestant, English Ontario. Admittedly, they seemed to have picked the more interesting province, if one were to believe what the Quebecers said; but he imagined that the Presbyterian gloom that supposedly still hung over Ontario might seem less oppressive to the English than it would to him, just as the high-pressure heartbeat and double pulse-rate that pounded through this province might seem less attractive to those trying to live out their ancient legend alongside an equally ancient rival than it did to a complete outsider like himself.

Old enemies, he concluded, make better partners than old friends. Perhaps, in the end, there was little real distinction between the two. (Verlaine and Rimbaud, Richard and Saladin: were they enemies or friends? He and Sally, if it came to that — was it love or was it hate?)

Putting his foot down on the accelerator, he continued at high speed until his progress was arrested by an outbreak of roadworks. Why on earth, he wondered in exasperation, did they have to dig up their highways at the one time of year when everyone wanted to use them? He realized they'd be unable to carry out repairs in winter – and, of course, those endless months of sub-zero temperatures must badly damage the roads – but still, why could they not do it in May, or in October? He tried to console himself with the thought that Sally must also have been held up and that she, being a much slower driver than he was, would have been less adept at negotiating these problem patches than he was. It did nothing to improve his temper, none the less.

Ahead of him, the low mountains of the Laurentian Shield rose darkly under a granite sky. It was a very hot evening, and the air was oppressive. Mosquito and blackfly hovered in their thousands, and the country was bathed in a sulphureous hue.

The road ahead was empty, but the sky was darkening so rapidly that by the time Philippe reached the foothills, he could barely distinguish maple from pine. To his alien eye, it was a sinister landscape. The woods on either side looked mysterious and unwelcoming; and there was something about the shape of mountains that made them look ghostly and old. Even the silence seemed ominous: it struck Philippe as unnatural. There was an animosity breathing in the darkness of which he was intensely aware. The forests seemed to whisper, as if seething with the irate spirits of dead Indians; and there was something evil about the way the distant ridges seemed to march along the skyline, as if preparing to wage battle against the coming storm.

Philippe disliked the unearthly quiet of this vast, empty world with its pitch-black forests and silent, watchful hills; but, rather than being discouraged by the menace he felt around him, it reinforced the dangerous edge of his already violent mood. Undeterred by the hush of expectancy which had fallen over the countryside, he switched on his headlights fully, turned up the radio till it was blaring, and continued to speed northwards in pursuit of his prey.

Glancing impatiently at signposts, he flashed past

Saint-Jérome and Sainte-Agathe; then headed in the direction of Saint-Donat, looking for the turning to Val-des-Lacs. As the darkness finally settled, the forest closed in on him until he felt caught in the ancient folds of the hills as if trapped in the folds of an enemy's cape.

He was relieved when he finally drove in to Val-des-Lacs, and triumphant to discover the garage open still. He pulled up beside the gas pump and was about to climb out when a sudden flash of lightning zigzagged across the horizon. He waited a second, then opened his car door, as the first crack of thunder echoed across the valleys and a surly-looking figure shuffled towards him demanding to know if he wanted gas.

'Yes, please. Fill her up,' Philippe replied, aware that the man was irritated by his accent. 'I'll just make a phone call while you're doing that, if you don't mind.'

He went to the phone booth, looked up the Hamiltons' number and dialled it. He did not intend to speak to Sally; he just wanted to check whether she was there. Had she answered, he would have replaced the receiver without saying anything, but, as it happened, he was greeted by the uninterrupted whine of a telephone out of order. He tried again, with the same result. Next, he dialled the Hamiltons' number in Westmount, replacing the receiver without a word as soon as he heard Louise's voice at the other end. At least she was safely back in Montreal, Philippe thought. He tried their local number for the third time, but the phone was clearly disconnected. Shrugging his shoulders, he replaced the receiver and made a note of the address.

It had started to pour while Philippe was phoning; and, within no time, torrents of water were cascading down the slopes. Running inside to pay for the gas, Philippe mentioned to the man (whom he assumed was Monsieur Dufour) that he had been unable to get through to the people he was trying to call.

'I expect the lines are down,' commented Monsieur

Dufour, who knew full well that this was the case, but who saw no reason to be pleasant to anyone speaking such ridiculously snobbish French. Assuming Philippe would be upset by this information, he added, in gloating tones, 'It's always the same. It happens whenever there's a storm.'

The French-Canadian accent always grated on Philippe. He felt like snapping at the man, but he needed his help. 'I've never been in this area before,' he said, trying to sound casual. 'I'm visiting friends – people called Hamilton.' He showed the man the piece of paper on which he'd written the address. 'You don't happen to know where this is, do you?'

'Sure,' the man replied. 'I know where it is.' He seemed disinclined to volunteer any further information, so Philippe produced a ten-dollar bill. At the sight of it, Monsieur Dufour gave him all the information he needed. Philippe handed him the money and rushed out into the rain.

Ten minutes later, he was driving up a steep dirt track that cut through the woods. On either side, the dark and silent forest stretched away. Philippe dipped his headlights and drove slowly. The track was full of potholes, and running with water; and his windscreen wipers were little help against the torrential rain. He could see almost nothing ahead of him and so was forced to drive cautiously, relying almost entirely on the lightning which, from time to time, lit up the way.

Suddenly, rounding a bend, he saw a glimmer of lights flickering dimly just ahead. He had been told that it was a private road and that there was only one house on this piece of land. Then he saw Sally's car and knew he had come to the right place.

He switched off his headlights and quietly inched his car forward, parking it on the grass under the trees. Opening the door quietly, he climbed out and made his way carefully through the downpour, keeping to the grass at the side of the track so that his footsteps would not be heard.

226

# Chapter Twenty-Seven

Sally, meanwhile, had had an infuriating journey. She decided to stop, about half an hour's drive out of Montreal, in order to telephone her mother and warn her she was on the way. She happened to choose the moment when Carson was speaking to Louise and, as soon as that conversation ended, Louise immediately picked up the phone again, first to try Sally's number and then to call Brock.

After five or six unsuccessful attempts to speak to her mother, Sally dialled the operator and demanded to know if there was something wrong with the phone. The operator, having checked, told her there was someone talking on the line. Aware that her mother was capable of chatting on the telephone for hours, Sally decided it was hopeless and returned, defeated, to her car. She had wasted fifteen minutes for nothing. It was always the same when she tried to call her mother. She was furious with Louise for spending so much time on the phone.

About ten minutes later, Sally encountered the first lot of roadworks. She could not believe it. They had only one lane functioning, and half the time that was given over to the cars heading the other way.

Twenty kilometres further on, the situation was worse. Here, the men seemed unusually keen to complete what they were doing before the rain started; and, once they had finished, kept everyone waiting while they manoeuvred their vast machines off the road. Exasperated, Sally climbed out of her car, marched towards the foreman, and complained. He replied, sarcastically, that perhaps she hadn't noticed that a storm was about to break. They had cleared the road and packed up for the night before Sally was able to drive on.

To cap it all, she discovered, as she was approaching Val-des-Lacs, that she had a slow puncture and that one of her car tyres was steadily losing air. It was, by this time, eight at night, and she knew it was unlikely she would find anyone to change it until the following day.

She toyed with the idea of stopping at the garage and asking for help, but she knew Monsieur Dufour was not the most amiable of men; and his mechanic would have left, she was sure: he always left at six. Anyway, the heavens were clearly about to open. She'd better try to reach home before the storm broke.

She drove slowly through the village, and on up the familiar road through the woods that she had known since she was a child. As she reached the entrance to the property she turned in through the gates, past the sign saying, 'Trespassers will be prosecuted', and eased her car cautiously up the track. Peering into the dark ahead, which seemed much blacker suddenly because of the density of trees on either side, she did her best to drive carefully, avoiding potholes, ruts and rocks. She skidded a couple of times, which frightened her, so she was grateful when the track finally widened and she drove out from among the trees. Pulling up as soon as she was within sight of the house, she switched off the engine with a sigh of relief.

There were no lights showing from any of the windows. Her mother must have gone out to dinner, she thought as, her bag flung over her shoulder and a flashlight clutched in her hand, she crossed the lawn and walked towards the house.

As she fumbled in her shoulder-bag, looking for her key, a rumble of thunder echoed around the hills. She glanced up at the sky for a second. She had made it just in time. Near by, in the woods, a whippoorwill called monotonously to its mate.

Sally felt irritated with her mother for being out. She was not worried – Louise often went to have drinks or dinner with friends locally – but it was hardly the warm welcome to which Sally had looked forward throughout her exasperating drive. She had envisaged a great wave of maternal sympathy; a decent supper, followed by a heart-to-heart; perhaps a nightcap, as they exchanged confidences, while an exciting storm raged overhead.

She went to the telephone, intending to call round the area, track down her mother and let her know that she had arrived; but to her fury, she discovered that the line was dead. She felt a surge of irrational anger with the telephone company; she felt cheated and annoyed. It struck her belatedly that she should have called her mother before leaving Montreal.

Flinging herself into an armchair, she sat brooding for a moment, as the thunder continued to mutter ominously, some way off, in the hills. She told herself that if Louise had just gone out for drinks, she'd be back at any moment. If, on the other hand, her mother had gone out to dinner, she would not be back for a couple of hours.

Deciding, after a time, that she might as well make herself something to eat, she went to the kitchen and fished about in the fridge. She had just found some ham when the lights went out. They came on again immediately, then flickered uncertainly, as a flash of lightning was followed by a huge crash overhead. Shortly after this, the deluge began.

Sally loved thunderstorms. She found them exciting. Her mother, who was nervous of them, had made sure that Sally, as a child, was unaware of the dangers and, in an effort to distract her daughter from any thought of forest fires or what might happen to wooden houses if they were struck by lightning, had invariably turned every storm into a party. If they occurred at night, Louise lit oil lamps all over the house, and Sally was allowed to sit in her parents' bed devouring candy and

Pepsi-Cola. If they occurred in the daytime, they wound up an ancient gramophone (a splendid relic of the thirties kept solely for these occasions) and, when the electricity was cut off, played games to the scratched accompaniment of Bing Crosby and Burl Ives. Only once had Sally questioned her mother about the possibility of their house being struck during a storm, and Louise had replied, with an admirable show of conviction, that lightning was only attracted to water. 'It won't hit us,' she said firmly. 'It will go for the lake.'

As a result of her early experiences, Sally had always enjoyed storms. With the onset of thunder, she switched into a party mood and, on this occasion, regretted being alone not because she was afraid, but because she could not share her enjoyment with anyone else. Since the electricity was always, sooner or later, cut off during storms, she temporarily abandoned the kitchen and went round the house lighting the plentiful supply of oil lamps that her mother had installed. The one thing that did not occur to her was to lock the front door. She felt as safe in the country as she had felt unsafe in the city; and since her parents only bothered, in the Laurentians, to lock the door if they were going out for some hours, the thought never crossed her mind.

Returning to the kitchen, she opened a can of soup and, while that was warming, went to the pantry to see if she could find some wine. (Her parents rarely drank wine, but Sally did: she always had.) Finding a case of Beaujolais, she extracted a bottle. She was about to sit down to soup, bread and ham when there was another crash of thunder immediately overhead. This time, the lights gave one last flicker, then died. Congratulating herself on having lit the lamps just in time, she uncorked the Beaujolais and poured some into a glass. At this moment, she heard the front door being opened, and sighed contentedly at the knowledge that her mother was back.

Not wishing to give Louise a fright, she called out, 'It's me, Mum, so don't panic. I'm in the kitchen having something to eat.' She heard footsteps crossing the hall and, struggling to make herself heard above the noise of the storm, shouted, 'I tried to ring you, but you were on the telephone for so long that I decided not to wait – and now, as usual, the phone has been cut off.'

As she said this, Philippe walked into the kitchen. Sally leapt to her feet, knocking over her chair in her haste, and glanced instinctively at the row of knives hanging on a magnetic board, above the sink, on the far side of the room. Philippe said nothing. Sally stared at him in terror, then took a couple of steps backwards, as he pushed the door shut behind him and stood looking at her without saying a word.

He was white-faced and dripping, and his eyes glittered strangely in the light cast by the lamp. Rivulets of water trickled from his hair on to his shoulders, and then on down, splashing in tiny droplets to the floor. He did not move, but his eyes followed hers, and a muscle twitched in his right cheek.

'Why didn't you tell me Carson was away?' he asked, after a minute. 'And why the hell did you send me on that wild-goose chase to your father's office? Why didn't you let me know you were coming up here?' Again he saw her glance in the direction of the knives.

(It would be difficult to walk round the table without being intercepted by him, she thought. She must keep calm. She must keep him talking until her mother returned.)

'You look wet,' she said, ignoring his questions. 'Would you like to change and have something to eat? You can borrow any of my father's things. There's a cupboard full of his clothes in the bedroom – first on the left at the top of the stairs.' He said nothing. She felt paralysed. She must make him relax. 'I've just warmed some soup,' she said. 'There's plenty for both of us – and, as you can see, there's lots of bread and ham. I'll lay another place.' He did not move. Nor did she. 'I'm afraid it's not very exciting,' she said faintly, 'but you're welcome to join me. I'm absolutely starving, for some reason. I don't know about you.'

'I'll wait,' he said. 'You eat. You'll need it. We've got a long journey ahead. If you want, you can make me a sandwich to eat in the car.'

'What do you mean? Are you driving back to Montreal tonight?'

'Of course not! I tried to call you to tell you: someone has lent me a house. It's way north, somewhere up towards Lac Saint-Jean. It's going to be a hell of a drive. We're leaving in twenty minutes, so you'd better hurry up and eat.'

Appalled, Sally stared at him. 'Well, I can't leave tonight,' she said, trying to sound calm. 'I've only just got here after a hellish drive. Anyway, my car's got a flat and I can't go anywhere until it's fixed.'

'We don't need your car. I'm taking you in mine.'

'Don't be silly,' she said, unable to hide the panic in her voice. 'How will I get back?'

'I'll bring you back.' He took a couple of steps towards her. 'Sit down and eat while there's time. You've got exactly sixteen minutes left.'

'Philippe,' she pleaded, terrified, 'I'm absolutely exhausted. I really can't face any more driving tonight.'

'You can sleep in the car,' he said. 'You'll have plenty of time. It's an impossible place to get to, judging by the map, and I've no idea what the roads are like. Even if they're good, we're going to be driving all night.'

'Let's wait until the storm is over. You can't possibly want to drive in this.'

'On the contrary. There will be no-one else on the roads.'

Sally cast about for some way of distracting him. 'I'll have to let Carson know,' she said pleadingly. 'I can't just go away without telling him. You must let me telephone him first.'

'The telephone lines are down, as you are aware,

since you were shouting about it when I arrived. In any case, as Carson is in Sherbrooke, he's hardly going to worry where you are for the moment. You can ring him when we arrive.'

'Carson isn't in Sherbrooke! What on earth are you talking about?'

'*Voyons*,' said Philippe, lapsing through fatigue and exasperation into French, 'there's no point in lying. Your father told me Carson had phoned when he was on his way there. He's addressing a dinner there, tonight – but I assume you knew that.'

'No, I didn't! I don't believe you!' Sally tried desperately to marshall her thoughts. Could Carson really have driven to Sherbrooke? He had no reason to go there, and he certainly wasn't supposed to be addressing any dinner. Either Philippe was lying, or Carson was . . . But Carson wouldn't lie – unless, of course, he was with a woman. Well, she couldn't afford to think about that now. He must have told her father about Philippe wanting to kill her. Why else would he have rung Brock? (She had not guessed, from Philippe's words, that it was her mother that Carson had rung.)

'Eat,' Philippe ordered her. 'Go on, sit down and eat.'

It would be a way of wasting time, she thought. She sat down and sipped a mouthful of soup. It was tepid. She stood up again, saying, 'I'll just warm this up.'

'There isn't time. Just drink it, or else leave it and eat the ham.' Philippe walked round the table and stationed himself halfway between the knives and the door.

Sitting down again, Sally pushed the bowl of soup away from her and helped herself to bread and ham. If her father knew about Philippe, and was looking for her, he'd presumably have the sense to call the police, she reflected. Her mother must return eventually, in any case: it was simply a question of playing for time. She ate in silence, taking as long about it as she could.

'How about a glass of wine?' she asked Philippe suddenly. 'Wouldn't you like a glass of wine?'

'I'm driving,' he replied. 'We can take the bottle with us. I'll have some when we arrive.'

'It does seem crazy to try and get there tonight,' complained Sally, trying to sound natural. 'Why can't we leave in the morning? It'll give me time to get my tyre changed, and phone Carson, and get everything sorted before we go.' She looked up expectantly but his face was impassive. 'Apart from anything else,' she added nervously, 'everyone will worry if I suddenly disappear – Carson, my parents, everyone. Supposing they call the police?'

'They won't call the police. Not tonight, at any rate. They know you're here – the porter in your building told your father – and if they try to telephone, they'll discover that the line is out of order, so they'll realize that you can't ring them to let them know you've arrived.'

'What if the telephone is reconnected and they find out I'm not here?'

'That eventuality had occurred to me, so I took the precaution of disconnecting the wire when I arrived.' Philippe smiled for the first time that evening. It was not a pleasant smile. 'Nobody will be able to get through, and I doubt if they'll bother to drive up here tonight. However, just in case they decide to set forth in this storm, I want to make sure that we leave before they arrive.'

Sally stared at him helplessly.

'Your time is up,' he said. 'Cork that bottle and we'll take all this stuff with us in case we're hungry when we arrive.'

Sally thought for a moment, then stood up. Philippe watched her in silence. 'OK,' she said, picking up the bowl of untouched soup. 'I'll just rinse these things and clear up before we leave.'

Philippe, sensing what she had in mind, took a couple of steps towards the sink. Sally walked slowly, with deliberation, bracing herself for a fight. Aware that Philippe was watching her, she tipped the soup down the drain, then turned on the hot water and let it run into the bowl while she carefully rinsed the spoon.

Lifting her hand, as if intending to turn off the tap, Sally reached instead for the largest of the knives hanging on the board. Philippe lunged towards her, and she found herself pinned against the sink. She managed to pull the knife from the board, but Philippe gripped her arm with both his hands and slammed her wrist down so hard against the taps that it was knocked from her hand. Sally gave a sharp gasp of pain as the knife clattered into the sink.

Spinning her round to face him, Philippe struck her a blow across the cheek. She reeled and put out a hand to steady herself, but he caught her arm in mid-air and held it while he hit her again.

Holding both her wrists so hard that it brought tears to her eyes, he stood looking at her in silence. He was shaking with rage. After a moment, he said, 'I advise you not to try that again.' He stared at her for a moment then, yanking her by the arm, dragged her, protesting, towards the door.

'My mother will be back in a moment and she'll wonder where I am,' Sally sobbed. 'She'll call the police immediately if she finds I'm not here.'

'Your mother is safely back in Montreal, I am happy to say. I telephoned your parents a few minutes ago, from Val-des-Lacs, to make sure.' He laughed. 'It's ironic to think that she must have set off just as you were leaving to come here.'

Sally let out a noise like the cry of an animal caught in a forest fire. 'Philippe, *please*!' she begged. '*Please*, let me go!' But Philippe ignored her cries.

She must not give in, she told herself in desperation. She'd thought it was all over last time, but he'd given up in the end. He'd become fed up with her struggling; he'd realized she would never love him. He'd given up completely and chucked her out. She'd make him give up again. She must try and convince him she had never loved him. Her only hope was to keep playing that last card.

As he dragged her across the living-room, she took a deep breath. 'I don't love you!' she screamed. 'I never loved you! I was only pretending. I'm in love with someone else.'

He stopped dead, with his back to her, still holding her by the arm; then turned to face her, his blue eyes suddenly as pale as arctic ice. 'I'm aware of that,' he said. 'You already told me that on the telephone. That is why we are making this journey. You're going to tell me all about it when we arrive.'

'I'm not going to tell you anything! I hate you! I wish you were dead!' Sally screamed.

Striking her with the full force of his anger, he watched her spin away from him and fall, unconscious, to the floor.

# Chapter Twenty-Eight

Sally woke to the sound of rain falling on the car roof. Her head was hurting, her cheek was bruised, and her right wrist was swollen as a result of being smashed against the tap. It took her a moment to realize that she must be lying in the back of Philippe's car. When she tried to change her position, she discovered that her hands and feet were firmly bound.

She opened her eyes and saw the back of his head. She tried to sit up, but he heard her and told her to remain lying down. 'I want you to stay out of sight,' he said, 'and I imagine you'd rather I didn't have to knock you out again.'

'I'm thirsty,' she pleaded. 'Please can we stop somewhere and buy a drink?'

'No,' he replied. 'If I were you I'd go back to sleep.'

It was very dark outside the windows. 'Where are we?' she asked. 'How long have I been asleep?'

'Not that long,' he said. 'We've still got hours to go.'

She dozed off again. The next time she woke, she lay in silence for a while, wondering how to make him stop. 'I need to go to the bathroom,' she announced suddenly. 'Can you stop at the next gas station, please?'

He laughed. 'Why a gas station?' he asked. 'You've got the whole damn country in which to pee.'

'It's pouring outside. I don't want to get wet.'

'You haven't much choice.' She felt the car slowing down; then he braked and leapt out. Pulling open the back door, he leant in and untied her feet. Leaving her wrists tied together, he helped her slide out. They were in a forest. It might be anywhere. There was not another car to be seen.

'Could you untie my hands, please?' she asked nervously. 'I can't do anything like this.'

'No,' he replied. 'That would be too easy. And don't try any more of your little tricks.'

Taking her by the arm, he marched her a few yards into the woods. 'OK. Get on with it,' he said.

'Do you mind turning your back?' she asked.

'Why the sudden modesty? Come on, get on with it. I dislike standing about in the wet.'

She felt humiliated. He knew damn well, she thought, that with her hands tied behind her back she would have to ask him for help. As if to embarrass her further, he held her arm tightly while he urinated against a tree.

In her mind, she was back in Paris and he was brandishing his penis above her face. He was going to do it again. She was sure, now. She could not face it, she thought. She simply could not go through that again.

'Why don't you kill me now and get it over, if that's what you want to do?' she sobbed as he marched her back to the car.

'Kill you?' he said pensively. '*Mais non, mon amour chéri. On va faire l'amour un peu, c'est tout.*'

She felt herself hovering on the borders of hysteria. 'Why are you talking in French?' she cried. 'I can't stand it! I don't want you to talk to me in French.'

'Oh, but you do,' he replied as he bundled her unceremoniously into the back of the car. 'We're going to re-enact your little fantasy and to do it properly we're going to have to speak French.'

She tried to kick his hands away as he took hold of her ankles and again bound them with a rope. Bending over her, he whispered, 'You should not have lied to me, *mon amour*. Do you think I don't know what you got up to in Paris in 1962?'

He saw her jerk. She was shivering, in spite of the heat. 'When we reach our destination,' he remarked, 'I shall prove to you that I can be the monster of your dreams. Don't think for a moment that you are the only one who can pretend.'

Sally lay, hour after hour, in a throbbing hell. Her nightmare visions had reached such a pitch that she screamed in terror when, some time later, Philippe again braked and climbed out of the car. 'For God's sake, calm down,' he said. 'There's no-one within miles, so you might as well save your breath.'

He pulled open the rear door and put his hand under Sally's head.

'I'm sorry to have to do this to you,' he said, as he undid the belt of her dress. Forcing a large handkerchief into her mouth, he used her belt to tie it tightly in place. 'It won't be for long. I'm going to have to stop and fill up at the next gas station, and I don't want any scenes.'

He pulled an old picnic rug from the back of the car and, throwing it over her so that it covered her head, said, 'I warn you, if there's so much as a peep out of you, I'll knock you out, so I advise you to lie still and keep quiet.'

Ten minutes later, he pulled in to a gas station and switched off the engine. Sally lay without moving, hardly daring to breathe, as he climbed out and slammed the car door. She waited while he filled the tank, calculating that the one moment when she might succeed in attracting someone's notice was when he went to pay for the gas.

The noise of the pump ceased and she heard the nozzle being hooked back into place. She gave Philippe a moment, then started to wriggle violently and kick her feet against the car door. She realized that her muted cries were likely to be inaudible to anyone standing outside in the rain so she concentrated on kicking the door as hard as she could.

Nobody came. Theirs was probably the only car there, she thought sadly, as she heard Philippe return.

He did not stop to remove her gag for what, to Sally,

seemed a very long time. 'It serves you right,' he said, when he finally undid it. 'I told you to lie quietly. You should have done as you were told.'

He climbed in the back beside her and propped her up. 'You said you were thirsty,' he remarked, holding a can of Coca-Cola to her lips. 'Go on. Drink it. I bought it for you.'

Through the long, dark hours that followed, Sally plotted her escape. It was clear to her that she would have to kill him. She had no other choice.

'Did you bring my bag?' she asked after a long silence.

'Yes. It's here on the seat beside me – but I left the knives behind, if that's what you want to know. Incidentally, don't try anything stupid when we get there. I could so easily lose my temper and kill you by mistake.'

Sally said nothing. Outside, the sky was gradually becoming light.

Philippe drove another 70 kilometres, then stopped the car and sat studying the map. *'Nom de Dieu!'* he muttered under his breath. *'C'est vraiment au bout du monde.* Right,' he said, setting off again. 'We should be there in about an hour.'

Sally felt the car swing sharply to the right. They must be on some rural route, she thought, hearing the scrunch of the tyres on pebbles and earth. If only she could see where she was. There must be a farm somewhere, surely, or a village she could run to for help?

'I'm feeling sick,' she said after a while. 'I'm going to have to get out.'

'We're nearly there. It's only another few miles.'

'Can't I sit up and lean my head out of the window? I don't want to be sick all over the car.'

'You won't be sick; and you can take it from me, there's nothing to look at – just water and trees.'

They bumped along for another half-hour. 'Well, here we are,' Philippe announced eventually. 'I'll just make sure this really is it.' He clambered out, slamming the door behind him, and she heard his footsteps walking away.

'Right,' he said, when he returned. 'I've had a quick look around the house and it all looks fine – very comfortable, in fact.'

Without untying her wrists or ankles, he pulled her out and carried her into the house. Taking her through to the kitchen, he deposited her on her back on the large, wooden table. 'Don't try to move or you'll fall off and hurt yourself,' he said. 'I'm just going to get the food out of the car. I'm famished and I imagine you must be hungry again by now.'

Sally began to weep. 'Please kill me,' she sobbed. 'Why can't you just kill me and get it over with?'

'You seem very keen to make me kill you,' he remarked. 'What makes you think you deserve to be killed?' He turned back at the door, adding, 'Anyway, I'm damned if I'm going to do anything until I've had something to eat.'

He returned in a moment carrying the food and the bottle of wine. Lifting her from the table, he sat her in a chair and undid the rope that bound her wrists. She tried to push him away from her as soon as her arms were free, hitting out with clenched fists, then clawing at his cheek with her nails.

He hit her hard across the face, knocking her back in the chair. Putting a hand around her throat, he squeezed it dangerously hard. After a moment, he let go of her throat and grabbed her by the hair. Jerking her head backwards, he used his free hand to pull off his belt and bring it down hard across her thighs. She let out a howl, then screamed as he hit her with it again and again.

'This will seem pleasant compared with what I shall do to you if you try that again,' he remarked, throwing his belt down on the table and picking up the rope that he had dropped when he untied her wrists. 'I can see I shall have to keep your hands tied the whole time from now on.'

Gripping her right wrist, he bound it securely with one end of the rope then, passing it under the seat of her chair, he tied the other end around her left wrist so that both arms, though firmly attached, hung loosely by her sides. 'That should be more comfortable,' he remarked, standing back to admire his work.

He made himself a sandwich and took a bite of it before sitting down. He ate in silence for a moment, then moved his chair so that he was sitting beside her and asked, 'Do you want anything to eat?'

'How do you expect me to eat like this?' she sobbed.

'I'm going to feed you. Come on, stop crying,' he said, producing a handkerchief and wiping her eyes. 'That's better. Now, how about a drink?' He poured out some wine, took a couple of sips, then held the glass to her lips. She did not want any, but he gave her no choice. 'Drink up,' he said, forcing her mouth open. 'There's plenty more where this came from. I took the whole case while I was at it. It's in the back of the car.'

Sally looked panic-stricken but said nothing. Guessing what she was thinking, Philippe nodded. 'You're right,' he said. 'We shall be here for some days; and it is possible that at some point I may wish to make you exceedingly drunk.' He was silent for a moment, then laughed. 'It's also possible, of course, that I shall feel the need to become very drunk myself before we're through. Who knows, after all, whether my enjoyment at inflicting pain will run out before you reach the depths of degradation to which you aspire?'

'Philippe, *please*,' she begged. 'Let me go. You don't understand. It's all been a mistake.'

'Not for me, I assure you. I've enjoyed every minute of it.' He rose to his feet, picked up his belt and said, 'Don't try anything stupid this time. I'm going to untie you while we go upstairs. But first, let me find a sharp knife. You like knives, don't you? Let's take one with us, just in case.'

He marched her upstairs, gripping her arm and holding a knife against her throat.

## Chapter Twenty-Nine

From morn to noon, from noon to dewy eve, as Mulciber cast over the battlements, she fell through that summer's day. Like Beelzebub, Belial and Moloch rolled into one, she at last understood the reality of life without love.

Philippe insisted that she speak only French; and because he, too, said everything in French, he sounded to Sally like the man who had attacked her in Paris, so she was doubly sure that they were one and the same.

*'Tu es une vraie salope!'* he shouted. *'Une vraie petite merde! Seize ans! Putain! Tu me dégoûtes! Qu'est-ce qu'il t'a fait qui t'a tellement plu?'*

When Sally, through fear or lack of French vocabulary, let slip a word or phrase in English by mistake, he hit her and made her repeat it in French. 'Come on!' he shouted. 'Let's hear you say it in French! I want to hear how you said it. Come on! Louder! You can do it! You did it before and you're damn well going to do it again!'

As the day wore on, he became more and more violent. 'I know what you did in Paris, so stop fucking well lying! You were only sixteen, for Christ's sake! How old were you when you started all this?'

Terrified and exhaused, beaten and bruised, forcibly violated in the most humiliating ways, Sally still would not talk. As far as she was concerned, he knew it all. He knew what he had done to her in Paris – he was doing it again. So she sobbed, 'You *know* what happened! I'm not going to tell you! Why should I, when you know? Anyway, I can't! I don't know how to say it in French!'

Philippe was amazed by her stubbornness and misinterpreted it, thinking it simply indicated her liking for being abused. It occurred to him, after a while, that she might be trying to protect the other man. The more Sally refused to answer, the more Philippe thought she was lying. 'What was his name? Where did you meet him? Who is he? Where does he live now?'

'I don't know!' Sally screamed in terror. 'I don't know! I don't know!'

'Liar! You're covering up for him, aren't you? You know where he is! I'm going to bloody well kill you if you don't tell me the truth!'

As dusk fell, Sally noticed something that had not caught her attention until then. The clue she had been looking for all those months – it was there in front of her, but she had never realized it until now.

Philippe was still shouting at her and shaking her, but suddenly stopped and became calm. *'D'accord, ma chérie. On va voir si tu te souviens.* Let's make love again, but differently this time.' He pushed the tip of the knife against her throat. *'Mais, si, mon amour . . . On va faire l'amour . . . Tu verras . . .'*

Sally watched her hands, as if they did not belong to her, tearing wildly at his chest; and she suddenly remembered. She had torn his shirt to shreds. She had plunged her teeth into his shoulder and lacerated his chest with her nails. She remembered vividly seeing great streaks of blood. But this was different . . . the chest was different; the skin was different. Why had she never noticed it before? 'Oh, my God!' she wailed. 'You don't . . . Oh, my God! What have I done?'

He saw her eyes focus for the first time for hours. She was staring at him as if she had never seen him before. Then, closing her eyes, she let forth a terrible howl.

Philippe dropped the knife and gripped her shoulders. 'Look at me!' he shouted. 'What is it? You've got to tell me! I have to know!'

Her eyes were wide with anguish when she lifted her head. 'You have hair on your chest!' she sobbed.

'Of course I have hair on my chest! I've always had hair on my chest, for God's sake! What's so odd about that?'

It was so smooth, she thought; such smooth, pale skin. She looked at Philippe, appalled. How could she have forgotten that? She stretched out her hand tentatively and touched his arm. It was not the soft, almost girlish, arm that she remembered clearly now. And his chest wasn't hairless. She remembered the bizarre effect it had had on her, that hairless torso under the thick head of hair.

Then she looked at her hands and saw Philippe's blood under her nails; and, suddenly, after all those years, she remembered his face.

'Answer me, will you?' Philippe was shaking her. 'What are you talking about? I've got to know!' He was shouting, but Sally had turned her head away and lay moaning to herself.

Grabbing the knife once more, Philippe leant forward and again pressed the blade against her throat. 'You've got to tell me, do you understand? I mean it. I'm going to kill you if you don't.'

He began to shake her so hard she thought her neck was going to snap. Suddenly, he hit her a sharp blow across the cheek, and she remembered the doctor slapping her face . . .

What was it he had said? 'You must forget what has happened . . . Whatever it was that happened, you must put it out of your mind. If you do not, believe me, you will destroy your whole life.'

Dragging herself back to the present, Sally tried to speak, but her voice was so faint that Philippe had to strain forward in an effort to hear her words.

'I thought you were the man . . . the man who . . . in Paris . . . I thought you were him!'

The knife fell from Philippe's hands. He thought he would explode. *'Putain de merde!'* he yelled. 'Am I never going to wipe that fucker out of your head? What did he do to you that you liked so much? Come on, tell me! What did he do to you that I haven't done? He tried to strangle you, didn't he? Is that what you want?'

She felt his hands closing around her throat and whispered hoarsely, 'Don't, Philippe! You don't understand. Don't! *Please!* Listen to me! I've made a terrible mistake!'

His fingers relaxed slightly. 'Go on,' he said. 'I'm listening. What did he do that made such an impression on you that you want to live it again?'

'I hated him!' Sally cried hysterically. 'Don't you understand? You think I loved him, but I hated him! I've hated him all my life! I was terrified because I thought you were going to do it again.' She was weeping so loudly he could barely understand her words. 'I'm sorry, Philippe,' she whimpered. 'I'm truly sorry. I really thought it was you.'

He stared at her. His hands unclenched and fell away from her throat. 'I don't understand,' he said slowly. 'Perhaps you would be kind enough to explain.'

'You said you knew what happened in Paris. That made me all the more certain you were him, otherwise how did you know? How *do* you know, if it comes to that? No-one knows, except Carson, and he'd never tell anyone, least of all you.'

'Your father told me.'

'My father? He couldn't have told you. I never told him or my mother anything. He doesn't know about it.'

'For God's sake, Sally! Try and tell the truth for once. He saw you in hospital, didn't he? Who on earth do you think you are fooling? Of course he knows!'

'He thinks I had a nosebleed. I never told him about that guy. I never told either of my parents that I was abducted and nearly raped.'

Philippe felt as though he had been hit with a sledgehammer.

'Someone tried to rape you?' he demanded. 'Are you saying you were attacked?'

'Well, you knew that, didn't you? You told me you knew!'

'How could I know, for God's sake? You never told me! How the hell was I supposed to know?' He was shaking. Was it true, he wondered. She had told so many lies, how was one to know? 'If you're telling the truth, you'd have told me this before.'

'I couldn't . . . Anyway, I thought you knew because I thought you were him.'

'You can't expect me to believe that!' Philippe shouted. 'I'm not a complete idiot! For Christ's sake . . . !'

'I did. I promise you. That's why I was so scared. I'm terribly sorry. I know it's an appalling thing to have thought . . . But I did. I swear to God, I was absolutely sure you were him.'

Philippe's face was drained of colour, and he seemed to be gasping for air. After a moment, he rose to his feet and began pacing about the room; then, suddenly, he turned to face her, shaking his head in disbelief.

'You wouldn't have had an affair with me if you'd thought I was him. You're still lying to me, aren't you? I swear to God, I'm going to kill you if you don't tell me the truth. I have to know the truth or I think I'll go mad.'

'I had to find out . . . I wanted to kill you, you see. I wanted to kill him – and I thought it was you. I was sure I'd recognize something . . . but I had to be sure. Before I killed you, I had to be a hundred per cent certain you were him.'

'I thought you said you *were* sure.'

'Well, I was. Almost, anyway. I mean, I was practically certain, but I wanted concrete proof.' Seeing his sceptical expression, she heaved a sigh. 'When I saw you at that party, I was absolutely certain; but then I didn't feel so sure once we'd been to bed. But I told

247

myself, you see, that you hadn't said anything in French, so I couldn't make up my mind whether you were him or not . . . Only, by then, I was in love with you and I didn't think you were him any more.'

'But you just said you *did* think I was him!'

'Not until the night before last; but then, when you said you'd kill me if I came to see you, and you said all those horrible things in French . . . You'd never spoken to me in French before, you see, and they were the same words. So I knew then that I'd been right in the first place and it *was* really you . . . I mean, that you *were* really him.' Her voice dropped, and she looked away. 'But I was wrong. It wasn't you at all . . . I've remembered him now . . .' She started to weep. 'I'm so desperately sorry, Philippe. I can't tell you how sorry I am. I'll make it up to you, I promise. I'll do anything . . . You can't imagine what a nightmare it has been.'

She was completely insane, Philippe suddenly realized. Her mother was right. She was off her head. 'Would you mind starting at the beginning?' he asked. 'I'm afraid you've lost me somewhere along the line.'

Her hands clenched and unclenched. It took some time, but she finally told him the truth – or the truth as she saw it then. Philippe watched her, listening in silence, and thinking she looked like someone trying to fight a duel in a fog. When she eventually stopped speaking, Philippe was at a complete loss for words.

After walking about the room for some minutes without saying anything, he went and stood by the window, looking out at the night.

'I need some air,' he said after a moment. 'I'm going outside for a bit. I need to think.'

Sally said nothing. Giving a great sigh, she turned over and buried her face in the pillow and sobbed.

Philippe was gone for over an hour. When he returned, Sally was sitting up in bed. She had stopped crying and was staring ahead of her, but turned and smiled at him as he walked into the room.

Philippe did not return her smile. He crossed the room and stood looking down at her, studying her as if he had never seen her before.

'You fool!' he said after a minute. 'You have ruined both your life and mine! I loved you, don't you realize? And now . . . What is left for either of us now?'

'It's all right,' Sally insisted. 'Don't you see? Now you know everything, it's going to be all right!'

'All right?' he exploded. 'What the fuck do you mean, it's all right? You've turned me into a monster! I've abused you; I've humiliated you; I've raped you and bloody nearly killed you, and you think it's all right?'

'But it doesn't matter any more. I understand why, now, so it doesn't matter. Let's just forget it and start again.'

'Forget it? How can we forget it? Can't you understand? You've changed me into something I would never have been without you?'

'But I love you! We love each other, don't we? Why can't we . . . ?'

'Love each other!' Philippe yelled at her in fury. 'How can we possibly love each other? After everything I have done to you, how can you pretend for one instant that you love me? And how can you imagine that I could possibly love you? Have you the faintest conception of what you have done to me? You have brought out the worst, the most degraded part of me – a part I didn't even know I possessed – and you've shown me the worst, most abject and degraded part of yourself.'

'But there's another side to both of us. You know there is. Why can't we start again?'

'It's too late, Sally. Can't you understand? You've given me a taste for violence which is something I shall have to fight for the rest of my life. I could have killed you, don't you realize, then gone off and raped other women and killed them too? I could have done it again and again. With your determination to think me a monster, you have turned me into one, and I can't ever forgive you for that!'

'Please, Philippe, try and forget it! I was terrified! You must understand that!'

'You did not forget what happened to you. What makes you expect others to forget? It is a vicious circle, my dear Sally. I would have thought even you could see that.'

'Then what is to become of us? What are we both to do?'

'You, at least, can return to your husband. As for me, God only knows!'

'I can't go back to Carson! He has left me! He doesn't love me any more, and he's guessed I've been having an affair with you, though I denied it. He walked out on me. He won't come back, I know. He's gone.'

'Well, that's your bad luck. It really doesn't concern me – and don't start blubbing again, for God's sake! You have only yourself to blame. Poor old Carson! If you don't feel regret for anything else, I hope you feel ashamed of what you have done to him.'

'Why? Why should I? He knew what had happened to me. He knew everything about it. I told him everything. He didn't have to marry me, did he? I told him before we were married. He was the only person I ever told.'

'Perhaps he did not realize that you were determined never to forget. That has been your mistake, my dear Sally. That single act has destroyed us all.'

He turned away and walked towards the window. 'I must go,' he said, thinking aloud. 'I must get back to Montreal. I shall have to resign from the university, get rid of both apartments. I have a hundred things to do before I leave.'

'You're not going to leave Montreal, surely?'

He turned to face her and eyed her coldly. 'You can hardly expect me to stay,' he said.

'I won't tell a soul, I promise. There's no need for you to go!'

'You don't seem to understand. I have no wish to stay.'

'Where will you go?'

'I have no idea.'

'You're not leaving here without me!' she cried, as he headed for the door. 'Wait! I won't be a minute.' She struggled to her feet and started to put on her clothes.

He looked at her. She was bruised all over; her cheek was swollen and her lip was cut. He could see it was painful for her to lift her arms. He stared at her for a second, then turned away in disgust.

'I'll drop you at the nearest bus station,' he said with his back to her. 'You can make your own way home from there.'

'There won't be any buses for Montreal from anywhere around here. How on earth am I supposed to get back?'

'There's got to be a local company somewhere,' he remarked without expression. 'You can take a bus to Quebec City and make your way back to Montreal from there.'

'You know perfectly well there won't be any buses at this time of night. There's only about one a day in these areas, if there's a service at all. I may have to wait nearly twenty-four hours before one comes. You can't just leave me . . .'

'Oh, but I can,' he replied. 'What's more, it'll give me time to return to Montreal before you. I intend to make myself highly visible before you reappear.'

'But what am I to tell my parents? They're sure to have found my car by the time I get back. They'll have the police looking for me. They'll probably think I've been drowned in the lake, or something. How am I supposed to explain where I've been?'

'Say you don't remember, that you've lost your mind – it wouldn't be far from the truth.'

'I can't say that! They'll put me in hospital. I must have an explanation that sounds credible.'

'I don't give a damn what you tell them,' snapped Philippe. 'It's not my problem any more. Get your clothes on. Come on, hurry up! I'll clear up downstairs and then I'm leaving, whether you're ready or not.'

Sally stood beside him while he locked up. 'Take this,' he said, handing her a plastic bag containing the empty wine bottle and the remains of the food. 'You can get rid of it on the bus. I'm going to throw the other bottles into a lake somewhere on the way back. Incidentally,' he added, 'I'm going to give these keys back to my friend and tell him I'm unable to take him up on his offer, after all. I warn you, if you attempt to tell anyone we've been together, I shall have you certified and put away.'

They drove in silence. It was too dark to see much. The track seemed to wind interminably between the black outlines of trees; and when they reached the road, it still looked the same. A couple of hours later, Philippe deposited her in front of a general store in a small village. 'Someone's bound to turn up here eventually,' he said, 'and you can ask them where there's a bus you can get.'

'Don't leave me,' Sally pleaded, as he walked round to her side of the car and pulled her out. 'I can't stay here all night on my own. Why can't you take me with you?'

'Because I can't stand your presence another minute. I can't stand what you have done to me and I can't stand the person you really are.'

She put out her hand and tried to take his arm, but he shook it free with an expression of distaste. 'Philippe, forgive me, I beg you. Please forgive me. I'll do anything to make amends.'

He turned his back on her and climbed into the car without a word. She watched as he drove off, staring after him into the dark as the car's lights faded and finally vanished among the trees.

It was a warm night and her legs and arms were already covered in insect bites. Blood, she thought, feeling a warm trickle run down her ankle; the blackfly were after her blood.

# Monsieur de Brillancourt
## Clare Harkness

'A JOY TO READ, LIGHT YET RICHLY OBSERVED,
WITTY YET ULTIMATELY TRAGIC . . .
RECOMMENDED'
Sandy Fordham, *Oracle*

Monsieur de Brillancourt has never married. Not that he
doesn't like women: he has simply not had much occasion
to encounter any. For most of his sixty-nine years he has
been quietly absorbed in his dusty library, studying
insects, plants and books.

His contentment would be complete, were it not for one
thing. He loves children and yearns to fill the halls of his
vast and ugly château in the Ardèche with the sounds of
childish laughter. When, one summer, Elizabeth
Hardcastle, a young Englishwoman, comes to stay in the
château with her three young children, his dream appears
to come true. In the enchanted days that follow, Monsieur
de Brillancourt's heart blossoms – and he falls fatally in
love.

Set against the dramatic and endlessly changing
landscape of the Ardèche in southern France, *Monsieur
de Brillancourt* is sometimes comic, sometimes tragic – a
novel of delicate emotions, richly described.

0 552 99467 7

## BLACK SWAN

# Time of Grace
## Clare Harkness

'SHE IS A MERCILESS OBSERVER OF CHARACTER . . .
THERE IS A LAUGH IN EVERY PARAGRAPH AND A
TEAR IN SOME'
*Molly Keane*

It was inevitable that Imogen and Jessica should become
friends. Both precocious and agnostic, arriving from
unconventional homes abroad to the same restrictive
English convent school, they were naturally singled out as
different from the rest and forced together in an alliance of
outcasts.

Years later the two women sit in the attic of a family home
on Lake Maggiore, surrounded by trunks and boxes from
which they dig out clothes, photographs and letters. As
they sift through the relics of eccentric school holidays,
life at the Sorbonne and the revolutionary atmosphere of
Paris in the late 1960s, years spent apart in Cambridge and
Milan, London and Washington DC, with husbands,
lovers and children, Imogen is at times doubled up with
laughter, at others, close to tears.

Clare Harkness's portrait of two women's struggle to find
fulfilment in the face of continuous and often hilarious
adversity forms a beautifully written, wise and moving
narrative.

'TRACES OF FRANCOISE SAGAN, FAY WELDON AND
MOLLY KEANE, WITH EVEN A HINT OF JUDITH
KRANTZ, WAFTED TASTEFULLY UP-SCALE'
Patricia Miller, *Evening Standard*

0 552 99387 5

**BLACK SWAN**

## A SELECTION OF FINE WRITING
## AVAILABLE FROM BLACK SWAN

THE PRICES SHOWN BELOW WERE CORRECT AT THE TIME OF GOING TO PRESS. HOWEVER TRANSWORLD PUBLISHERS RESERVE THE RIGHT TO SHOW NEW RETAIL PRICES ON COVERS WHICH MAY DIFFER FROM THOSE PREVIOUSLY ADVERTISED IN THE TEXT OR ELSEWHERE.

| | | | | |
|---|---|---|---|---|
| ☐ | 99564 | 9 | JUST FOR THE SUMMER | Judy Astley £5.99 |
| ☐ | 99537 | 1 | GUPPIES FOR TEA | Marika Cobbold £5.99 |
| ☐ | 99488 | X | SUGAR CAGE | Connie May Fowler £5.99 |
| ☐ | 99467 | 7 | MONSIEUR DE BRILLANCOURT | Clare Harkness £4.99 |
| ☐ | 99387 | 5 | TIME OF GRACE | Clare Harkness £5.99 |
| ☐ | 99449 | 9 | DISAPPEARING ACTS | Terry McMillan £5.99 |
| ☐ | 99480 | 4 | MAMA | Terry McMillan £5.99 |
| ☐ | 99503 | 7 | WAITING TO EXHALE | Terry McMillan £5.99 |
| ☐ | 99551 | 7 | SUFFER THE LITTLE CHILDREN | Lucy Robertson £5.99 |
| ☐ | 99506 | 1 | BETWEEN FRIENDS | Kathleen Rowntree £5.99 |
| ☐ | 99325 | 5 | THE QUIET WAR OF REBECCA SHELDON | Kathleen Rowntree £5.99 |
| ☐ | 99529 | 0 | OUT OF THE SHADOWS | Titia Sutherland £5.99 |
| ☐ | 99460 | X | THE FIFTH SUMMER | Titia Sutherland £4.99 |
| ☐ | 99574 | 6 | ACCOMPLICE OF LOVE | Titia Sutherland £5.99 |
| ☐ | 99130 | 9 | NOAH'S ARK | Barbara Trapido £5.99 |
| ☐ | 99056 | 6 | BROTHER OF THE MORE FAMOUS JACK | Barbara Trapido £6.99 |
| ☐ | 99494 | 4 | THE CHOIR | Joanna Trollope £5.99 |
| ☐ | 99410 | 3 | A VILLAGE AFFAIR | Joanna Trollope £5.99 |
| ☐ | 99442 | 1 | A PASSIONATE MAN | Joanna Trollope £5.99 |
| ☐ | 99470 | 7 | THE RECTOR'S WIFE | Joanna Trollope £5.99 |
| ☐ | 99492 | 8 | THE MEN AND THE GIRLS | Joanna Trollope £5.99 |
| ☐ | 99393 | X | A SENSIBLE LIFE | Mary Wesley £5.99 |
| ☐ | 99258 | 5 | THE VACILLATIONS OF POPPY CAREW | Mary Wesley £5.99 |
| ☐ | 99126 | 0 | THE CAMOMILE LAWN | Mary Wesley £5.99 |
| ☐ | 99495 | 2 | A DUBIOUS LEGACY | Mary Wesley £5.99 |
| ☐ | 99591 | 6 | A MISLAID MAGIC | Joyce Windsor £4.99 |

*All Black Swan Books are available at your bookshop or newsagent, or can be ordered from the following address:*

Corgi/Bantam Books,
Cash Sales Department
P.O. Box 11, Falmouth, Cornwall TR10 9EN

UK and B.F.P.O. customers please send a cheque or postal order (no currency) and allow £1.00 for postage and packing for the first book plus 50p for the second book and 30p for each additional book to a maximum charge of £3.00 (7 books plus).

Overseas customers, including Eire, please allow £2.00 for postage and packing for the first book plus £1.00 for the second book and 50p for each subsequent title ordered.

NAME (Block Letters) ................................................................................................................

ADDRESS ................................................................................................................

................................................................................................................